To remember what you've read, write your initials in a square!

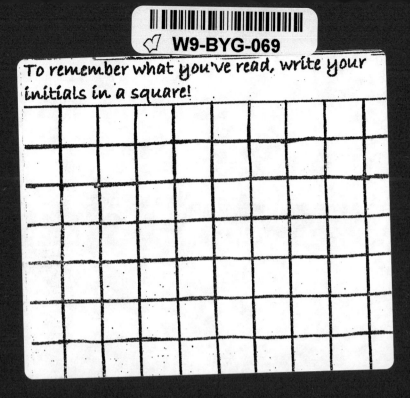

DATE DUE 6/16

THE
SWORD
OF
MIDRAS

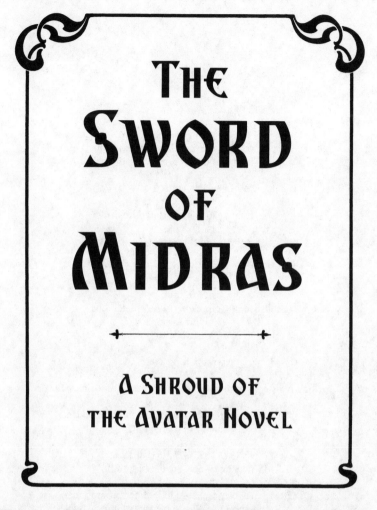

THE
SWORD
OF
MIDRAS

A SHROUD OF
THE AVATAR NOVEL

TRACY HICKMAN AND RICHARD GARRIOTT

TOR

A TOM DOHERTY ASSOCIATES BOOK
NEW YORK

THE SWORD OF MIDRAS

Copyright © 2016 by Portalarium, Inc.

Map by Portalarium, Inc.

A Tor Book
Published by Tom Doherty Associates, LLC
175 Fifth Avenue
New York, NY 10010

www.tor-forge.com

Tor® is a registered trademark of Tom Doherty Associates, LLC.

The Library of Congress Cataloging-in-Publication Data
is available upon request.

ISBN 978-0-7653-8230-6 (hardcover)
ISBN 978-1-4668-8680-3 (e-book)

Our books may be purchased in bulk for promotional, educational, or business use. Please contact your local bookseller or the Macmillan Corporate and Premium Sales Department at 1-800-221-7945, extension 5442, or by e-mail at MacmillanSpecialMarkets@macmillan.com.

First Edition: June 2016

Printed in the United States of America

10 9 8 7 6 5 4 3 2 1

CONTENTS

Contents

THE
SWORD
OF
MIDRAS

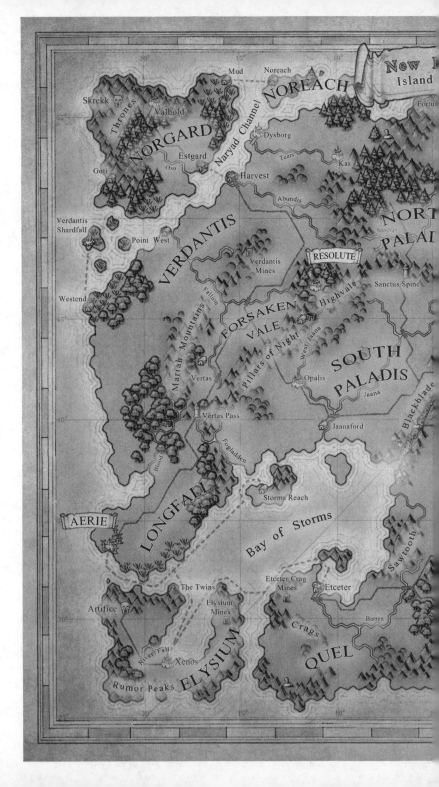

PROLOGUE

❖ ━━━━━ ❖

The Destiny Pool

The End is the Beginning of us all.

Hear the soundless lamentation of the ages lost! The past is hidden from the eyes of the weary, blanketed beneath ash and tears. The old world is passed away, its mountains shaken, its rivers torn from their courses, its plains rent with fire and the shining towers of man tumbled to ruin. The orb of night is broken, its black shards tumbling from the dome of night to fall as judgment's cruel, black rain. The music of daughters fails to resound, the proud boasts of men are as dust in their mouths, and fear reigns in the dark silence that follows. The flesh is turned to dust, and all that we once were is forgotten and lost in the shuttered past.

Where are the Virtues of the world now fallen? Were they taken from us or were we taken from them? Were they abandoned or were we orphaned by them? Was this not the blade of too fine an edge that cut between the light and night, between me and thee? Avatars of our dreams or nightmares, did you steal away from us in the night or did we lose you by the wayside, sightless in our pride?

How, then, are we to look forward when we cannot look back?

Only in the obsidian darkness can we comprehend the bright truth. The Fall has sown the seed of our redemption, that we may harvest its fruits, harness its might, and rise again from the blanketing ash of a past that has been cut from us as sharply as a malignant growth.

Tomorrow is to be forged anew from a molten chaos by those who seize destiny's hammer and strike with uncompromising will.

—Sariah the Blind, *Lamentation of the Fall*

The man reluctantly closed the thin metal sheets of the small book. Each page was slightly bent and wavy from use, and the edges were rusting despite his constant care. They were bound by six wide leather thongs along the left edge and a thick cover of tooled leather after the style of the northern Grunvald binders, and the book was barely larger than the size of his hand when he closed it. Still, the rune letters engraved on each page were as clear to his eyes as when he had first stolen the volume as a young boy. He no longer remembered where he had stolen it or even why it had seemed important to him at the time. He had not even known how to read then, an orphan of a village on the River Meino just outside of Rhun.

He had survived on magic. He had a natural talent for conjuring and shaping that was of no small use to the farmers who kept him fed and sheltered in exchange for his urging their crops to grow or coaxing a troublesome boulder out of the way of their plow, but it was not until this book that he felt there might be more to his life than surviving.

It was this book that had been his companion in learning to decipher the meaning from the runes with the help of the occasional minstrel that might mistakenly pass by such an inconsequential place. It had changed his life in such profound ways. He ran the fingers of his right hand over the tooled leather artwork of the front of the book as though caressing the cheek of a lover.

If, indeed, he had ever loved at all.

"Only in the Obsidian darkness can we comprehend the bright truth," he murmured.

It was the book that had led him to cross the Vaughban Mountains and into the Grunvald Plain. It brought him to the first of the Shard Falls. The shining crystalline stone, black and enormous, stood plunged like a dagger into the vast flatness around it. Everywhere else into the distance the grass was brown in the cold winter air, but around the Fall were a variety of plants and animals and even what the young man had thought were both plants *and* animals weaving and reweaving themselves into strange and wondrous forms, only to shift again into new shapes, both chaotic and ordered at once.

It was the heart of a magic the likes of which the young man had never before experienced, and he was drawn to it without ever once questioning the wisdom in doing so.

The man had had a name in that time before, but he decided

that, like the world in his book, his old self should pass away and a new self should take its place. So he abandoned his name and became, instead, simply "the Obsidian Eye."

In the years that would follow he would come to understand that the wild magic surrounding the Shard Fall had all been a sign to him of bringing order out of chaos. He embraced the magic and its intoxicating power. Over time more and more men and women with the gift were drawn to him as his reputation spread, each learning and expanding upon the craft of Obsidian magic, but tempering it all with the glorious book in his hands as a touchstone to order amid the chaos.

"It has shown me so many things," he said as he gently set the book down on the stand next to the high-back chair on which he sat. It was in the center of a room whose walls could not be seen in the opaque darkness around him. He knew the place well, for it was his own chamber deep beneath the fortress of Desolis—a ruin from before the Fall that his young order of sorcerers had claimed for their own. It was near enough to the Shard Fall that magic could be wrought here and far from the prying eyes of the petty warlords who were constantly battling one another in the wake of the world's collapse. He turned to face the floor before him. "And now we shall see even more."

In the floor was set a circle of stones around a dark, still pool. There was not a ripple in its surface, and it looked to be of infinite depth.

The Obsidian Eye cocked his head slightly to one side. "Markus? Are you ready?"

"Ready, my master," came the answer echoing through the chamber. Markus Dirae was an acolyte among the Obsidian

Sorcerers, and the Obsidian Eye knew he was far too lowly among the ranks of their order to attend him. Undoubtedly, the nervous Markus was more perplexed at being here than any of those of higher rank and status who had thought to be here in his stead. The Obsidian Eye smiled. The presence of Markus was a matter of destiny.

"Attend me." The older sorcerer's whisper carried throughout the hall. "We have never before looked into the Destiny Pool, but is not a thing created such that it might be used? It is time we know our fates."

The Obsidian Eye stepped down from his throne to the edge of the pool. He heard Markus take up his stylus behind him. There were several soft clay tablets arrayed on a table next to him within easy reach.

The Obsidian Eye reached down.

Was this not the blade of too fine an edge that cut between the light and night, between me and thee?

He stopped his hand short of the mirror surface of the pool.

"Have you read *The Lamentation of the Fall*, Markus?"

"Yes, my master," the acolyte answered at once. "We all have, Master."

"Of course," the elder sorcerer said, and sighed.

He extended his hand and touched the surface of the pool.

The placid surface erupted at once into a frothing, roiling madness. The Obsidian Eye stared at it for a moment and then began to speak. His own voice came to him as from a distance, being everywhere in the hall and nowhere at once—outside of himself.

"The world is fallen . . . fallen into chaos . . ." he heard himself say.

There was a dim awareness that Markus was inscribing runes into his tablet in some faraway place.

† † †

The world is fallen, fallen into chaos.
Men reached up in anger and shattered the sky.
Its blackness falls to Earth like a rain of dark, immutable
*   glass;*
The ordered customs and rows of society are shattered.
All men stumble
In the blinding light of a bloodred dawn.
Sightless who will not see.
Deaf to the truth they will not hear.
Mewing and wailing of and for themselves.
They kill with discordant and untamed shouts
The melodic order of their better selves.
Yet from the Obsidians' fall shall arise
Seen only by the ordered Eye
The blade that shall render order in their midst;
Silence the voices who screech outside the ordered tune;
Darken the eyes of unwelcome vision;
And bring one vision, one voice, one song
To a world reborn in perfect twilight.
Supreme and ordered once more in its flawlessness.
Of one thought and purpose born and died.
Until only the night remains.

—Prophecy of the Obsidian Eye

† † †

The master sorcerer withdrew his hand from the pool.

"Master?"

It was Markus behind him, near his chair.

He could not stop his hand from shaking.

"Master?" came the voice, more urgent this time.

"Yes," the Obsidian Eye answered hesitantly.

"What . . . what does it mean?"

"It means the world must be ordered," the Obsidian Eye said with a smile as he gazed at his still shaking hand. "And that it is our destiny to order it."

PART I

THE
OBSIDIANS

CHAPTER
1

Midras

Aren Bennis, captain of the Westreach Army of the Obsidian Empire, looked out for the heads of his archer ranks toward the remains of the city of Midras.

"Why does bringing order demand such a mess?" he mused as he scanned the splintering stockade wall for the remaining defenders behind it. "Such a beautiful, glorious mess."

The city—or what passed for a city in these times, Aren corrected himself ruefully—lay under the pall of a large column of smoke billowing from the still burning barracks on the far side of the city. The smoke rose to mar the otherwise clear sky overhead. Aren could see the forward lines of battle against the stockade wall that stood between him and the interior of the city beyond. This was the third breach in the defenses he had commanded that day. Parts of the city were already being looted because of his two previous successes. Now, once more at his orders, the satyrs had regrouped into a concentrated force and were tearing down another section of the defensive wall. The fauns were grouped here as well in support of the satyrs, their special song loosening the mortar between the timbers. They had been the key to the fall of Midras, penetrating the timbers that stood against them in a number of places. It allowed the main force of human warriors to sweep through the breach and collapse the city defenses. Now the city had fallen to them as the captain knew it would.

The captain knew nothing of the city's history nor did he particularly care. He could see there were walls and columns that predated the Fall in various places about the city. One area of these on the eastern side looked as though the ruling warlord of the city was trying to restore it to some semblance of its original form. Now the building was a ruin again following their assault. The warlord had been dislodged. Blood soaked the ground, and the city was being pillaged. Securing the city from vengeful pockets of warriors, under the mistaken belief that they could still win a victory through resistance, would be difficult and long—Aren had seen that time enough before—but the rule of order and law under the Obsidians had once more reclaimed part of the world from ignorance and the petty squabbles with its equally petty neighbors.

Aren smiled.

It was a beautiful day.

"Captain!"

The call came from behind him, barely carrying over the clash of steel, the death cries, and the battle shouts that filled the air. Aren turned only slightly in response, not wanting to miss the battle raging before him. "What is it, Halik? I'm a little engaged at the moment."

Nik Halik saluted after the manner of the Obsidians, slamming his fist against the center of his breastplate. "General Karpasic sends his compliments—"

"Nik, General Karpasic *never* sends a compliment," the captain observed, his eyes still on the battle. "At least not without demanding payment for it."

"Of course," Nik replied with a shrug of his steel pauldrons at both shoulders. Halik had dark, close-shorn hair and preferred to keep his face shaved bare. His dusky complexion only made his smile brighter. "Did you think our glorious commander would send me out here just to tell you how pretty you are?"

"So you've come to tell me the general thinks I'm comely?" Aren snorted. "Now we both know how much that's worth!"

"So you'll be asking me for a receipt?" Nik flashed an easy smile as he patted down the breastplate. "Oh, must have lost my parchment and quill during the battle. You'll just have to take my word for it then. . . . The general sends his compliments, and you'll owe him for it on account."

Lieutenant Halik was wearing his full battle armor as he approached. Aren looked him over once with approval. The lieutenant wore the armor of a Westreach warlord that looked nearly identical to Aren's own: blackened plates trimmed in bright silver, with bloodred accents.

Aren smiled at the memory of the original design, when he had first seen the sketches made over a year ago by General Karpasic. The helmet looked like it had more horns and spikes sticking out of it than a thistle. The shoulder pauldrons and gardbraces were similarly sculpted into spikes and points and, it seemed, at every other available point. It looked impressive and fear-inspiring, but it was completely impractical in battle. A warrior would not be able to exit his own tent in such a ridiculous contrivance, let alone engage in combat. True, an enemy's weapon could easily get caught up in the pointy bits, and he might even do himself harm should he be so foolish as to impale himself on his opponent. More likely, however, the enemy weapon would simply do more damage by directing the blow *into* the armor rather than *away* from it. Aren managed to work with the armorers and, in the end, convinced Karpasic that a design with fewer spikes and more deflecting curves would be more effective. The one concession was a single large and spikey gardbrace attached to the pauldron of the right shoulder, which became a symbol of rank among the warlords based on the shape and design. Aren made certain that the gardbrace could be detached during combat. Warriors could then at least shed this spiked contrivance when necessary. Only General Karpasic's armor was ornamented with six such ornate gardbraces, with three at each shoulder. Aren knew they were showy and practically useless—not unlike the general himself.

Aren smiled with satisfaction as he saw that Halik's armor was stained, and a number of blade strikes marred the finish. Aren had no use for army staff who kept their armor bright.

Which explained why his own armor was so badly damaged.

"I'd rather not owe the general anything for his compliments, on account or otherwise. You don't suppose the general would consider our ledger balanced now that I've taken the city for him?" Aren mused as he turned toward a message runner who was rapidly approaching from his left.

"No more than he credited you with the previous two cities, or any of the engagements in between," Halik rejoined. "His ledger is a bit one-sided."

"Elf of Blood-Cleaver Legion reports that the tower ruin on the left flank has been occupied by enemy archers, sire!" the runner reported slightly out of breath. "The elf requests the captain order the support of the west-flank archer units for his assault to retake the tower!"

"Tell the elf to pull his forces back westward along the battle line until they are out of range of the tower," Aren said pointedly to the runner. "He is to support the breaching force until we're through the stockade wall."

"But, sire," the runner replied, his eyes blinking nervously as he spoke, "the elf said he has orders from the general to take the tower and eliminate the threat."

Halik rolled his eyes.

"What the elf has not appreciated is that we don't *need* to take the tower," Aren replied, his voice attaining a dangerous, calm quality as he spoke. "If we isolate the tower by breaching the wall first, then we completely take them out of the battle and make them irrelevant to our victory. Tell the elf, further, that he *will* take the tower as instructed by the general—but only *after* the wall is breached and the city is secure. Do you understand?"

"Yes, sire!" the runner replied.

"Then get back to the elf with my orders before he charges the tower without permission and gets a lot of my forces killed without reason."

"Yes, sire!" the runner said again with more conviction, before turning and running westward back into the conflict.

Halik cleared his throat loudly. "The general sends his compliments and requests that you—"

"Nik, my time is occupied at the moment with keeping this army together and seizing the city," Aren said as he rubbed his tired brow with his fingers. "What does the general want?"

"Simple"—Halik sighed—"he asks that you accompany me to the command tent."

"The command tent?" The captain could barely accept the possibility. "When?"

"Now."

"I'm conducting the battle right now!"

"And your fine work is appreciated so much"—Halik nodded—"that he wants you to stop doing it and report in person on how well it is going."

Aren closed his eyes, trying to keep his temper in check. "He means it, doesn't he?"

"Oh yes." Nik nodded. "And, uh, we're already late."

"Captain Hart!" Aren yelled.

Hart was Aren's second in command of the assault. Aren believed that what Hart lacked in creativity, he made up for in determination. Though they were of equal rank, Hart always deferred to Bennis's judgment on the field of battle.

"Yes, sire!" Hart reported.

"You are in command," Aren said as though the words tasted of bitterness in his mouth. "Continue to concentrate on breaching the wall, then have the force move into the city in pursuit of the defenders once the breach is complete."

"Yes, sire!"

Aren turned to Lieutenant Halik. "Let's go. Hopefully, this won't take long."

"You never know with the general," Nik observed.

"Yes, you never know." Aren sighed as he turned away from the battle and stalked off toward the north.

† † †

The column of smoke from the city was far behind them to the south as Captain Bennis and his companion approached the Westreach Army encampment. The sentinel guards recognized them both at once and let them pass the sentry line unchallenged. They both moved quickly between the warrior tents, mess kitchens, and weaponsmiths, toward the oversize tent near the center of the camp.

"How are the second-version elves in combat?" Halik asked as they walked toward the general's tent.

"Somewhat better than the first versions," Aren observed. It was good to talk about anything except the general and the meeting that was coming nearer with every step. "But they are still a problem."

"I thought the improved eyesight and reflexes would be an advantage," Halik said. "And their tactical savvy should be something you above anyone would appreciate."

"I do like the idea of their being able to demonstrate independent action as commanders of small units, but they're still too aggressive," Aren said, shaking his head. "That, and they're completely unstable. I'm getting reports daily of elves abandoning their commands, forming independent cells, and then attacking both their enemy and their own troops."

"How many elves do you have?" Halik asked.

"Eight," the captain replied. "It's all the Obsidians would send us, and I'm just as glad. I try to keep them separated in different groups as much as possible. It seems to help. I am more impressed with the satyrs and the fauns. At least they follow orders. The satyrs have limited use and have to be caged once the battle is over. The fauns are easier to manage, although you have to goad them into the fight. At least they have a calming influence on the satyrs. We were fortunate to figure that out."

"It's a mixed bag," Halik agreed. "Do you think these 'crafted warriors' are ever going to make a difference?"

"Is *that* what they're being called now?" Aren smiled. He could already see the guards standing to either side of the command tent's entrance. "I thought *monsters* was the accepted term among the rest of the army. The Obsidians may have a talent for crafting life into more useful shapes, but I'm not certain their efforts to create new forms of life are paying off on the battlefield."

"You mean like the undead?" Halik almost laughed.

"Now there's an example of misguided thinking," Aren replied, grimacing. "Sure, one could easily think that an army of warriors who were already dead would be invincible. The Obsidians let loose their great magic, and now the dead spring up where we wish to serve our cause. No one considered that the dead hate all the living and would attack both sides when the magic called them back to life. We only recently gained any semblance of control over them, only to discover that the dead are as stupid as posts when it comes to anything outside their own life experience. You can't command them or direct them to where you need them to go. As a weapon, they're nearly useless."

"The Obsidians have promised that the next incarnations of

their wizardry would be functionally better," Halik said, though his tone belied his doubt.

"As they always do," Aren said, chuckling. "They love to shape new creatures first and then promise to fix the monsters later."

"Don't you have a friend among the Cabal of the Obsidians?" Halik asked. They were approaching the enormous tent of the army command. Pennants were flapping from the tent poles, clearly demonstrating that General Karpasic was holding court within. "Perhaps you could ask him when we might get a version of these creatures they like to summon that is actually useful in battle."

"Assuming I *have* a friend among the Obsidians," Aren replied as he stopped just short of the tent entrance, "would you really think it wise to ask a mutation sorcerer why the magic of his cabal is so flawed?"

"Don't want to be transformed, eh?" Halik laughed.

"I'd hardly be able to serve the empire as a frog, would I?" Aren said. He cast a cynical eye on the tent flap of the entrance. "Are you coming in with me?"

"In there? I'd rather hit my own head repeatedly with a large rock," Halik said. raising an eyebrow. "You wouldn't make that an order, would you, Captain?"

"No." Aren sighed with resignation. "But that large rock is sounding very attractive right about now."

Aren stepped inside the tent. He was momentarily blinded as the brightness of the day gave way to the dim confines of the command tent. His eyes quickly adjusted to the darkness inside.

General Milos Karpasic sat on his ornate chair opposite the entry flap. It was like Milos in a way, Aren thought: so large that its usefulness was literally outweighed by its inconvenience. The general had the porters for the army carry the monstrosity everywhere the army went and insisted on it being set up on its matching carpet almost before the tent pegs had stopped ringing from being driven into the unforgiving ground. The army did not eat until the general's "throne" was settled. The chair itself was designed to fit on a large wooden dais that elevated the eye level of the general above anyone who stood before him. Milos claimed that the presence of the chair struck awe into the hearts of those who came under the rule of the Obsidians, and that it was a symbol of inspiration to the troops under his command. Aren thought it simply demonstrated the arrogance of a man who preferred image over substance and truly believed there was no difference between the two.

The vision he presented now confirmed every opinion Aren had of the general. He sat wearing his "battle armor." The gardbraces mounted over the pauldrons on either shoulder were oversize and completely impractical, their sweeping points threatening to poke out the general's eye if he moved his head too quickly to either side. The ornate filigree on the breastplate, with the fanciful image of the head of a one-eyed dragon, shined even in the dim light within the tent. Every inch of the armor gleamed, and not a single scratch could be seen anywhere on its surface. His helmet, also forged to look like the head of the same one-eyed beast, sat on a stand to his right, which he had designed especially for the purpose. The black armor was framed by a luxurious crimson cape attached at his shoulders and flowing over the frame of the throne.

As for General Karpasic himself, he had a square face and, at first glance, no neck. He looked as though he were trying to pull his head back down between the shoulder gardbraces of his armor. His black hair he coifed back from the low slope of his extensive brow, and his dark beard and mustache were trimmed into a very controlled Vandyck-style. With small dark eyes and a playful smile he looked back at Aren, though Aren knew fully well how quickly that placid facade could be turned into tempestuous rage.

"Captain Bennis!" the general's voice boomed so everyone else in the tent could take notice that Aren had come at Karpasic's whim. "A triumph for the Obsidians once more! Have you brought us all news of our victory?"

Aren turned slightly, noticing that most of the command staff were standing near the sand table set up on the left side of the tent. Aren sighed inwardly. Schnell, Odman, Gerald, Gorn . . . each of them should have been at their commands at the front, maintaining control over their forces still assaulting the city. But instead they had all been summoned, just as he had been, to the general's tent.

At least Aren was pleased to see that Syenna was there as well. The Midmaer woman was tall and sharp featured, with almond-shaped eyes that seemed to take in the world at a glance. Her skin was deeply tanned. She wore leather breeches— much to the disapproval of the general—and dressed more like a man than the custom of the Midmaer region usually dictated. She had long, honey-colored hair, bleached nearly white by the sun, and it reached her waist in a tightly woven braid down her back. Syenna had been the scout for the army of the Westreach since they rescued her from the trade caravan in the western Grunvald. Much to Aren's delight, the woman proved to be not only familiar with the land but remarkably knowledgeable of the region's stories and people. She also was the one person in the entire force who would argue with him when she thought Aren was wrong.

And, thought the captain with a rueful smile, Syenna always thought Aren was wrong. Their arguments were the one pleasure with which Aren indulged himself. The captain nodded his acknowledgment to Syenna and accepted the slight dip of her chin in return.

"My lord general," Aren said, turning toward the throne and the occupant who demanded everyone's attention. "The legion under my command is engaged against the guardians of the city. We were breaking through the stockade battlement when the general summoned me here."

"Then our victory *is* complete!" the general insisted with a wave of his thick hand.

"No, sire, our victory is assured," the captain said, sighing. Aren played politics well, but it was not a game he enjoyed. "It is not yet complete. I must beg your leave to return to my command and oversee the general's full victory."

"Nonsense, Captain!" Karpasic chuckled as he waved a dismissive hand. "The priestess of Midras is dead, and the guardians of her order are all dead with her. The wall has fallen, and the deed is done. Now it is time we revel in the spoils of our triumph!"

"Sire, there are still significant pockets of resistance in the city." Aren knew it was probably a hopeless argument, but he had to try. "There are any number of places among both the newer buildings and the far more extensive ruins where smaller, independent pockets of Midras guardians could remain hidden."

"Insignificant rabble." Karpasic wrinkled his wide nose in disdain.

"The Guardians of Midras are a well trained and disciplined cadre of warriors devoted to their priestess and their city," Aren pressed on. "They are far more cunning and skilled than the general defenders of the city and will continue to be a source of danger to our occupation until we deal with them."

"They are defeated and dispirited rabble," the general said, and sniffed. "They are of no concern."

"Nevertheless, sire," Aren continued, "I would recommend that you permit me to organize a number of smaller units to methodically sweep through the city—"

"What are you doing, Bennis?" The general's demeanor had changed in an instant. He cast a baleful eye on the captain.

"Sire, I am trying to help you to victory in occupying the city of Midras. . . ."

"Are you deliberately trying to make me look bad?" Karpasic frowned.

"No, sire!"

"This isn't all about you, Captain!" the general spoke in low, pointed tones. His small eyes seemed almost feverish as they stared back at Aren. "Do you think the Obsidian Army of the Westreach has the luxury of waiting for you to 'sweep through' the city? There are objectives to be met! Schedules to maintain! The Masters of the Obsidian have expectations of us all, Captain, and they will *not* be disappointed!"

Aren held his silence. He knew better than anyone the expectations and objectives laid out by the Obsidians for General

Karpasic and his army. This tantrum had less to do with Aren and far more to do with the general himself. It was a tempest he had weathered before.

"Our victory *is* complete, Captain Bennis, because I declare it so!" The general was in full rage now. "These people are under the benevolent rule of the Obsidians as of this moment, and no one, not these barbarian guardians you are so afraid of, nor even my own quivering command staff will make it otherwise!"

"Yes, sire," Aren replied with all the self-control he could muster. "My apologies, sire. I should not have doubted you."

"Quite right, Bennis," the general replied. "Let that be a lesson to you all!"

Aren had to find a way out of the tent before his bile rose in his throat. "You summoned me, sire? To what purpose do you require my service?"

"Yes, well . . ." The general fumbled his words for a moment as he settled back into his throne. It came to him at last, and the thought of it made him smile. "As our victory *is* complete, I believe it would be in the best interest of our warriors for us to hold a March of Triumph!"

"A . . . parade, sire?"

"No, Bennis, not a 'parade,'" the general repeated. "A March of Triumph. We will march our triumphant army in formation down the widest street of Midras so its inhabitants can fully understand the might and glory of those who have liberated them from their oppressive priestess and her false teachings. It will also lift the spirits of our warriors to hear the accolades of freed citizenry. What do you think of that, Bennis?"

"As thoughtful and brilliant a plan as you have ever made, sire," Aren forced himself to say with a straight face.

"I'm glad you see it my way." The general smiled again. "You are to go out at once and find a suitable street for this celebration within Midras, and then report back here to me so we can plan the elements that will make up the celebration of my victory."

"But my command is still engaged in breaching the northern wall of the city," Bennis said. "Perhaps Captain Schnell is more suited at this moment to—"

"Am I not clear, Captain?" Karpasic glowered. "I mean for this to happen now, and I mean for you to do it. Your little monsters and men will manage without you."

Aren drew in another breath to respond but decided against it. Instead he asked, "May I have the assistance of Syenna? She may be helpful in discovering the most advantageous place for the general's processional."

"Syenna again, eh?" The general cast a leering gaze toward the tall woman. "You seem to require her skills more often of late, but I could hardly deny you the use of her. Just don't get lost for too long among the ruins, Captain. I'll want your report back here within the next two hours. . . . A most detailed report, understand?"

"Yes, sire." Aren glanced at Syenna. "Then, as time is pressing, may we have your leave to go now, sire?"

"Yes," Karpasic replied with a casual, dismissive wave. "Find a proper setting for our triumphant march, Captain. Our warriors deserve it."

Aren turned, hoping Syenna was at his heels.

He could not leave the tent quickly enough.

CHAPTER 2

Ruin

A beautiful day for a walk, isn't it?" Aren said in a casual, if hushed, tone. He crouched slightly as he moved.

Syenna spared only a short, humorless laugh at the captain's joke. "If death's specter is to your liking, then yes, this could qualify as a beautiful day."

The two of them moved with measured steps down the remains of the city's main thoroughfare. Behind them, one side of the main gate was all that remained standing. Every other part of the city wall that once supported it was now thrown down. The smoke from the smoldering remains of a row of buildings on their right drifted across their path, making it difficult to see much farther in front of them. The abandoned shells of buildings looked silently down on them from either side of the road. At their feet, shattered stone and splintered wood were mixed with broken limbs. Stilled bodies occasionally stared back at them through sightless eyes. The main assault force had broken through here, and the extent of their brutality had been unchecked. The warriors had surged into the city like a tide, sweeping away anything in their path. Now the western part of the city was an abandoned landscape, its buildings empty of the living, and its rubble-strewn streets and alleys still.

Disquietingly still, Aren thought as he picked his way down the wide avenue. *Keep talking, and you won't have to think.*

"Have you ever noticed how our enemies bleed the same color as our allies?" Syenna said as they passed another in a seemingly endless succession of crimson that stained the white cobblestones on the ground beneath their feet. The towering column of smoke from the barracks fire to the south still cast a shadow over the city's remains.

"All the more reason they should be part of the Obsidian Light," Aren said. "That's what we bring to these squabbling, selfish, and disorganized tyrants in their petty little city-states: an efficiency, unity, and purpose they could never attain on their own. The price is paid in the lives taken on both sides— but how many more lives do we save, and how much more suffering do we relieve once these people are brought under Imperial Law? We silence the shouting chaos of dissent with order. That's a proper peace."

"I would agree that you have brought silence." Syenna paused and looked around at the deathly stillness of the abandoned and smashed buildings around her. "I doubt the dead would be grateful to the Obsidians for quieting so completely their voices."

"The dead no longer care. Believe me, I've tried talking to

them," the captain said as he stopped and then dropped down to one knee. At Aren's feet before him were a pair of dead combatants, one clothed in the dark robes of the Midras Guardians, and the other in the armor of an Obsidian warrior. Each had died still locked in grip of their struggle against each other. Aren gestured at the two of them with the tip of his drawn sword. "Both of these men fought for something they believed in. Whether it was for or against some cause is not what impresses me."

"What does impress you?" Syenna asked as her eyes searched the deep shadows beyond the shattered windows.

"That they valued their lives less than their duty to that cause for which they fought," Aren replied. "That is something I can honor. That their cause happened to be in conflict with each other does not lessen the value of their lives, or the sacrifice they made for it. It was the price of their honor that both of them paid. And, on balance, it always ends up that one side pays more than the other in war. Our cause has paid less and won more. What I believe is that both of these men paid that highest price of all so the world might be a better place for them having been here."

"You presume to speak for them, then?" Syenna asked.

"I presume to live for what makes sense of their deaths." The captain stood up and stepped over the bodies with a long, careful stride. "Not that it matters to them any longer."

They followed the road toward the center of Midras. The newer structures gave way to the more ancient ruins near the center of the city. They came to where the avenue ended in a circular plaza in the center of the town. Here it was evident by the carnage that the fighting had been the most intense. On the east side of the plaza, an enormous tree rose up out of the ground. It had once been part of a small garden in front of the doors entering the ancient temple. Now the gates into the ruins were missing, and the tree had overgrown the garden. Its thick roots had broken up the paving stones and cracked an ancient wall behind it. Broken scaffolding was strewn about where the recent attempts at restoring the walls and towers had fallen once more to the ground.

Syenna followed Aren into the shadow beneath the wide-spreading branches of the tree.

"The road is ruined," Syenna commented as they quietly surveyed the streets leading to the north and south.

"But with an organized effort, that western avenue may be suitable enough for the general's parade," Aren observed as he sat down at the base of the tree. The silence was getting to him as well. "How long ago were these cobblestones put down, do you suppose?"

"They predate the Fall," Syenna said with solemnity. "Avatars may have walked these paths."

Aren chuckled.

"Do you doubt it?" Syenna glared at him.

"That there were Avatars or that they walked this road?"

"You choose."

"Then both, actually." Aren's smile was all indulgence. "Myths to frighten small children into obedience . . . and to make sense of the Fall to equally bewildered adults."

"The Avatars brought us purpose and a better way!" Syenna stated with unquestioning belief. "They brought us the Virtues!"

"For all the good it did them . . . or us." Aren chuckled,

shaking his head. "These legendary Virtues didn't prevent the Fall and, for all we know, they may have caused it. And what are these great, vaunted 'Virtues' anyway? Everyone likes to talk about them, but no one seems to remember exactly what these Virtues were supposed to be."

"They were lost to us in the Fall," Syenna said with conviction.

"A rather convenient loss," Aren said. Something down the western street caught his eye, a flash of light on polished metal. "And why is it that those who *do* remember them only remember Virtues that profit them? If they don't know a Virtue off which they can make money, then they seem perfectly willing to make up a suitable one that can. Our hope doesn't lie in the failed past, Syenna. . . . It lies in the future of one voice, one truth, one thought, one purpose, and one destiny: that is us. Our destiny is the only one that counts."

"Because you bring order to the world?" Syenna asked.

"Because we bring order to the world." Aren nodded.

"This city brought order to the Midmaer Plain. It brought your straight lines, order, and purpose," Syenna observed with a toss of her head toward the ruins. Then she put her hand on the trunk of the tree. "Yet this tree still stands here, Captain, after all the battles raged around it. Its roots break up the stones. Its branches push over the walls. This tree and the trees from its seeds will be here long after the stones have been crushed into sand and the walls erased beneath the enduring force of its nature. This wild and natural thing will always defeat the order of these walls, Captain, given enough time."

"And yet our Obsidian sorcerers command nature itself," Aren countered. He was enjoying the challenge Syenna so often provided him. "They shape it to our will."

"Like the elves?" Syenna cast a cool, dark eye in the captain's direction. The lift of her brow indicated to him that she was fully engaged in their fencing words.

Aren scowled as he picked up a fragment of broken stone and tossed it casually across the plaza. "What about the elves?"

"Your Obsidian sorcerers used their powers to shape them from enslaved humans," Syenna said as she leaned down toward him in the shade of the tree. "They did the same to create the satyrs and the fauns. They have even unleashed magic to raise the dead from their graves. Who knows what they might try next? All of it done that they might more fully serve the cause of the Obsidian Light."

"What's your point?" Aren fixed his vision on the bright flashes of light he could see down the ruined roadway they had just passed over. It was getting closer.

"My question is whether they have souls," Syenna said.

"Souls?" Aren looked up in surprise.

"Yes, souls," Syenna reiterated.

"You're joking!"

"Is there something remaining in them that rebels against your control and your order," Syenna pressed on. "Do they have a will of nature that makes them want to *be* rather than simply *exist*? These monsters your empire is shaping with their magic may become something more than just animals in a harness to do your bidding. If they can *think,* then what happens when they start thinking for themselves? They might *think* they don't want to follow your straight lines. They might determine a 'greater good' of their own. Have you ever considered that—"

"Wait," Aren said, holding his palm up. He stood slowly, his eyes fixed down the road.

A lone warrior was approaching. He was clothed in the dark robe of a Midras Guardian. His hood was pushed back, revealing his shaved head. Aren knew from previous encounters that the tattooed sigils that began at the center of his forehead ran continuously to the back of his neck. They were supposed to delineate the miraculous capabilities granted to the individual Guardians by their priestess. The magic appeared to have failed this particular Guardian, as he was bleeding from a long gash at the side of his head, yet his ice-blue eyes remained fixed on Aren with a fanatic single-mindedness as he approached. His short sword bore similar markings to the tattoos down the blade. It flashed in the sunlight. The tip of it swung listlessly before the Guardian as he staggered toward the captain and his guide.

"What does he want?" Aren asked. "He's alone."

"Guardians are *never* alone," Syenna said under her breath. She reached a hand slowly across her body to wrap her long fingers around the hilt of her sword. "And they never come at you from the front."

Aren glanced around from where he stood by the tree.

He was startled to see a figure through the sundered temple gates.

There was a beauty about her despite the dark smudges on her skin and the haggard look to her face. She wore the tattered remains of a robe that showed her to have been a priestess of the lower ranks. Her dark hair was disheveled and in a hopeless tangle, but she carried herself with a clear, confident poise that beamed through her countenance despite her physical appearance. And there was a deep sadness about her too, which startled Aren. Her large, watery eyes looked back at Aren with a fixed, pleading gaze.

Aren watched as the woman shifted that gaze upward past where Aren stood. The strange priestess gave a start and then disappeared into the darkness of the ruins beyond the temple entrance.

Aren turned to follow the woman's gaze to the rooftops on the far side of the plaza. A crooked smile came to his lips. "I think we should be more concerned with what's at our rear. We might consider a hasty offering in their temple."

Syenna drew in a breath, her grip tightening on her sword. "Must you always offend local customs everywhere you go?"

"Only the ones I don't know about," Aren said. "Ready?"

"Yes."

"*Now!*"

Aren and Syenna turned as one, dashing past the tree toward the broken doors of the temple beyond. Aren had taken only three steps before he heard the whistling behind him. He dug in his booted heels and turned his shoulder into Syenna's body, halting her flight.

A dozen arrows stabbed the ground in front of them, forming a curved pattern before the temple doors.

"Go! Go now!" Aren propelled Syenna ahead of him. The shafts of the arrows splintered under their boots as they rushed through the missing doors. Aren had already drawn his sword as he passed into the ruins of the temple.

The hooting calls of the Guardians followed them as they plunged into the shadows of the hallway. Aren had once heard a pack of wolves on the Midmaer Plain as they pursued their prey. The sound of the Guardians was entirely too similar.

The ceiling overhead had collapsed in places, allowing sparse sunlight, filtered through the ruins above them, to fall into the hallway. The hall ended in an empty alcove with branching hallways to either side. Syenna slid to a halt at the alcove, Aren nearly running into her from behind.

"Which way?" Syenna demanded.

The priestess glanced back at Aren from the end of the left hall, vanishing from view as she fled.

"She's gone this way!" Aren called to Syenna.

"Who?" Syenna called back.

Aren was already running down the hall toward where he had just seen the priestess. She would know her way around these ruins, he thought. She knows the way out.

Aren could feel Syenna at his heels as he burst into the large open space. He could only guess at its function. It was several stories high, and its roof was missing entirely. Two galleries ran around the second- and third-floor spaces circling the room, each choked with vines that wound around the pillars of the colonnade.

The dark robed forms of several Guardians ran along both galleries overhead, searching for a way down to their prey. One of them stopped, pulling a bow from off his shoulder.

Aren glimpsed a flash of priestess robe in the dark archway to his right.

"That way!" he yelled, shoving Syenna toward the arch.

Again he plunged into the darkness after her. Syenna cried out. Aren heard the cacophony of her armor and weapons crashing ahead of him, and in moments he nearly fell himself as the hall suddenly ended in a steep, downward stair. He descended in quick steps.

"Are you all right?" he called, his eyes quickly becoming

accustomed to the reduced light. There were fewer breaks in the ceiling here, making the available light sparse.

"Yes," Syenna called back to him from below. "But I think I've broken my pride."

"Well, at least it's something easily repaired," Aren replied. The calls of the Guardians sounded closer and louder in his ears. "Keep moving!"

Syenna was running in front of him. "There's more light ahead."

They passed into a small circular chamber. The room was nearly thirty feet high, with a domed ceiling. Part of the dome had collapsed, allowing light filtered through leaves of vines and trees to spill into the room.

"The Guardians!" Syenna said in hushed tones.

"I know," Aren whispered into the sudden silence. "Their calls have stopped."

A second archway opened on the far side of the circular room. Syenna stepped through it, Aren right behind her.

He reacted instinctively to the motion to his left.

Aren's blade rose, parrying the blow from the Guardian lurking at the side of the arch. Aren stepped back and then quickly thrust in riposte. He felt the blade slide along the Guardian's armor and under his robes, but he followed up with his armored left glove to the Guardian's face.

A quick glance revealed Syenna in a similarly desperate battle with a second Guardian. She had managed to draw both her sword and main gauche dagger. The dagger had trapped the Guardian's blade as she slashed at him with her sword.

The Guardian before Aren staggered back against the ancient wall. The unstable structure shifted behind him, a number of remaining tiles tumbling down from the groaning ceiling overhead.

The Guardian tried to push away from the wall, but Aren kicked him hard in the chest, sending the man once again to stagger backward, shifting the wall stones even farther.

Syenna's main gauche was still locked with the second Guardian's blade. She twisted him around, her own back now to the opposite wall.

Aren could hear shouts of more Guardians approaching from the plaza beyond the entrance. He reached for the Guardian wrestling with Syenna and, gripping him with both hands, pulled him backward and away from his guide. Aren then threw him with all his strength across the narrow hallway and into the body of the first Guardian still struggling to regain his balance.

Aren reached out, gripping Syenna's wrist as he plunged farther into the hall.

The weight of the two Guardians fell a third time against the wall. It gave way, the stones bowing out and then collapsing completely. The ceiling overhead cascaded downward, crushing and choking the entrance.

Aren continued to run down the corridor, Syenna's wrist firmly in his grip. Faint light shone in shafts from the breaks in the ruins above them, bleeding into the hall where they were now being choked with dust.

The rumble of the collapsing ruin walls continued to be heard down the corridor from which they had just come.

"Now, that wasn't so bad, was it?" Aren laughed.

"It wasn't so good either, Captain." Syenna coughed. "I don't think they were out to kill us. . . . I think they wanted to take you prisoner."

"Well, I'd rather they didn't. Who would find a route for the general's parade if they did?" Aren smiled. The rumbling down the hall increased. "All we have to do now is circle around through these ruins and . . ."

The hall suddenly shook.

The stones beneath their feet gave way.

They were falling into darkness.

CHAPTER 3

The Blade

Aren rolled over with a groan as much born of anger as of pain. He lay on his back for a moment, the broken stones under him pressing uncomfortably into his back despite the armor. He felt the warm wetness of his own blood on the side of his head. Nevertheless, he held still. He felt disoriented from the unexpected plunge through the weakened floor. The drop felt like an eternity, and he had no idea how far he had fallen.

His eyes were adjusting to the darkness. The filtered daylight of the ruins was bright compared to this subterranean night, yet the darkness was not complete. There was some light here, and Aren was already beginning to distinguish shapes emerging from the shadows that surrounded him.

Strategy depends on knowledge, he thought. *A wise man*

waits; only a fool rushes into what he doesn't understand. He lay quietly for a moment, taking in his surroundings.

The faint glow from a series of globes gave scarce illumination to the ancient chamber around him. Each sphere had been mounted in ornamental frameworks on a series of columns that supported the dome of the ceiling. This vague light was further obscured under a layer of rust-colored dust. Still, it was enough; he could soon make out the extents of what had been an oval-shaped chamber beneath the ancient ruins. Almost directly above him, part of the dome had buckled downward, breaking through an upper gallery that looked down into the chamber. Debris from the collapse had fallen into a slanting pile. Aren, in turn, had fallen down the face of this debris and come to a halt on its slopes a few feet above the floor.

A massive, dark shape sat atop a dais of concentric steps in the center of the room, but Aren was still having trouble making it out. He listened for the sounds of pursuit but was greeted only with silence. Satisfied, he slowly sat up.

"Are you all right?" Syenna said in a hushed tone. She stood, leaning against a pillar near the base of the debris from the collapse. Her right hand was clutched over a wound on her left forearm.

"Yes, I believe I am," Aren replied, keeping his voice low. Just because he could not hear his enemy did not necessarily mean they were not listening. "And you?"

"Well enough, although I would prefer to be somewhere else," she replied. There was something odd in her voice, something Aren had not heard before.

"Why?" Aren asked as he stood up, checking his armor and

sword more out of habit than need. "Once you've seen one ruin you've pretty well seen—"

"Because it's a tomb," Syenna said, her voice sounding suddenly dry.

Aren was seeing much better now under dull light from the wall globes. The object in the center of the room was an enormous stone sarcophagus of dark granite inlaid with gold, jade, and cut gems. The massive lid had been shifted off the stone box, lying across the stone stairs next to it. There appeared to be some sort of ornate figure carved into the lid.

"So it's a tomb." Aren shrugged. "You once told me that before the Fall such things were common."

"Not like this," Syenna answered. There was a quaver in her voice. Aren had never known her to be the least bit hesitant or concerned when death was on the line in battle and was surprised by her sudden nerves. She pointed at the base of the sarcophagus box. "This is different. The symbols are . . . Just look at the symbols."

Aren stepped cautiously toward the stone box atop the raised dais, peering at its base. A large symbol was inlaid into the base of the sarcophagus. Three curved blades were intertwined as though delineating three linked circles. The grips and guards formed a triangle in the center of the symbol that surrounded a large, clear gemstone. Six additional gemstones—each of a different color—were fixed about the sword hilts, forming the outline of a bowed triangle.

Aren placed his foot on the bottom step of the dais.

"Captain, please!" Syenna pleaded. "Stop!"

Aren froze. "Syenna? What is it?"

"Stay away from the crypt, sire!"

"Why? What's wrong?"

"Look around you," Syenna said breathlessly. "That symbol . . . it's everywhere!"

Aren turned. The columns and the curved walls behind them were all carved in ancient runes mixed with hieroglyphics—but each prominently displayed a carved rendition of this same three-bladed symbol. Aren could also see now that there were three doors exiting the lower level of the chamber, each of which was sealed closed under this same sign.

"It means someone really liked curved swords." Aren shrugged.

"No, Captain." Syenna swallowed hard. She was having trouble speaking. "I've never actually seen this symbol before, but there are warnings about it in a number of ancient texts and a pair of songs sung by bards in the Drachvald. Warnings about this symbol are found in most of the tribes of the Midmaer and the coasts of the Bay of Storms. It's one of the lost symbols, coming into use just before the Fall, and some say that it *caused* the Fall—"

"Enough, Syenna," Aren cut her off. "It's a symbol . . . a symbol of what?"

"The Avatars," Syenna said, seeming to breathe out the words.

"Avatars?" Aren smiled. "You're saying this is an Avatar's tomb?"

Syenna only managed to nod, her eyes wide.

"It seems like someone went to a lot of trouble and expense for this Avatar." Aren chuckled. He turned back toward the dais, stepping up the stairs to the edge of the sarcophagus. "The least we could do is pay our respects."

Aren peered down into the open stone box. His eyes narrowed as he tried to penetrate the darkness within. He frowned with momentary frustration and then suddenly reached down into the coffin, feeling about its interior.

"Captain! No!" Syenna gasped.

"Huh!" Aren straightened back up, his fists set on his hips. "Empty! Well, if your Avatar was ever here, he didn't have the good manners to wait for us to pay him a visit. More likely tomb robbers decided to liberate both him and any of his wealth that happened to be buried with . . ."

Something next to his feet caught his attention.

"Captain?" Syenna took a hesitant step forward. "What is it?"

The lid of the sarcophagus rested on the stairs next to Aren. Beneath a thin layer of dust, the top of the stone slab was intricately carved into what he presumed was a life-size relief depicting the personage who was supposed to have occupied the crypt. It was the figure of a man in a full suit of armor lying on a bed of beautifully carved flowers. The armor was unlike any that the captain had seen before. There was elegance to the bands of overlapping plating that was both functional and handsome at once. The head was compelling, with an exquisitely depicted goatee beard and mustache—both carefully trimmed—and a single, narrow braid of the figure's hair extending from the back of its neck down onto the left side of the breastplate. There the braid ended, where was carved another of the tri-bladed symbols that everywhere ornamented the crypt chamber.

But it was what was under the grip of the carved hands resting at the base of the carving's breast that drew Aren's immediate attention.

It was a magnificent longsword.

It gleamed in the faint light. No dust had touched its blade nor had any corruption of rust tarnished its surface. The fuller channel of the blade had intricate runes etched into the polished surface of the metal, though in this light he could barely make them out. They vaguely reminded Aren of the runes on the blades of the Guardians' swords, and he wondered for a moment if this was where the priestess got the idea from in the first place. The cruciform guard was pitched forward so as to capture any strike and direct it into the shoulder at the base of the blade. The grip looked old, and yet the leather was still supple and intact. The circular pommel at the base of the grip was larger than more recent custom would dictate, the disk of which was inscribed with the same three-bladed symbol, etched there in black.

Aren smiled. The sword was a delightful puzzle of contradictions: shining as though new and yet obviously of ancient make. Found in a tomb sealed beyond the memory of men, and yet its blade still displayed a keen edge. It was entirely consistent and completely out of place all at the same time.

He reached down for the sword.

"*No!*" Syenna cried out.

Aren hesitated.

"Don't touch it!" Syenna's words were a rushed warning. "It's an Avatar blade!"

"So?" Aren was becoming annoyed with Syenna's superstitious nonsense. "This dreaded Avatar obviously isn't at home, and I don't suspect he'll be coming back for it anytime soon."

"The Avatar may not be here, but his weapon may still be cursed," Syenna said, swallowing hard as she took another hesitant step toward the dais. "Avatar blades are legendary, and each legend speaks of a curse associated with the weapon. The symbols in this room are certainly related to the ancient Avatars. But I've never seen this particular symbol before, so I cannot tell you what form the curse will take! The carving on the lid of the coffin might animate and take its revenge on you . . . or you might turn to stone for touching it . . . or any of a thousand other dreadful things we cannot even imagine! Before we even think about touching this terrible artifact, we need to examine the writings on the walls, understand the dangers it presents to us and . . ."

Aren cleared his throat, reached down, and wrapped his hand around the sword's grip.

"Captain!" Syenna drew in a deep breath. Her words fell to a whisper that carried through the empty tomb. "Don't pull on it! If the blade is fused to the stone, it could trigger . . ."

The blade slid easily from the stone grasp of the knight carved into the crypt's lid. It rang slightly as Aren held it up in front of him.

A wave of dizziness passed over Aren as he stood up. For a moment he wondered if the blade did, indeed, carry a curse. He felt suddenly aware of himself and his surroundings as though the world had turned under his feet, and he alone had remained standing still. The feeling passed almost at once, however, and Aren silently chided himself for mistaking standing up too quickly after hitting his head on the rocks for some ancient Avatar curse.

"It's very cooperative for being cursed," Aren said dryly. He looked down the length of the blade and smiled. The edge was unerringly straight. He swung the blade with his wrist, carving circles in the air on either side of him, and then stopped, admiring the blade once more. "It is remarkably balanced— almost effortless. There's weight to the blade, too, but you don't seem to feel it in hand. Wait. That's odd."

Aren gazed curiously down on the blade as he held the grip of the sword in his right hand and gingerly cradled the blade in front of him with the palm of his left. The captain turned the blade over in his hands, examining both sides with intense interest.

"What is it?" Syenna asked with dread even as she crossed quickly to where Aren stood.

The runes on both sides of the blade now glowed with an intense purple hue that Aren found difficult to focus on. Stranger still, the runes appeared to shift before his eyes, twisting and settling into new shapes as he watched, only to shift and change again a few moments later.

"Can you read these?" Aren asked, turning the blade over once again for Syenna to examine.

"No," Syenna replied almost at once. "I can hardly look at them as it is. Captain, please, put this sword back where you found it. Leave it. It's magical in ways we don't understand; it's cursed from before the Fall by Avatars and far more powerful than we are and—"

"And it is *mine*," Aren finished for her with delight as he smiled down on the blade once again. "What's more, I think this would be a rather fitting tribute to feature in this ridiculous parade we're arranging for our lusterless General Karpasic. A captured blade of an Avatar! What more fitting symbol of our triumph?"

"I agree it would be a symbol," Syenna said, her own gaze

fixed on the shifting runes of the blade. "Of what, we do not yet know."

"Then by all means, let us get out before the Guardians figure out a way to make this tomb our own," Aren said. "Look! That archway over there on the other side of the crypt. The seal is broken, and it looks to be slightly ajar."

"Strange neither of us noticed that before," Syenna said in dry tones. "Conveniently miraculous, isn't it?"

"I'll take the convenience," Aren said as he looked down once more at the blade. "The miraculous, I'll leave up to you."

Their eyes drawn once again to the glowing runes, neither Aren nor Syenna noticed that one of the blades etched in the pommel of the sword had changed from black to bright silver.

CHAPTER
4

Messages

"Captain Bennis!"

Aren awoke with a start, sliding his feet over the edge of the cot and coming to sit in the familiar gloom of his tent. He'd awoken at once, though he now noted he was feeling a few aches and pains that were unfamiliar to him. He still wore the tunic and the breeches from the previous day. He reached for his nearby boots, dragging them on even as he spoke.

"I am here," he called out, his voice still a little hoarse. "What is it?"

"General Karpasic requests that you come at once!"

The captain stopped what he was doing immediately, dropping the second boot and then running his hand back through his untamed hair. The cascade of actual emergencies that had suddenly flooded into his mind along with each of their dire and immediate responses fled from him. "And did the general say what it was he wanted?"

"He . . . He would like to inquire as to just how soon the March of Triumph might begin." The voice from beyond the tent flap was young and high-pitched. Aren felt some sympathy for the young warrior. Few soldiers in the army of conquest received a message from the general with politeness.

"The March of Triumph?" Bennis shook his head in disbelief. "Is the general in some particular hurry?"

"The general has received orders from the Obsidians," came the muffled voice beyond the canvas of the tent. "We are to leave a garrison force, but the bulk of the army is to strike the encampment and prepare to march."

"So the general has received orders to move the army, but he still insists on having his parade," Bennis muttered, shaking his head once again. He raised his voice slightly so the messenger could hear him clearly. "Please inform the general that I will report to him shortly."

"Yes, sir! And . . . Er . . ."

"What is it, boy?" Aren could hear the hesitance in the voice outside.

"The general asks that you bring the tribute you discovered in the ruins yesterday," the warrior said, tripping over his words.

Aren sat up straight on the edge of his cot. His eyes moved to the sword, which still rested on the folded blanket next to his cot where he had laid it the previous night. Even in the dim light of the tent, it was a truly beautiful and remarkable weapon, a true prize. In all the sieges and conquests in which he had participated and, by and large, commanded personally to victory, this was the one treasure he had wanted to keep. Aren sighed. He supposed it was inevitable. Word of such a prize would, no doubt, have spread like a grass fire throughout the encampment.

"Please convey to the general my compliments," Aren forced himself to say, "and tell him that both my prize and I will attend him shortly."

Aren sat still for a few moments, listening to make sure the messenger had moved safely away. Satisfied, he reached for his second boot and pulled it quickly on. He stood up painfully, stretching to work out the aches in his muscles from the battles of the previous day. Combat with any sword was strenuous work. No matter how strong the arm or how experienced the warrior, there were only so many blows you could swing before your arm got tired and your mistakes became more frequent. Yesterday had been one of those days when his limits had been tested, and he was feeling the effects of it.

Aren cast his gaze about him. His war chest lay to one side, containing some extra pieces of miscellaneous armor, a few of his personal weapons, and such miscellaneous tools and supplies as he had managed to acquire for himself along the road. Next to it stood his battle armor, held erect on a framework. Aren took a moment to critically eye the damage to the suit, making a mental note to see the armor smithy later in the day. He knew General Karpasic would expect him to wear it in his presence, but for the moment he was loath to put it on. There was a pair of campaign flags that hung down from cross poles on the other side of the tent. The saddle and bridle for his horse lay atop a pile of canvas sacks, one of which lay open, spilling out a dirty pair of his hose and his stained cloak.

Aren began to whistle. It was a low, quiet tune with an unusual rhythm. Five notes, then three and three again. Aren leaned forward, placing his palms on his knees as he continued to whistle louder this time. Five notes, then three and three again.

He heard a high-pitched scree.

"Monk!" Aren said sotto voce. "Come out now. I've a job for you."

Nothing moved in the tent.

Aren repeated eleven notes once again. He heard the scree once more.

Aren kept his eye on the bag of clothes beneath the saddle. "I've no time for this nonsense, Monk. Come now!"

The dirty clothing shifted slightly. Aren could see the small, dark face peering back at him from under the folds. Its features looked more like shadows; the crest of its head obviously bore a crest of horns. The eyes were like burning coals.

"Come here, Monk," Aren urged, his fingers motioning the creature toward him. "I think it's time you and I had a little chat."

The homunculus glanced furtively about and then, satisfied, it leaped out of the cloth, spreading its leathery wings as it rushed toward the captain. Its span was barely two feet across, while its body, not counting its whipping barbed tail, did not measure more than a hand and a half in length. Its skin had a quality that was difficult to look at, as though focusing upon it would be arduous if not entirely impossible. It had something of a pushed-in snout, with two pairs of opposing fangs protruding from its lips. The palms of its hands were long, as were the soles of its feet, with talons protruding from its fingers and toes.

Aren had long ago learned the hard way the importance of keeping those trimmed.

Aren held his forearm in front of him, providing the homunculus a perch on which to land. As the creature settled on his arm, Aren reached forward with his right hand and rubbed it under its chin. The homunculus responded with a deep, satisfied rumble from its chest.

"Monk, my old friend," Aren said, and sighed. "It is time to pack our gear once again. See to it that all this is packed up, won't you? Oh, and settle my debts for me and saddle my horse."

The glowing, red pinpoints of light ablaze like glowing embers stared back at Aren without comprehension.

"No? Well, sometimes I wonder why I keep you around," Aren chided. "Perhaps, because you are such a sparkling conversationalist."

The homunculus blinked.

"Well, you are good listener, at any rate." Aren shrugged. He gave a slight lift of his arm, and the homunculus took flight once again, perching on the crossbar of one of the pennants. Aren looked over at the armor once more and, with another shrug, efficiently began securing the various pieces around him. "No, don't worry about me. It is all for the good of the Obsidian Empire, is it not? I'm just a captain—relatively unimportant in the scope of things, and quite frankly, I prefer to leave it that way. I have a job to do, and all I really want is for people to get out of my way and let me do it."

Aren snatched the helmet from the top of the frame and then paused. He turned and looked down upon the blade still cradled in the blanket.

The captain reached down, wrapping his fingers around the

grip. He lifted the sword up in front of his face, examining the shifting runes in the fuller of the blade. As he did so, he was suddenly struck with the tawdriness of his possessions, for compared to the sword in his hand, everything else he owned seemed cheap and pitiful.

"And what about you, my new friend?" Aren whispered to the blade. "Are you also a good listener, or are you trying to tell me something? Sadly, I don't think I'll have the time to find out."

Aren slid the blade into the scabbard at his waist. It had originally been made for a much larger sword, and the blade rattled slightly as he moved. The captain stepped forward and pushed aside the tent flap with the back of his hand.

The homunculus watched Aren leave, a shadow within the shadows.

† † †

The captain had originally looked for the general in his accustomed command tent, only to find it had already been struck and was being loaded into supply wagons for transport. It had taken him nearly half an hour to find General Karpasic, who had already situated himself and most of the army at the western gates of the city. It was fortunate, Aren mused, that he had left orders with Halik the night before to properly apportion garrison troops about the city and secure the avenue for the March of Triumph before morning.

"Captain Bennis!"

Aren turned toward the all-too-familiar voice, composing a blank look on his face as he did so. He had no problem communicating with the general, but it was never a good idea to let him know what he actually thought of him.

"Yes, General. How may I serve you?"

The general sat atop his throne once again, which in turn sat atop a litter being held aloft on the shoulders of a number of Midras merchants who had been pressed into the service. The clothing of each of these was relatively opulent and clean, considering the circumstances, but the men and women wearing them were bowed and miserable. Aren wondered in that moment whether their condition was affected more by the weight of the unreasonably large chair, its occupant, or the defeat their city had just suffered. Their condition was not helped in the least by the general's insistence that he remain held aloft despite the delay in beginning the procession.

Worse, clouds had formed above the city and now stretched to the distant horizons. These wept rain down on Midras. It was a miserable drizzle; too persistent to be ignored, yet too light to either cleanse the streets of the stench or hide from the eyes the wreckage that once was Midras. Everyone, it seemed, was miserable with the possible exception of the general, who seemed to take the weather as a personal insult.

"What is the delay now, Captain?" The general snapped from his perch. His cape, which was meant to be billowing behind him during the parade, was now soaked and hung with a leaden quality off his back. "Why are we not moving?"

"It has taken some time to properly assemble the citizens of the city," Aren answered, "as per your orders, sire. I am awaiting Halik's word that the street has been properly cleared. Once he is returned, then we may proceed."

"And why is my person being borne through the streets by the shopkeepers?" the general demanded. "I thought I made it clear that I wanted to be carried on the backs of Guardians."

"Sire, such was the determination of the Guardians that there were not enough remaining to properly man the litter," Aren responded with a slight bow, although he could feel both of his fists clench. "Those few Guardians who are in our custody would be a danger to yourself and, almost certainly, make unfortunate ruin of this procession."

"They would have looked spectacular," grumbled the general.

"They would have slain you in front of the remaining citizens of Midras," responded Aren, keeping his vocal tones even as he bowed slightly. "This would not support the message of strength you are trying to convey. Now, if you'll excuse me . . ."

Aren turned to leave for the head of the procession.

"One more thing, Captain . . ."

Aren stopped in his tracks, clenched his teeth, and turned once more. "Yes, sire."

"I hear you found something of a treasure," said General Karpasic, his face splitting into a knowing grin.

Halik, Aren thought. *He must have been bragging about it to the general staff.* "Hardly a treasure, sire. Just an old sword buried in the ruins."

"Nevertheless, I think it would do nicely as a symbol." The general grinned back at him, and leaned over the left side of his chair, causing the merchants on that side to groan under the added weight. The general reached across himself, his right arm and hand extended toward the captain. "It will show the people of Midras that their power is now our power. I shall bear it down the street so everyone may see the tribute they have given to the Obsidian Empire."

Aren drew in a breath, hesitating.

"The sword, Captain," General Karpasic insisted, the fingers of his right hand urging Aren's compliance. "For the greater good."

Aren permitted himself a slight sigh and then reached for the hilt of the sword. It slid out of the scabbard with a bright ringing sound.

Aren's eyes were drawn to the merchants supporting the litter. There were eight of them on either side, each of them doing their best to support the weight of the general, his armor, and his opulent chair. It was for Aren as though he had seen them for the first time even though he recalled choosing them himself only the evening before. All of them were men from the city's major trade houses, but now he remembered each of them in turn. The tall one in the front with the long, clean-shaven face but eyes that still burned with defiance. He was a textile merchant who had also been a member of the priestess's closest circle of advisers. His lower lip trembled with humiliation, his eyes were fixed forward, but his back was straight and unbowed. Behind him was a shorter man, soft and in poor health. He, too, came from a long-established family of Midras, although, Aren recalled, it was his wife who actually owned the cooperage. Aren, in his haste to organize the procession, had ordered the woman to be one of the litter bearers, but her husband—who by all appearances had never done a day's work in his life—had insisted he take her place and spare her the shame of it. Already the shorter man's arms were shaking from the burden but a satisfied smile played about his lips, welling up from some secret thought of his own.

In just a few days we have taken from these people what it took them a lifetime to build, Aren thought. *And still they stand, unbending before us.*

"Captain Bennis!" the general insisted.

Aren shook himself from his reverie and offered the weapon hilt first to the general.

A smug and victorious grin spread across the broad face of the general as his eyes took in the vision of the sword. He reached down again from atop the litter, causing even greater groans to come from the merchants. His broad hand wrapped around the grip. Aren took a step back.

The general lifted the blade up in front of him, eyeing the weapon with open avarice.

Then, in an instant, the general's face transformed into a look of abject terror. Karpasic stood suddenly on the platform of the litter, suspended between the two long poles. The merchants staggered under the suddenly shifting weight, struggling to keep their feet under them.

General Karpasic shook visibly as he gaped about him, his face a reflection of horror. He gripped the sword so tightly, the blood appeared to have drained from his fingers. His mouth opened and closed as though he were a fish suddenly pulled from the stream. Sounds and words began to form, low at first, but soon rising in fear. "No . . . You can't . . . You can't look at me that way! I *order* you to stop looking at me that way! *I'm* in command! I'm the one you have to respect! You think I'm weak. . . . You think you can take my place and no one would care one way or the other. . . . Because . . . Because . . ."

Karpasic realized he was still holding the sword. His eyes shot to look at it as though he were holding his own death in his hand.

General Karpasic flung the sword away from him and fell back into the chair. The merchants again struggled to steady the weight on their shoulders as the sword tumbled through the air and fell with a dull thud into the mud of the road.

For a moment the only sound was the patter of the rain.

Aren quickly stepped over to where the sword lay, snatching it out of the mud.

"You did this!" the general screamed.

Aren turned toward the sound.

The general lay slouched back in his chair, his breastplate rising and falling rapidly with his quick breaths. His thick finger pointed back at Aren in accusation.

"You . . . You deliberately set out to embarrass me!" Karpasic snarled. "I've known it all along. You've been jealous of me and my position from the very start! Well, it will do you no good, Captain Bennis, and I don't care how many friends you have among the Obsidian sorcerers. No doubt they helped to conjure up this cursed sword as some sort of vicious joke, but no one is laughing, Captain Bennis!"

"Sire!" Aren protested. "I swear to you I didn't—"

"I won't hear it!" The general was in a full rage now. "You're a fine enough officer, but you need to learn your place. You are my subordinate in every way, and until you learn that, you are relieved of your combat command. Go back to the encampment and take charge of the supply caravans. Maybe if you follow my army long enough, Captain, I may let you lead some of it again."

Aren drew in a deep, calming breath before he responded. "As you will, sire."

"Yes, as I will," the general hissed.

† † †

It was a long walk back to the encampment from the city gates. Aren heard the drums of the March of Triumph diminishing behind him, but with every step, he grew firm in his resolve as to what he must do. Each footfall brought with it the faces of the merchants, the faces of the crowds dragged forth to give their heartless cheers, the faces of his own warriors far from their homes and struggling to find purpose in being there, and the face of the woman who led them into the ruins and to this strange and wondrous blade. And he saw the faces of the dead—especially the dead who had given their lives in exchange for . . . what? General Karpasic's parade?

Aren held his rage until he pushed through the folds of his tent. He had barely stepped inside before he turned and threw his helmet with such force, its spikes embedded themselves into the side of his wooden war chest. At once, he threw wide both arms, his fists clenched and shaking in the air as he threw his head back and roared against the world at large.

Aren closed his eyes and struggled to control his breathing. It took him a few minutes, but still, he knew what he had to do. It was essential he be calm. When at last he was ready, he opened his eyes and began to whistle.

A shadow shifted behind the cot.

"Well, Monk," Aren said evenly. "I have a little job for you."

The emberlike eyes peered back at him from behind the cot.

Aren whistled again, holding his left arm in front of him. The homunculus flapped its leathery wings and settled obediently on the captain's arm near his wrist. It faced the captain with its pointed ears swiveled forward in anticipation.

"Personal message to Obsidian Evard Dirae," said Aren, gazing into the eyes of the homunculus. "Our old friend, General

Karpasic, has relieved me of my command duties over the army and has decided to relegate me to the supply wagons at the end of the column. This after insisting on holding a March of Triumph celebrating his own immense self in a city that is not yet secure and, I believe, at the expense of our promptly following the orders conveyed to us from the Obsidian Brotherhood. All this was brought about because of a relic sword I discovered in the ruins of—"

The homunculus suddenly started screeching and beating its wings. Aren stopped speaking, and the creature calmed down almost at once.

"Damn, I'd forgotten how limited these things are." The captain sighed. He cleared his throat, determined to try again. "Personal message to Obsidian Evard Dirae. General Karpasic relieved me of combat command and is living up to our worst expectations. I am now in charge of supply caravans. This army would benefit from your guidance in person."

Aren paused for a moment. The message had conveyed everything he meant to say, but he felt there was enough room in the tiny brain of the homunculus to add a little more.

"Recovered an ancient blade from the ruins here—possibly Avatar in origin. Come soon."

As soon as Aren stopped speaking, the claws of the homunculus's feet began anxiously kneading the captain's forearm. Aren stepped outside the tent, and the small creature instantly spread its wings, pulling itself swiftly into the sky. Aren watched it for a minute as it disappeared to the east, then turned back into his tent to pack up his things.

CHAPTER 5

Dark Horizon

The last to leave Midras were the caravans and their escort warriors under Aren's command. The column of heavy wagons laden with food, equipment, tents, and all else needed to support the army wound northwest across the plains, the road running close beside the meandering course of the Shimano River. Before them always was the dust cloud raised by the bulk of General Karpasic's army with which they struggled to keep up. The dust would have been unbearably choking during the dry season, but the recent rains had dampened the ground before them and granted something of a reprieve to the teamsters at the end of the column. Behind them, the towering column of smoke from the still burning Midras continued to remind them of where they had been and what they had done.

Aren, astride his horse, found himself looking back often.

Of course, not everyone under Karpasic's command was leaving Midras. Nearly one out of five of their warriors had been left behind to garrison the city. The Guardians of the priestess had proven to be both resourceful and tenacious. While General Karpasic had declared Midras pacified, no one among the army's command staff, including the general, was so foolish as to believe it to be true. The city itself had been built upon the ruins of the previous city, and its roots were honeycombed with passages, chambers, and tunnels in which rebellion could fester and flourish. While they had dispatched many of the Guardians, there was no way of knowing for certain whether all them were dead.

And it was not just a question of keeping the priestess from retaking her own city. Weakening the defenses of Midras sufficiently enough so it could be taken by the Obsidian Army meant it was now ripe fruit to be picked by others as well. Midras had been the greatest city-state in the Midmaer region, far too strong to be challenged by any of the petty clans and kingdoms scattered across the plains. But now, having proven itself weak, it was subject to any number of jackals wishing to prey upon its carcass. Even Ardoris, the next great city-state to the southeast, might rouse itself for such a prize as Midras, its people emerging from where they cowered on the Perennial Coast. It would surprise no one if they were marching even now across the Brightbone Mountains and north along the upper Shimano River on the chance of "liberating" the city and nearly doubling their own landholdings in the process.

Aren reminded himself that far more than a quarter of the army was left behind. The siege of Midras had proven to be a difficult and more costly a task than Aren or any of his fellow commanders had thought. Nearly two in ten of his comrades in arms had bled their last drop of blood among the walls of Midras, and an equal number again were too wounded to continue traveling with the campaign.

Aren shook his head vigorously, trying to throw the thoughts away from him as a wet dog might throw water off its back.

The river twisted around the low set of grassy hills, turning slightly to the north. Trees lined the riverbank to his left, their leaves whispering with the wind along the river. The wagons had crowded into a single file as the road narrowed. Aren saw the trampled and shredded remnants of what had been tall grass that had swept down the embankment to the river's edge, and here and there a bright petal from the wildflowers that must've grown here before the army trampled them under its feet. Aren smiled slightly. It might have been a beautiful spot, he thought.

And, he realized, it would be again. Once the might and glory of their warriors had passed, once the drums had all been beaten and the sound of the trumpets had passed beyond the hills and memory, the grass would return. The flowers would take root again once the resolve of men had passed over them and would be gone and forgotten.

Aren smiled warmly at the thought. There was a triumph in patience that no temporary application of force could conquer.

And Aren was a patient man.

He was pulled from his reveries by unusual movement farther on in the column ahead of him. A rider was coming back down along the side of the road. Aren recognized the figure at once.

"Well, this is a good day," he said, chuckling to himself.

Syenna reined in her horse as she approached, swinging around to ride beside him. She waited for the captain to address her first, but all he did was whistle happily to himself. They both continued in this way for some time before Syenna decided she could speak.

"What *is* that tune you're whistling?" Syenna asked casually.

"Oh, just something I picked up in Grunvald," Aren replied. "You know, sometimes a tune just stays with you. You never know when it will come to cheer you up."

"And you need cheering up?"

"Hardly!" Aren grinned.

"Well, you are looking rather sad to me," she said, and chortled, examining him with a critical look. "I don't believe that a single piece of the armor you're wearing—what little there is of it—came from the same armor. And where did you get that lobster-tail helmet?"

"Do you like it?" The captain turned to look at her, a smug grin on his face. "Picked this up during the Drachvald campaign near Rhun. We had even captured the armorer who made it, so he put it back into pretty good shape, I think."

"It's hardly regulation for the Army of Obsidian Triumph," Syenna said with a raised eyebrow.

"Have you ever tried to wear one of those steam kettles while riding over a long stretch of road?" Aren shook his head. "They are beautiful, awe-inspiring statements of authority that chafe terribly after the first half hour on horseback. Their principal function on the road, so far as I can tell, is to draw about five pounds of sweat from its occupant and boil him in it at the same time. Don't get me wrong; I cherish my 'Armor of the Night . . .' So much so, I have it safely packed on that wagon over there so it will remain sufficiently clean and odor free for when I need it next."

"And are you expecting this look to get you back in Karpasic's good graces?" Syenna said with a barbed smile.

"My attire today is practical, functional, reasonable, and logical." Aren bowed slightly from the back of his horse. "None of those qualities either impress or apply to General Karpasic, as you well know."

"You shouldn't say things like that." Syenna looked away with a frown. "Someone who doesn't understand you the way I do might hear you."

"Captain! Here, Captain!" The shout came from the caravan just ahead of them. Aren spied a familiar wagon among them.

"Ah, my command skills are required." Aren urged his horse forward even as he beckoned Syenna to follow him. "Come on!"

They both drew up alongside the driver's bench of an enormous supply wagon.

"Jester!" Aren called out. "How are we doing?"

"How are we doing?" The man gripping the reins at the front of the large wagon scowled back at him. He was an enormous, broad-shouldered teamster who looked as though he might have loaded every wagon in the caravan himself. His wide, red face was framed in a bushy white beard that extended up over his ears and around his bald head. His name itself was something of a joke, as there was nothing jocular about the man. When he wasn't ranting of the other teamsters in the caravan, he was bemoaning the perpetually impending doom he believed with fanatic devotion was his unbending destiny. "How might we be doing on such a terrible day as this? I've had no word from my home since we crossed the Grunvald, and me leaving the wife with the grumble-wombles and all. Them healers in the Drachvald could manage it well enough, I'm thinking, but them Obsidians insist on doing the healing themselves. Even in service of the army, I can't be afford'n' no healing from an Obsidian."

"Grumble-wombles?" Syenna asked.

"A mysterious malady that, I understand, is only suffered by Master Jester's wife," Aren answered with a nod, and then turned back to the teamster. "What do you need, Jester?"

"It's that Murdoch! He's driving that team of his too close behind me," Jester fumed, his face turning a deeper red as he spoke. "Every time I look back, I see the face of his oxen nigh onto brushing my tailgate, and his stupid face big as a pie staring back at me. As though I could be in the way!"

"Well, Master Teamster, if you just didn't turn around to look—"

"If a wolf or a bear, or dragon maybe, were to jump out in front of my team, and I'd have to stop all sudden like"—the teamster's words were rolling now and had momentum—"then Murdoch's oxen would come crashing into the back of my wagon and maybe jar those wheels right off!"

"I see your point but—"

"And it wouldn't do them oxen any good either!"

Aren's hand unconsciously touched the hilt of his sword.

Syenna gave a short laugh.

Aren drew in a deep breath, withdrew his hand from the sword's hilt, and held it up in an attempt to stop the avalanche of Jester's complaints. "Jester, you're absolutely right. It's shameful the disrespect he is showing you. I'm going to put an end to this right now."

Aren wheeled his horse around and, with a short gallop, came face-to-face with the puzzled Murdoch, leaving Syenna with Jester.

"He's a right man, that captain," Jester said.

"As right as you can be in this army," observed Syenna.

"Now there's a man who could protect a woman." Jester grinned a gap-toothed smile at the army scout. "Keep her sheltered from the troubles of the world and make sure she's fed and warm."

"Keep her?" Syenna's eyes narrowed as she looked sideways at Jester. "You mean like a dog?"

"Well, a maiden needs protecting . . ."

"You do realize I regularly kill men bigger than you," Syenna said, an icy edge to her tone.

"All I'm saying is, he'd be a right good c-catch for anyone," the teamster stammered.

"Well, if you like, I can let him know you're interested," Syenna said as she raised both eyebrows.

The teamster's mouth opened, but no words came out.

Behind them, Murdoch pulled his reins, and the oxen dragged his wagon out of line with the caravan, opening a large space behind Jester's wagon. Aren trotted his horse forward and rejoined Syenna next to Jester. "I've taken care of it for you, Jester. He won't be bothering you again for a while."

"My thanks to you, Captain," Jester said with a nod. "For all the good it will do you or any of us. Each turn of these wheels is taking us toward that dark horizon. It's always takes me farther from home, but it never seems to get no closer."

Aren gave a short bow and a quick salute to the teamster and then urged his horse away from the column. Syenna followed him on her own horse, riding side by side for a time in silence.

"So this is your new command," Syenna said at last. "It doesn't make much sense."

"You're supposed to be a scout for the Obsidian Army," Aren observed, "and you appear to be leading us from the back of the advance. How much sense does anything make? Do you know where we are going?"

"For now we're headed toward a trading post called Kiln," Syenna said. "Follow the Shimano River that far and then intersect with the southern trade routes. From there, our orders are to cross the Midmaer Northwest to the Blackblade Mountains and report at Hilt."

"Hilt." Aren considered this news for a moment, gnawing at his lip. "That's the gateway to the Paladis and the Western Lands. And what are we supposed to do when we reach Hilt?"

"The army is to be reinforced," Syenna said as she looked about them to be certain they were not heard. "Warriors from Drachvald and, so I hear, new Fomorian creatures from Desolis."

"Indeed?" Aren brightened at this bit of news. "So the Obsidians have come up with some new toys for us to hurt ourselves with. Well, if we're getting reinforcements at Hilt, then that means the Obsidians plan to push into Paladis. It means we have just finished one campaign only to begin another."

They came to the edge of the Shimano River. They paused there for a moment, allowing the horses to drink. Beyond the wide, slow-moving river, the Midmaer Plain rolled into the distance. There, at the horizon, stood the jagged teeth of the Blackblade Mountains beneath gathering, ominous clouds.

Aren sat back in his saddle and began whistling his tune once more.

"Do you think Jester was right?" Syenna asked quietly.

"Who?"

"Jester—the teamster—do you think he was right?" Syenna gazed at Aren with a furrowed brow. "Are we chasing a horizon we can never reach? Are we never getting closer but only farther from home?"

Aren gazed at her for a moment and then turned his eyes back toward the west. Once again, he began whistling his tune.

"So you have no glib and easy answers you can fire back at—"

The sudden rustle of wings and movement between them startled Syenna. Aren felt the claws scrabbling at his shoulders and eventually finding their perch.

"Hello, Monk," Aren said to the homunculus clinging to his back. "I was wondering when you might find me."

Syenna shuttered. "I don't think I'll ever get used to that thing."

"You should be grateful to it." Aren smiled as he reached back to rub the creature under his chin. "Unless I miss my guess, Monk here may have just helped us bring that horizon much closer than you think."

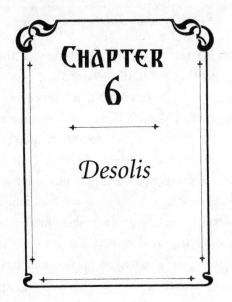

Chapter 6

Desolis

The homunculus known as Monk flapped its wings with determination as it rose higher and higher above the Midmaer Plain. It had left the arm of Aren, its master, from the edge of the Midras ruins two days before and had been making its way eastward beneath daylight and starshine ever since. The homunculus was not a rapid flyer or, for that matter, a very good one, as its wings had been shaped by magic rather than by nature and were barely sufficient to support the miniature, humanlike body suspended beneath them. The barbed tail provided insufficient directional control even in the slightest crosswind. But for all that, the homunculus could unquestionably lay claim to two solid Virtues. Its wings, poor as they were, would never tire, and it was single-mindedly relentless in performing its assigned task. The homunculus would die before it would fail.

Monk flew eastward from the still burning ruins toward the Shadowed Hills that led to the western slopes of the Spectral Peaks. It might not have been the most direct route to Monk's objective, but within Monk's altered and engineered mind, the homunculus knew that the rarefied air at the crests of those mountains would not support its flight or permit its aerial passage. Had Monk been capable of it, it might have felt frustration of the knowledge, but instead its red eyes caught the bright ribbon the River Pashal shining far beneath it in the rays of the morning sun, and the creature wheeled on its wings northward to follow it. Before the sun had set on the same day, Monk had reached the confluence of the Pashal and Shimano Rivers. Just to the northwest of the confluence, the homunculus could see the burned-out ruins of a small town, its stockade walls shattered and charred. The ruins were cold; the fires had long since gone out, and no smoke rose from among the dead. The homunculus did not care; curiosity was not part of its current mission. Its only concern, if the term could properly be applied to the creature, was the building storm clouds to the northwest that were moving with uncharitable swiftness toward it. Monk turned eastward climbing higher as best it could with its eyes on a dark line on the fading horizon, known to its masters as the Sentinel Forest—the boundary between the plains of Midmaer and the Grunvald Prairie.

Monk pushed on through the sky, the storm gaining upon the creature with every beat of its wings.

The tempest overtook the creature in the night. Monk's eyes were more efficient in the darkness—reading variations in heat was far easier for the homunculus than the visible spectrum of light—but the turmoil of the conflicting wind gusts, the torrential downpours of cold rain, and the almost constant veins of lightning crackling through the cloudy blackness made it impossible for him to proceed. The homunculus descended, but even in the caution that it took, the storm still managed to hurl the creature through the upper branches of the hardwood trees and slam it with painful force against the trunk of an oak tree. The homunculus clambered for some purchase with its clawed hands and feet across the wet bark, and managed to arrest its fall within a few feet. There, with the ground an unseen distance beneath it, Monk clung to the tree as the storm raged around it in the darkness. The homunculus rocked itself slightly through the night, trying to comfort itself as it was caught between its unquenchable need to fulfill its master's command and the storm that made its progress toward that objective impossible to fulfill.

The rain was still falling at midmorning when the homunculus took to the skies once more. It had crashed the night before on the western edge of the Sentinel Forest. Who had given the forest that name or why was of no concern to the creature. All it knew was that the storm was moving off toward the south so that it might exhaust itself against the Spectral Peaks. That meant that the skies would be clearing above the forest and gratefully permit the homunculus to continue.

The leathery winged messenger flew high above the treetops of the Sentinels through the rest of the day. By the time the sun was once again setting to the west, Monk was leaving the eastern edge of the forest behind him. The great, billowing clouds piled up around the small monster as it flew eastward, but through the occasional breaks, Monk caught glimpses of the Eylo River to the east. This filled Monk with a sense of anticipation. It was familiar territory and, if it could be said that the conjured being had a home, it was nearing that place with every beat of its wings.

Once again, the sun fell below the horizon behind its flight. Monk flew through towering salmon-colored clouds beneath the twilight sky, but the beauty of it was lost on the creature. The glorious colors soon faded, and the more familiar darkness surrounded it. Monk welcomed the starlight shining down through the clouds, for it helped it to navigate. This part of the journey was at once more difficult and yet more familiar to the creature. There were few landmarks that broke up the monotony of the prairie below, but Monk knew where its flight led and with the help of the stars, could find its way.

Late that night Monk flew over the very source of the magic that had given it form: a great rent in the otherwise featureless plain where a piece of the sky had fallen and seeded the essence of magic into the ground. The homunculus did not even notice its passing. The creature simply crossed over it in the night, its thoughts and its being intent on the sunrise that was to come, and on delivering the message to the one man who could release the creature from the ecstatic agony of its mission.

It would take the creature another full day to find him.

† † †

Personal *message to Obsidian Evard Dirae. General Karpasic relieved me of combat command and is living up to our worst expectations."*

Evard Dirae leaned back in his chair, his elbows on the armrests on either side. He pressed the index fingers of both hands against his lips as he listened carefully and considered the homunculus that perched on the stand before him. This was not an unusual event; the creature had returned to Evard from Aren with reasonable regularity every week or two since Evard had given him the creature at the beginning of the current campaign. Aren had even joked about the gift, saying it was just like Evard to give a gift that would constantly return to the giver.

"I am now in charge of supply caravans."

Evard stood up in nervous agitation. Pacing in the small chamber that had been assigned to him would be out of the question given the limited space. When it had first been shown to him, he had thought it charmingly compelling. The scarred walls and the partial frescoes had a sense of history and connection to a time that was now lost. The ancient civilization that had once lived here in opulent splendor was arrested in all its glory when the sky fell, not terribly far from here, and punctured the crust of the world. The floor of the once verdant plain had buckled and heaved before its fury. The unnamed city had been buried and swallowed up by the ground, leaving only a number of domes of earth and stone to mark its grave. Centuries later the Obsidians had been drawn to the shard that had fallen from the sky, but it was in the discovery of the lost city under the mounds and its connection to the power of the shard that determined where Desolis, the home of the Obsidians, would be established.

Since that time, a number of the slaves of the Obsidians had been pressed into carefully recovering the ancient glory of Desolis room by buried room and street by buried street. The reality was that living in these rooms was generally cold, dark, uncomfortable, and a bit depressing. However, it was considered a sign of status among the Obsidians to be given quarters among the old ruins within one of the mounds, a connection to the glories of the past that the Obsidians had hoped to reclaim as their own future. Where your rooms were located in Desolis was a strong indicator of where you stood regarding your position in the cabal. At the moment, Evard reflected, his position was improving.

Evard brought his mind back to focus on the problem at hand. The honor of sleeping in rooms where people had died horribly centuries before was not nearly as important at this moment as the problem and opportunity that his old friend had just laid at his feet.

"This army would benefit from your guidance in person."

"Yes, I am sure it would." Evard smiled. "But I'm going to need something more than just your demotion to justify what I have in mind, my old friend."

The homunculus stopped talking.

Evard shrugged and frowned. He had just opened his mouth to begin dictating a return message when the homunculus abruptly began speaking again.

"Recovered an ancient blade from the ruins here—possibly Avatar in origin. Come soon."

Evard took in a breath. "Repeat that last."

"Come soon."

Evard shook his head. "No. Before that."

"Recovered an ancient blade from the ruins here—possibly Avatar in origin."

A knowing grin slowly formed on Evard's face. He turned and threw open the dull and dusty black trunk that sat at the foot of his bed. The contents had all been very neatly and carefully placed, allowing him in a moment to put his hands on the black cloth of his dress robes. They unfolded as he lifted them up. It was an elegant robe, carefully embroidered with metal thread designed specifically to bring to mind to any sorcerer the exacting nature of their craft. They were most often used, Evard reflected, when one presented themselves before the lords of the Obsidian Council.

Or at funerals.

"And sometimes both," Evard said aloud to himself as he straightened the robe settling on his shoulders. "I wonder which one this will be?"

He was about to step out of his room when he suddenly stopped and turned toward the creature waiting expectantly on the perch. He reached forward impetuously and rubbed the homunculus's forehead between his tapered ears. "Thank you, Monk, but I think you need a rest."

Evard glanced at the embroidered symbols on the sleeve of his robe to confirm the patterns of the spell. He reached within himself, connected with the magic within the homunculus, and unbound it.

Monk's form suddenly lost cohesion. The creature dissolved at once into a settling cloud of dust.

"I'll call you when I need you," Evard said as the dust drifted toward the floor.

The sorcerer stepped out of his small quarters and into what had once been a paved street. The ancient street had a stone sky: a mixture of dirt and cold lava flow held in place by rough-hewn timbers set as reinforcing beams. This particular mound had been one of the first excavated, and while the section that survived the ancient upheaval amounted in this case to only a handful of streets in what had been a residential district, it remained the most prestigious of residences to the Obsidians. There were few occupants of the section and the street before his room was deserted.

He could hear great winches turning in the distance and headed in the direction of the sound. A few turns of the road and he could see the light of the outside world streaming into the tunnel that the old avenue had become.

The sorcerer stepped past the pair of guards flanking the entrance to the mound known as Old Market, squinting into the morning sun. There were a number of these small, low mounds that looked like ocean swells formed out of the prairie earth. Each had been given a name largely associated with some feature that had been discovered during the excavations beneath them—Temple, Canal, Millstone, Old Market, or Tombs—but all these were dwarfed by what the previous inhabitants of the region had called the Epitaph. It was a mountain plateau of stone that had been thrust up from the ground at the time of the ancient Shard Fall and had carried a great deal of the surface skyward in the process. It was largely comprised of sandstone infused with the ruins filled with ash and marbled with cold volcanic flow. It was the latter, however, that gave the site special significance to the Obsidians, for the lava tubes that had formed carried the power of the Shard Fall directly into the caverns beneath the Epitaph.

To Evard, however, it was one thing more. It was also home.

"Master Evard!"

The sorcerer winced inwardly upon hearing his name. The voice calling it was entirely too familiar to him. Evard stepped quickly away from the entrance to Zinas Mound from which he had just emerged and strode purposefully toward the primary entrance into the Epitaph. Much of the Vaughban Guard, one of three elements making up the Northreach Army, were encamped around the base of the Epitaph. He had the faint hope he might lose himself of pursuit amid the confusion of the five thousand warriors still sorting themselves out after their long march from the Drachvald.

It was a hope quickly crushed.

"Master Evard!"

"Yes, apprentice . . . uh . . ." Evard knew the man's name but wanted to at least pretend that he could forget it.

"Acolyte Tren," the young sorcerer in training said, falling into rapid step next to Evard. "I'm serving under Mistress Norn."

"How fortunate for Mistress Norn," Evard replied dryly. He had encountered this particular parasite far too often. Out of the several hundred acolytes being trained in the depths beneath Desolis, he wondered if he were actually being plagued by this sycophant or if it just seemed that way because the mere sound of his voice was annoying to him. "Is there some purpose in your finding me or is this just a coincidence of the stars?"

Evard kept up his rapid pace, slipping between warriors and even a few tradesmen who were trying to sell the soldiers some of their goods. The hoarse shout of voices, punctuated with occasional bursts of loud laughter or swearing, made it difficult to hear, but it did not prevent the acolyte from speaking.

"My mistress asks if any further progress has been made toward the shaping of the ogres," the acolyte begged. There was an implied accusation in the question that Evard had not done enough to move the experiment forward.

"You may remind your mistress that I am not counted among the Obsidian Central Circle," Evard replied with as much patience as he could muster. "Indeed, you may remind her that I answer to the Central Circle only, and not to any of its individual members."

"My mistress is most keenly aware of that, Craftmaster," the acolyte continued as he kicked and stumbled for a moment over a helmet. The soldier began to swear loudly at them but, realizing who was passing, quickly choked back his words. "She wishes me again to express her regrets at the early passing of your mother and looks forward to the day when you may ascend to her place in the Central Circle."

Evard held his tongue. His family had been at the center of the Obsidian Empire for four generations. Markus Dirae himself had written down the Prophecy of the Obsidian Eye at the edge of the Destiny Pool. He had ascended to the Central Circle and taken the place of his master upon his passing. His son, Doran, had followed to take his father's place as Obsidian Eye. His daughter, Malam, came to the council upon Doran's death and retained her own family name in marriage as a symbol of the dynasty she hoped to build. His mother's death had been a most carefully orchestrated event and was as plausible in its appearance of accident as it was convenient for the ambitions of several remaining masters and mistresses of the Central Circle.

Their one problem, however, was Evard, the son of Malam. His inevitable ascension to the Central Circle threatened the place of any grand master or mistress who might ally themselves with him. At the same time, none of them wished to cross him. As a result, the seven-member council that was the

Central Circle and from which the reigning Obsidian Eye was sanctioned and elevated to position of emperor or empress, was more than willing to utilize his talents and fortify their position of authority so long as it did not threaten them personally. Evard was a prince of the Obsidian Order, whose influence was unquestioned despite his having no clear authority from the Central Circle, nor any single member of that council to whom he answered.

It was an awkward position for Evard, and he had long been searching for a way of distinguishing himself in such a way that the Central Circle could no longer deny him his rightful place in the Circle—as soon as a vacancy could be arranged.

"Convey to your mistress my appreciation at her concern for my future," Evard said. He noted with gratitude that they were approaching the gates of the Epitaph. The stone on either side of the entrance had been reworked into representations of dragon heads, each facing one another as stone guardians of the inner reaches of the Obsidians' might and power. The acolyte, he believed, had no authority to pass these stone sentinels, and Evard would soon be rid of his questions. "Tell her also that the problems with reshaping the ogres continue. More slave subjects will be required for the experiments."

"My mistress would be most grateful for any increased diligence you might exert in this matter," the acolyte said quickly, also noting their approach to the gate. "And, as the craftmaster appears to be on urgent business, may I inquire on my mistress's behalf how she might help you in your current efforts?"

"No, you may not," Evard said with relief as he strode between the statues and into the darkness beyond.

CHAPTER
7

Chamber
of
Souls

vard's steps were familiar to him. They brought him past the Sentinels that lined the long hallway of the Maw, every step taking him farther beneath the Epitaph. They carried him into the Cavern of Night where the Old City's layers were exposed around a funnel of stone piercing deep beneath the mountain. Obsidian Falls could be heard more than seen in the darkness, its waters roaring on his left as they tumbled down the northern wall. His eyes quickly adjusted to the darkness, the only illumination coming from the lamps lining the Long Stair on the opposite side of the enormous cavity. It formed a great, descending arc back and forth along the eastern curve of the natural shaft plunging into the darkness beneath him. He could see movement down that staircase: another line of slaves being forced down the steps toward the laboratories of the Obsidian reshapers. Their flesh and bone would be twisted into forms and purposes more suited to the objectives of the Obsidian Cause: the will of the Central Circle and the vision of the Obsidian Eye.

If, Evard reflected, it worked.

And, as caveats go, it was a very big *if*. The truth was that Obsidian magic, despite its roots in the ancient Fall and generations of study, remained an imprecise and largely unpredictable craft. Its power unquestionably emanated from the shards that plunged violently from the sky at the time of the Fall, rending the Earth and transforming its features. Yet despite the presence of this power in the world for centuries, and the many decades in which the Obsidians had been studying and practicing to understand and harness its seemingly limitless capabilities, the power itself remained a mystery and its effects volatile and mercurial. Even when the Obsidian craft-sorcerers managed to stumble upon a magical configuration that gave reasonably consistent results—such as the shaping of elves—and even when those forms proved to be stable as living creatures, they had proven to be difficult to maintain under any kind of discipline. Most forms simply failed, ending either in misshapen creatures at best, or agonized monstrosities lashing out at their shapers in the throes of their suffering.

Despite all that, the Central Circle had been adamant in the continued research into shaping the living into a powerful army of creatures under their command. Evard wondered if it was because refugees and captives were easy to conquer but difficult to control. Transforming them into monstrous creatures that fought for you rather than against you, perhaps, seemed like solving two problems in a single stroke.

It's just as well they don't know what awaits them, Evard

thought as he stood at the top of the Acolyte Stair, the nearer staircase that descended into the Cave of Night. The legend taught to the acolytes was that these steps followed the original path taken by Heb-Shar, the first Obsidian, when he first found the towering stone butte he named Epitaph and followed the siren call of magic through a crack in the stone wall and down into the darkness below. Evard glanced at the stair and, with a shrug, stepped up onto the stone railing and leaped out over the plunging shaft below.

He murmured into the darkness and felt the rushing wind around him slowing. Magic was precious, and the expenditure would cost him, but he was in a hurry and did not want to appear at his appointment as though he had rushed to arrive. The air around him got cooler, and the lamps of the grotto floor below him were drifting closer. His feet touched gently to the stone just as he murmured again to release the spell.

He looked down another stair, this one straight as it led to a series of landings. To the left of the staircase were the Cascades, the lower part of the underground Obsidian Falls, tumbling over rocks. Evard stepped easily down the stairs, passing a number of acolytes and several craftmasters along the way. At last he came to the courtyard at the foot of the stairs, and gazed out over the mirror-still surface of a lake.

This was Fate's Lake, where Obsidian magic was first forged. Of course, the actual shard from which the magic emanated was now known to have fallen more than a day's ride to the west of the Epitaph, but somehow its powers were carried by the channel of an underground river to this place. It was easy to imagine magic flowing from this hidden lake underground and, in fact, it was easier to channel the powers of magic here than from the surface. It was, he reflected, why he felt so free in using his powers to float down rather than walk the distance. Here, at least, he could recover quickly.

He would do so too, but first he had an appointment to keep that, he suspected, would be much to his purpose.

Evard turned and glanced up at the Obsidian Keep. It was set into the cavern wall, its polished black stone gleaming in the faint light of the lamps.

In this place, he thought, *my ancestor stood by the Destiny Pool. In this place my forebearers built the foundations for an empire of sorcerers who would bring order to a world in chaos. This is mine by right. My destiny. My fate.*

Beyond these final gates lay the heart of the Obsidian Empire.

"A dark heart." Evard smiled to himself as he strode into the keep.

† † †

Ah, my dear Evard." The voice was nasal and high-pitched, echoing slightly in the large hall. It came from a tall, thin man in a crimson robe with golden filigree patterns embroidered throughout its cloth. "What has brought you to extend this invitation?"

The Chamber of Souls was a large rotunda with an upper gallery supported by a colonnade. Below, accessed by the single stair, was a stone floor at the edge of which sat seven high-backed thrones. The gallery had been used in previous decades for witnesses to the proceedings of the Central Council, but since the departure of Evard's mother, the council had not seen the need for any further general witness to their proceedings.

At the top of the stairs stood Doran Valsond, a member of the Central Circle. It was rumored that he was incapable of growing hair on his head at all. His appearance was skull-like with sunken hollows beneath prominent cheekbones and deep-set eyes. Those eyes, however, were of a most pale blue that was at once both startling and piercing.

"News, my lord of the cabal," Evard replied. "News that has come to me that you will find most profitable."

"Evard," Valsond said, stepping softly down the narrow staircase that descended from the gallery into the round room. "How could I decline?"

"Indeed." Evard nodded as the sorcerer came to stand before him. "You could not."

"I see that the rest of the cabal was not included," Valsond observed, glancing around at the empty chairs.

"I thought our conversations were best kept between us," Evard replied.

"Are we meeting here, Master Sorcerer," Valsond continued, "because the words spoken in this chamber remain in this chamber?"

"The Chamber of Souls?" Evard doubted with raised eyebrows. "The names of every Obsidian Eye who had served and every member of the Central Circle who has ever served and died in our cause—betrayed or otherwise—are inscribed in these walls. Surely, the very name of this place would suggest that they are taking an interest in the results of their handwork."

"The past does not concern me," Valsond said with a wave of his hand. "The dead are gone. My thoughts are on the future, as should yours be also, my friend."

"I assure you, my lord, my thoughts are very much on the future," Evard observed quietly. "As in I prefer to have one—a future, I mean."

"A most sensible attitude," Valsond agreed. He stepped over toward his chair, the second from the right of the one designated for the Obsidian Eye, and sat down on it. "You certainly are a man with a destiny."

"Do you know that for a fact, my lord?" Evard asked coolly.

"If you are asking if I saw it in the Destiny Pool, you know that is not possible," Valsond replied. "Only the Obsidian Eye may gaze into that artifact and be able to sort through all the pasts, presents, and futures that converge there. No, I'm speaking of the *man* Evard Dirae, whose rightful place on this cabal has been denied him by those members whose jealous hearts have prevented him from attaining the greatness his family name deserves."

"Those *other* members, you mean," Evard corrected.

"Yes." Valsond sniffed. "Precisely."

Evard nodded casually and stepped over to the chair opposite where Valsond was sitting. He ran his hand along the upper edge of the chair as he spoke. "You are wrong about one thing, my lord: the past should concern you very much."

"I fail to see why." The lord sorcerer chuckled.

"Because very often the past is the gateway to the future," Evard countered. "Take the Avatars, for example . . ."

"Avatars?" Valsond laughed heartily. "*That* old ghost story? Really, Evard, you surprise me."

"Yes, my lord, that old ghost story," Evard continued. "It's a lie, a fable, and a myth. But it is a story that is told and known in every city-state to which we have laid siege. It's sung around every refugee campfire, and it's whispered among the slaves."

"So what of it?" Valsond leaned back in his chair, spreading his hands out before him. "Let them believe that their nonsense heroes will return to save them."

"But what if *we* were those heroes?" Evard asked quietly.

"You're not making sense." Valsond sighed in a way that showed he was getting bored.

"I know a man in the service of General Karpasic," Evard continued. "I have just gotten word that during the siege of Midras, he discovered an artifact that, by all indications, is a sword once used by an Avatar."

Valsond gazed back at Evard for a moment with a questioning look. At last he responded. "You're out of your mind . . . or he is . . . or both of you are."

"I am not trying to tell you that this blade he found is actually *from* an Avatar. . . ."

"I should hope not!"

"But what does it matter, so long as our enemies *think* it is a relic from an Avatar?" Evard concluded. "If we, the Obsidian Empire, are the bearers of the Avatar's might of old, who will stand against us?"

"But it is nonsense," Valsond said slowly.

"And yet, what does it matter," Evard said quietly, "so long as our enemies are foolish enough to believe it? A sword can slay a single soul . . . a symbol can cause thousands of souls to lie down before us."

"And by *us*," Valsond said, "you mean you and me?"

"We are the only ones in this room," Evard said, slipping into the chair opposite Valsond. "Send me to Hilt, and I can retrieve this souvenir for our use."

"Hilt?" Valsond snorted. "Why Hilt?"

"My friend is with General Karpasic's force and is currently being resupplied," Evard said, failing to mention that it had taken him considerable effort to arrange the army to be ordered there through other members of the cabal. "Hilt is where he and this sword will be waiting for me."

CHAPTER
8

*Treacherous
Paths*

Within a few days' march, the army under General Karpasic's command had reached Kiln and, with barely a moment's hesitation, had passed it. The village proved to be a miserable collection of buildings clustered around a central stockade. The self-styled warlord within seemed almost eager to surrender the place to the protection of the Obsidian Army after word had come that Midras had fallen to the south. Kiln, however, was beneath the notice of General Karpasic; the place would have cost him more to secure it than he could gain through plundering it. So, in sad wonderment, the mighty warlord of Kiln was left to watch the great army pass by his town.

Syenna returned from a scouting sortie ahead of the advance. She pointed out to Karpasic a less-traveled road that led to the northwest. It departed from the main trade routes that followed the Shimano River to the northeast in the direction of Port Crucible before intersecting with the east-west trade routes. Following the main roads meant that the army would have to take a circular route to its objective. Syenna assured him that the less-traveled road would more closely follow the roots of the Black-blade Mountains with an easy ford across the River Cascade, and thereby saving them nearly a week's march in getting to Hilt.

The perpetual storm above the Blackblade range appeared on the horizon a full day before the peaks themselves were evident. Dark and roiling, the black clouds rose so high into the air that the tops seemed to flatten against the dome of the sky. They seemed like an angry, living thing with sporadic pulses of lightning beating somewhere deep within.

By the next day, the saw-toothed peaks of the Blackblade Mountains themselves were evident. The enormous, towering granite showed the same slanting thrust from north to south. This was violence on an unspeakable scale, where the rock had been torn up out of the ground into a dark and forbidding wall, five thousand feet above the prairie floor.

Syenna had been proven correct. The wide ford at the River Cascade was easily traversed, and within another day they had rejoined the western caravan route.

All they had to do was follow it west into the forbidden canyon of Hilt.

† † †

W ell, Jester, have you ever seen the like of it?" Aren grinned as he rode alongside the teamster on the wagon.

"Never have, and I hope to say, I never will," replied the red-faced man, though his eyes were filled with wonder.

The towering walls of the winding, narrow canyon, which moments before seemed so close as to fall upon them, suddenly opened up into a mountain bowl nearly a mile wide. General Karpasic's army was already organizing into its encampment, but it was the site on the north side of the narrow valley that had captured their eyes.

Set back into the bow of a branching box canyon was an enormous construction site. A succession of terraces carved from the rock itself gave the impression of looking at the bow of a boat from inside. The method was ingenious, for as each terrace was being excavated, its stone was removed in blocks for construction of additional walls, battlements, and structures. Each terrace provided another level of defense, for Aren could see there was only one road leading to the top: a set of switchbacks on the left-side terraces that were not only exposed to the defensive fire from the levels above, but to archery, ballista, and magical fire from the levels on the opposite wall of the box canyon. A channel cut down through the right-side terraces, where a succession of waterfalls cascaded between sluice gates at each level and emptied into the meadow below. Undoubtedly, those sluice gates could be raised as needed to flood the approaches of each level as Aren perceived a slant in each terrace from east to west. Each terrace ended both on the east and west corners of the canyon in magnificent sheer columns of solid rock, nearly two hundred feet high. The top of the westernmost column was still shrouded in scaffolding, but part of it had been removed on the east, exposing the shaped likeness of an Obsidian warrior. When completed, they would face each other, looking down on any who dared approach.

Atop the uppermost terrace, the carved, stone framework of

the great gate rose to an arched peak. On its left, the shorter side, a magnificent curtain wall had been completed nearly twenty feet in height with crenellated battlements along its crest. To the gateway's right, the much longer side of the wall, the scaffolding was still in place, as it was far from complete. Beyond the scaffolding stood the keep itself, its lower section carved directly out of the granite mountain face. The keep, too, was almost entirely obscured by scaffolding and its associated ramps, as the upper portions were being laid by stonemasons at an unprecedented height. Numerous other buildings, some completed and others still being built, were grouped around the base of the keep beyond the defensive wall.

Aren hoped he would have a chance to speak with the master mason. What he could see only hinted at the glorious magnificence the structure might achieve. He would love to know and appreciate what the final, intended form would be. Nothing on this scale had been attempted since the Fall, and he suddenly felt great pride at being part of making it happen.

Then, as he looked closer, he could see the movement along the scaffolding, the quarries at each level, and the ramps up to them. Dark figures that moved in streams like ants, only he knew that they were not ants. These were slaves, pressed into service as the Obsidians added the conquered regions of the Drachvald.

It is the price of progress, he thought to himself even as he frowned.

"Why do they call it Hilt?" Jester asked.

"I asked Syenna that just the other day," Aren replied. "She told me that before the Fall, there was a great battle between the Gods of Man and the Avatars. It raged all across the face of the world. One of the Avatars saw that they could not win and so, rather than fight the gods, he plunged his blade into the world, desiring to kill the thing that the gods loved most; their creation. The edge of the sword tore through the fertile lands of the world, opening a great and terrible wound. It was here, then, that the gods in their wrath stopped the Avatar and cast him back into the abyss from which he came. But the damage had been done, and the gods, in their wisdom, left the hilt of the blade exposed until such time as some legendary hero from some other nonsense legend were to come along and heal the world. That's what that southernmost peak is supposed to be: the hilt."

"The gods, you say?" Jester said, gaping at the captain.

"Yes," Aren replied, nodding seriously.

They both burst into laughter.

"Well, that's what she said!" Aren grinned as he shook his head.

Jester closed one eye as he considered the peak. "It don't look like no hilt to me."

"It's a legend, Jester." Aren chuckled. "How much sense do you really expect it to make?"

"About as much sense as anything else in this army." Jester sighed. "If you don't mind my saying so, Captain, I don't have much use for legends. They don't put food on my table, they don't cure my wife of the plague, and they don't give me a minute's more peace for myself."

"Your wife," Aren said, looking askance at the teamster. "She's had the plague for about, oh, what now, eight months?"

"Aye, that she has," Jester moaned, shaking his head.

"And you sent her extra coins from your compensation every month in order to help pay for an Obsidian healer?"

"Aye, Captain, every month."

"Eight months . . . That seems like an awfully long time to have the plague, doesn't it?"

"That it is, Captain"—Jester nodded with conviction—"and proud I am that she's put up with it this long. And, say, speaking of companions, where is your creepy little friend?"

"Monk? I have sent him to watch over my possessions," Aren replied. "Sometimes things go missing off the wagons."

"Never!" The teamster blustered. "If their owners are too casual with their valuable and useful items, whose fault is that?"

Aren smiled and was about to say something when the teamster interrupted him again.

"Captain! Isn't that your scout friend?"

Syenna was approaching quickly down the length of the caravan column, waving her hand. She drew up alongside Aren, her words coming in a rush and slightly out of breath. "Captain Bennis, I bring the compliments of General Karpasic . . ."

"And what does the general want this time?" Aren asked.

"What he wants is to reinstate you to the command staff," the scout said quickly. "You are hereby relieved of your responsibilities to the caravan and are ordered to report at once to the general for reassignment."

"Now that sounds official," Aren replied, his eyes narrowing.

"I just bring the message, Captain," Syenna said. "Follow me, and I'll take you to him."

"Very well," Aren said, and nodded.

Syenna turned her horse back toward the base of the Hilt fortress.

"So, Captain," Jester said with a gap-toothed grin, "is this a good thing?"

"I'll let you know," Aren said as he spurred his horse to follow Syenna.

† † †

The general's command tent was located near the pool at the base of the fortress. This was unquestionably a beautiful spot, although the construction work of the fortress was ongoing, and the occasional crack of chisel against rock fell down upon it from above. Aren wondered if the general had hastily chosen the spot without regard to how it might affect his sleep.

Aren glanced down at himself. He was still wearing his makeshift armor and his dusty tunic. There was no help for it; while he knew that the general would disapprove of the captain's appearance, his equipment was still loaded somewhere in the caravan wagons. Syenna was already gesturing him into the folds of the tent. With a sigh, he patted off as much of the dust as he quickly could and stepped into the tent.

"My dear Captain Bennis," the general gushed from his elevated throne, his thick arms open wide in a welcoming gesture. "It has been too long since we have had the pleasure of your company!"

Aren almost took a step back. He had seen this in the general before. Karpasic could be cruel, vengeful, and duplicitous with others but afterward, when he found it would be to his benefit to be on good terms with them, he would simply treat them as though nothing had ever been amiss between them. It was a strange, twisted trick of his mind. Somehow the evils he had done to others were twisted into evils they had done to him. Those, in turn, he could forgive magnanimously and thereby turn his cruelty into benevolence. He would then forgive himself and require those whom he had harmed to forget.

Aren knew that the general was at his most dangerous when he was appearing benevolent.

"Yes, sire," Aren replied with a slight bow. "It has, indeed, been too long."

Aren glanced around him. Most of the command staff was present, wearing their ubiquitous Obsidian armor. Halik was among them, doing his best to avoid eye contact. Syenna stood near the door, her arms folded in front of her.

"I see you have managed to retain your prize," Karpasic said, his eyes falling to the hilt of Aren's sword.

"A prize, sire, that remains in your service," Aren said carefully.

"I confess it would be difficult to determine just in whose service you are in, given your present state of dress," Karpasic responded, the edges of his smile taking the more vicious aspect.

"My deepest apologies, sire," Aren said quickly with another slight bow. "The caravan wagons have not yet had the opportunity to unload the—"

"It is no matter, Captain," Karpasic said with a dismissive wave of his hand. "You have been relieved of your responsibility to the caravan. An opportunity has presented itself for you to demonstrate your service to the Obsidian Cause. What do you know of the Nightshade Pass?"

"I know we are in it," Aren answered. "It is the only passage through the Blackblade Mountains between the Midmaer Plain and the lands of South Paladis."

"Quite correct, Captain." Karpasic nodded. "There are no known passages to the north even beyond Port Crucible—"

"And the Hellfire Rift to the south extends as far as the Storm Sea," Aren interrupted. "That is why the Obsidian command is building this fortress; it controls the only invasion route between Midmaer and—"

"That may not be true," Syenna said.

Aren glanced back at the scout as the general continued. "Syenna has informed us of a local legend—something called the Paths of the Dead—that may provide additional passages across the Hellfire Rift. Should such paths exist, they would represent a serious threat to our southern flank."

"Not to mention, that their existence would largely invalidate the reasons for building this magnificent fortress," Aren said, nodding.

"Not to mention it," the general said, chuckling. "Your orders, Captain, are to accompany the scout southward into the Blackblade Mountains toward the Hellfire Rift, determine if these so-called Paths of the Dead exist, then return and report your findings to me."

Aren considered this for a moment before speaking. "General, if these mythical Paths of the Dead do *not* exist, how am I supposed to determine that?"

"By the evidence, Captain," Karpasic replied as though stating the obvious.

"The evidence of something that is not there?" Aren pressed.

"Then the lack of evidence." The general glared at him. "Must I think for you as well, Captain?"

Aren drew in a slow breath. "No, sire. So, you're asking me to go look for a path that we don't believe exists and only return when I can prove that it doesn't."

"Precisely!" The general was genuinely pleased. "And while you're about it, I would suggest you comport yourself as a proper Obsidian warrior . . . properly attired."

Aren cleared his throat. "In proper armor, of course."

"Of course." The general smiled, reminding Aren of a snake. "And be grateful, Captain, for this opportunity to redeem yourself."

"Yes, sire," Aren said, though his mouth was dry as he spoke. "And may I thank you, sire, for the opportunity."

"Well, don't thank me." The general shrugged. "This was entirely Syenna's idea."

Chapter 9

Awry

"Is it night?" Aren asked.

"I'm tired enough for it to be night." Syenna sighed. "So it might as well be."

Syenna and Aren stood on an outcropping of rock at the top of the cliff face that overlooked the Hellfire Rift. It was, perhaps, the most inhospitable terrain Aren had ever viewed. The jagged peaks thrust upward as sharp as finely honed knives on either side of what passed for a wide valley floor of the Hellfire Rift. The rift itself was a bleeding wound in the world that never healed. Shifting pools of lava sputtered and spit molten rock into slow-moving rivers that glowed with unspeakable heat and shifted down their courses only to cascade back into crevices once more. In the far distance, through the dreamlike shimmering of the heat waves rising from the molten floor and the haze of ash and smoke, Aren could see a shattered mountain.

Great plumes of smoke and ash rose from its maw, feeding the perpetual storm that raged overhead, and blotting out the sun and sky as far as he could see. Lancing webs of lightning were being woven among those terrible clouds, constantly fed by the ash and the heat from below. Any forests or vegetation that might once have been here had long since burned away, leaving only the raw stone, sand, and occasional steamy, acidic rain.

It was raw and powerful, angry and forbidding.

And promising. Aren smiled to himself at the thought. *If you could master such a place as this, who could possibly stand against you?*

"What can you possibly be smiling about now?" Syenna stared at him in disbelief. She wiped the sweat from her brow with the back of her hand. "Especially in that ridiculous armor."

Aren glanced down at himself. He was wearing the breast and backplate of his Obsidian armor, as well as the shoulder pieces and the greaves, but had left the rest of it with the packs on the horses. His trousers and boots he had deemed sufficient from the waist down, and the sleeves of his tunic took up the space between the gaps in his armor. He gave the scout a lopsided grin. "You heard the general: a warrior in the service of the Obsidian Cause must demonstrate his allegiance with said ridiculous armor at all times. Besides, Syenna, all this was entirely your idea as I recall, including wearing this armor."

"I suspect you're not wearing the armor only out of a desire to please General Karpasic," Syenna observed.

"No," Aren said. He turned to look back into the sand grotto of the small mountain bowl just down the ridge behind them. Their five escorting warriors were busy setting up tents for their small encampment. "I think it is more out of a desire to remind them that we serve the same master."

"Our escort?" Syenna said with a raised eyebrow. "You do not trust them."

"Do you honestly think I *like* wearing this armor in this heat?" Aren chuckled darkly. "No. I do not trust them."

"Has your Avatar blade warned you about them?"

Aren shook his head with a slight grin. "I don't need some ancient divining rod to tell me when a man won't look me in the eye. I have never worked with these warriors before; they weren't under my command, and I don't recall seeing them in camp. They have come on this outing, but not out of loyalty to me. One never knows what might happen on an expedition such as this. Accidents happen all the time, and I would just as soon not be part of one."

"You're rather sure of yourself," Syenna said as she stretched the ache out of her arms.

"Well, there are only five of them, and I've got you at my back, so I think the odds are slightly in our favor." Aren smirked as he raised his chin. "And your talents as a scout are quite re-markable. I'd prefer to think that finding this most fortunate campsite was more than blind luck."

Finding the sand hollow was, Aren reflected, a fortunate thing indeed. It had formed a natural collection bowl for the recent rains and allowed them to replenish their stocks of fresh water. The pack horses, already skittish in the hot and alien landscape, were taking in the waters of the small pond and seemed to be calmed by it.

But their escort was another matter. In truth, Aren had considered several times drawing the Avatar blade out of his scabbard so that he might know something about the strangers. Each time he reached for its handle, he stayed his hand, telling himself it was only superstition. Yet, even that was only partially true; there was part of him that was simply loath to draw the blade, for perhaps, he really did not want to know. The scout had mentioned that the escort had been chosen by General Karpasic himself, and that it seemed odd to her that he should be involved in so trivial a matter.

"Well, I prefer to think of that as a compliment," Syenna said, her eyes also fixed on the warriors securing the horses farther down the ridge. "And I can certainly understand your not wanting to trust our escort."

"Haven't you been telling me for days not to trust anyone out here?" Aren said, turning his gaze back over the desolate, fiery vista. "Why you thought I would want to get back into Karpasic's good graces is beyond me."

"And I suppose you'd rather go back to being commander of the caravan?" Syenna had become increasingly irritable since they had left Hilt. "If I hadn't spoken to the general and convinced him that I needed you for this, you'd still be back at camp, feeding the oxen and trying to laugh at Jester's jokes."

"Hey, I'll have you know that those oxen are pretty good listeners when they're well fed," the captain said, chuckling. "And what Jester's jokes lack in originality, they more than make up for in sheer repetition."

"How can you be this way?" The fires of the valley below were suddenly reflected in Syenna's angry eyes.

"What way? What are you talking about?"

"How can you not care?" Syenna sputtered. "For three days we have pushed our way through these peaks and down along the edge of this accursed rift, and in all that time and all the words between us, you haven't said a single thing that would make me believe that *you* believe in anything!"

"So I'm supposed to convince you that I believe in something?" Aren asked, then shook his head. "Why should you care whether I believe in anything or not?"

"Because everyone has to believe in something," Syenna shot back. "It's at the heart of who we are, of why we do the things we do. And here you are, a warrior like none I have ever met before. And you have a gift for commanding others in battle better than anyone I have ever heard of in all the legends of the Midmaer. And yet you'd rather trudge along with the supply wagons than fulfill a greater destiny."

"I've always been rather suspicious of destiny," Aren said, folding his arms across his armored chest. "It always seems to serve other people's politics and plans."

"And yet you support the Obsidian conquests," Syenna said, holding her hands open before her as if hoping to receive an answer. "You do their bidding and follow their orders in support of what they claim to be their destiny."

"The Westreach Army under the glorious command of General Karpasic serves my purposes," Aren replied, a stern firmness underlying his voice. "Not the other way around."

"Your purposes? Do you even know what that purpose is?"

Aren tilted his head, considering the question as he squinted up at the dark and thundering sky.

"Why, to make possible these delightful conversations." Aren beamed back at her. "And, of course, to avoid any unpleasant surprises that our mutual friend the general seems to plan for us along the way. So, if you happen to know how to find this legendary passage across impassable terrain, then I suggest the sooner we do so, the healthier it will be for all us."

Syenna glared back at him with a look that might have chilled him had they been standing in any other place. Then, with a growling sound from deep within her throat, she stepped past him, back onto the ridgeline and down toward a ravine that led toward the valley floor.

"A blade of an Avatar," he heard her mutter as she passed him. "An ancient relic of ultimate good . . . And it had to pick *him* as the chosen one?"

† † †

The northern section of the rift proved to be too volatile for any possibility of a crossing. Most of the valley floor was composed of molten lava flow surging, slipping, and occasionally exploding from the open source of the world. Syenna continued to lead them along the maze of ridges, and for three days, they wound their way southward along the edge of the inferno. The rift was widening—areas where the molten lava had cooled into solid, dark patches like islands in the midst of a fiery ocean. Syenna found a passable ravine that allowed them to descend toward the edge of the lava field. They made their way, skirting the base of the vertical mountains, red flows that had cooled into larger areas webbed by lava streams flowing through jagged fissures. Here and there, the lava had solidified over one of the streams, forming bridges between the black, hard ground. Steam and fumes rose from the crevasses between the dark patches.

Aren, weary from the interminable night beneath a perpetual storm, watched as Syenna quite suddenly dashed ahead, disappearing around the edge of a cliff face. Aren reached up, wiping the sweat that poured profusely from his brow away from his eyes. The heat radiating from even the cooled lava field was intense, draining him. Nevertheless, he drew in a deep breath and charged forward after her. He turned around the base of the cliff, panting in the heat, and nearly ran into her where she stood.

Aren followed the scout's gaze, and his jaw dropped in wonder. It was not the flows of stone that had arrested Aren's attention but, rather, what was jutting upward from their surface, towering above them.

The statue of a woman was over a hundred feet in height, though only the form above her hips remained exposed above the surrounding lava field. She had been built of carefully fitted stone with a craftsmanship beyond anything Aren had seen in his time. The stone carving had been fashioned so expertly that it gave the illusion that one could see through diaphanous fabric to her beautiful figure beyond. Her left hand rested casually against her hip, although a section of it was entirely missing just below the elbow. The right arm was only slightly damaged, shaped as though crossing her bare chest, her hand covering her left breast in a fashion both modest and alluring. The stone head, too, was intact, and she appeared to gaze impassively across a land that once had thrived but was now desolate. There, however, her humanity ended, for twin horns twisted backward from the hair near her forehead. Moreover, enormous dragonlike wings stood poised on her back, their broken, jagged edges reaching around her.

Before them, an enormous, square column had fallen, forming something of a ramp out of its ruins. Syenna stepped onto its slope, climbing upward. Aren followed her to its upper edge to get a better look.

Beyond the towering statue, throughout the lava field, stood the shattered walls of a lost city. The carvings on the face of the ruins were obscured by drifting smoke, and the walls were broken and jumbled. Here and there, dark doorways beckoned them like open graves. Aren could make out at least one additional statue through the smoke much farther down the lava field, whose silhouette was similar to the one looming above him. Square columns had also fallen in various places, some of which spanned the fissures beneath them.

"Alabastia," Syenna said breathlessly. "The City of the Sky."

"You know this place?" Aren asked in wonder.

"Rumors . . . stories . . . It was a great place before the Fall, a city of the plains." Syenna pointed upward toward the statue. "You see the horns on her head and leathery wings at the back? Those were said to be symbols of flight beyond the circles of the world. It was the hope of the priests here that they might find a way to leave the world and follow the Avatars to their home among the stars. This was a blasphemy for which the heavens exacted their terrible justice. The bards usually tell of this place as a civilization of decadence and selfish conceit. Some said that the world swallowed it up at the Fall; others that the moon broke in the sky so that it might crush it out of its sight."

"And what do *you* say, Syenna?" Aren spoke in almost reverent tones.

"I look upon this great woman, and I want to weep." There was a catch in Syenna's voice. "There is no one left to remember her name. All the might and the glory of the past has taught us nothing. The Avatars are gone, their Virtues with them, and we are left with the broken relics of their hopes and dreams."

"Dreams are for the living, Syenna," Aren said. "The dead are gone, and their dreams are gone with them."

Syenna turned toward him, a look of fierce determination in her eyes. "Unless their dreams live in us."

The sound of metal rang behind him. Aren turned at once toward the sound and immediately reached for his sword.

"It's the escort!" Aren yelled in warning. He glanced around quickly at the maze of the surrounding lava flows, then suddenly grabbed Syenna's wrist and pulled her toward the edge of the column. "This way!"

He leaped from the far end of the column, Syenna with no choice but to follow. They landed on the hardened lava rock, its surface stinging his hand as he touched it. Aren cried out as he stood up, pulling at Syenna as he ran toward steaming ground, weaving between the lava flows.

"Where are we going?" Syenna screamed as she dashed with him.

Aren let go of his sword hilt and pointed with his free hand. "There! That narrow doorway. If we can make it there, we can make a stand. We can take them on one at a time as they come through the door, and even the odds. . . ."

Aren's tunic was soaked with sweat. He was having trouble breathing in the heat as he ran. Behind them, Aren could hear shouts of the warriors as they charged after them. The narrow doorway seemed impossibly far away.

Aren let go of Syenna's wrist, leaping over a narrow lava crevice and into the pitch darkness of the ancient doorway. He slid to a stop just within. Syenna slipped past almost at once as Aren turned to face their pursuers.

Aren could see the warriors moving toward the doorway across the lava field.

He reached down for the hilt of the sword, drawing it in a single motion from its scabbard.

Something within Aren changed. He wondered in that moment if perhaps the feverish heat were getting to him. Yet, as he looked to the doorway, he could see clearly the warriors as they approached not just as they appeared but as they *were*. He had traveled for days with these men and barely knew their names yet now, sword in his hand, he *understood* them.

The first among them was a large, broad-shouldered warrior by the name of Arnel Courts. He was a quiet man despite his size, who often kept to himself. Aren suddenly realized that this was because of the pain Arnel carried from being torn from his family, and a deep longing for home. His strength and skill of the blade was his curse, for the general had taken notice of him and would single him out for tasks that were not to his liking. He had nothing against Aren and was heartsick at the idea of killing him. But he feared the general, he feared for his family, and he was only looking for a way home.

The second was a thief from out of the Grunvald who had often plied his trade as a highwayman along eastern trade routes. He looked to most people as cocky and self-assured since he had come into service of the Obsidians. But his attitude sprang from the coals and anger that had burned within him since his father had abandoned their family when he was barely old enough to grow a beard. And so he would fight and brawl for whoever would pay him, trying to satisfy a thirst that could never be quenched and a raging fire that would never go out.

Aren staggered slightly, resetting his stance.

The third of the warriors had been beaten as a child.

The fourth had gone to war to win the heart of his sweetheart.

The fifth would hide himself from the others each night to weep for the lives he had taken.

Aren glanced at his sword hand.

It was shaking.

"Syenna!" Aren called out. "Stay behind me. If any of them get past me you'll have to . . ."

The blow to the back of his head threw him forward, sprawling Aren face first onto the stone threshold at the base of the doorway. His mind was reeling, spinning in confusion and pain. He tried to push himself up, his hands pressing against the blistering heat of the stone beneath him. He managed only to roll onto his back, his right hand still clenching the hilt of the sword. His vision was blurred, but despite the pain he could understand the voices.

"What now, Syenna?"

"Wrap the sword in the oilcloth, but be careful not to touch it." The voice was Syenna's and seemed to come from a great distance. "It's the prize that will take us home, boys. Home with honor."

"And what about the captain?"

"He comes with us." Syenna's voice was getting farther away as Aren lost his fight for consciousness. "Shackle him and make sure the bindings are tight. Someone, after all, will have to carry the sword."

PART II

THE FALLS

CHAPTER
10

Hilt

vard Dirae, Craftmaster of the Cabal of the Obsidians, rode his horse through the last and grandest of the gates of the fortress at Hilt. The challenge that the guards tried to voice at his approach died on their lips, each falling silent at the passage of a sorcerer.

Evard kept his cold, pale-green eyes forward as he passed into the upper courts of Hilt. He did not need to look back down over the multiple concourses that formed the fortress. He had taken them all in with mounting anger as he rode up the various switchbacks, passing through each gate with increasing disdain. Now, as he passed through the final gate, he felt entirely too familiar with the grand structure and, so far as he was concerned, the true reasons for its existence were all too evident.

What had once been a small mountain bowl nestled above a

steep, stony canyon, was now an unfortunately crowded construction site. A grand tower keep, far more impressive than
practical, was nearly complete toward the front of the bowl just
behind the still incomplete defensive curtain wall. The five cascades from the surrounding peaks contributed to the deep gla-
cier lake at the back of the bowl. This, in turn, emptied into the
swiftly moving river that plunged through a gap in the curtain
wall and down its restricting channel over the concourses
below. In every other reasonably dry spot, buildings of various
size and design were evident in every conceivable state of in-
completeness. Some were cleared ground only, whose foundations had barely been laid out. Others had their walls partially
completed with stone pillars standing free, either in their intended place or on their side. A very few others appeared to be
nearly complete, only lacking in a few finishing details such as
a roof or doorway. The shod hooves of Evard's horse rattled
against the newly laid cobblestone paths that wound between
the structures.

Such a pointless waste, Evard thought. *A monumental conceit
that served no real purpose.*

Evard tugged at the reins of his horse, riding the creature
across an ornately carved bridge to the other side of the mountain river. There he could see the one structure that he knew to
be complete, due in no small credit to the help of the mountain
itself. Carved directly out of the face of the cliff, it had the
appearance of a stone building with six columns in the front.
Between the columns on either side, the likeness of two thirty-
foot-tall warriors had been carved from the stone in relief. The
armor depicted in the carvings was obviously modeled after
the Obsidian design, with the ornate filigree in the breastplates

and the menacing spikes at the forearms and shoulders. Each of the depicted warriors held a sword in front of them, its tip touching the ground and their hands folded over the pommel. Evard noted that each was depicted without a helmet, and he suspected that the faces were intentionally carved in the likeness of the four generals of the Obsidian Army.

The sorcerer considered the third of the likenesses. He had ridden for nearly a week in order that he might meet with the much smaller and equally dull version of the carving.

Evard slowed the horse and then dismounted as they reached a small grassy patch just before the doors. The sorcerer immediately caught the reluctant eye of the nearest of the two guards standing watch on either side of the door.

"You," Evard said, pointing at the guard.

He was resplendent in Obsidian armor, its black surface polished like a mirror, its red and silver markings shining even in the nearly perpetual shadow of the mountain. Despite evincing an outward calm, the guard's eyes were blinking furiously, and his voice broke slightly in his reply.

"Yes, sire?"

"Your assistance is required," Evard said in quick, flat tones. "You will take my horse. You will walk her. You will keep walking her until I come and tell you to stop."

"Yes, sire . . . But, sire—"

"My suggestion is that you take her to that lake at the back of the canyon where, it seems, it is the only place large enough to do the job properly."

"Yes, sire . . . I understand, sire. . . ." The guard stammered. "It's just that—"

"I see." Evard nodded, his eyes looking not so much at the

guard as through him. Evard was tall—just slightly over six feet—which allowed him to look down slightly at the guard as he stepped uncomfortably close to him, his deep voice mumbling quietly as he spoke. "What is your name?"

The guard swallowed hard. "Garvin, sire!"

"You are, no doubt, the most diligent guard in the service of the Obsidian Cause and a devoted warrior who, assuredly, would never, ever abandon his post. As I understand it, your duty is to prevent unexpected people such as myself from disturbing the peace of your commanders ensconced beyond the doorway. However, as you see, I am a sorcerer of the cabal who has come on Obsidian business with your general. I don't suppose you would care to know exactly what my business is with the general, would you?"

The guard shook his head in such violent denial that Evard thought his helmet might come loose.

"You are quite right; you most certainly do *not* want to know my business. You may be thinking *that* abandoning your post would almost certainly incur the wrath of your general. On the other hand, *not* taking care of my horse and trying to prevent me from seeing the general will most certainly incur *my* wrath. And so now I am standing here wondering just which wrath a guard named Garvin would prefer?"

Evard knew he was taking a luxurious amount of time with this young guard, but watching him squirm was the only pleasure the trip had afforded him thus far.

Besides, it was good practice for what was about to come.

"S-sire," the guard stammered quietly. "I believe I was ordered to walk this horse over by that small lake. With your permission, I'd very much like to do that right now. And oh, sire?"

"Yes, my wise friend Garvin?"

"Would that order also include my brother?" Garvin gestured to the second guard standing with the petrified stillness equaled only by the stone statues to the left of him. "It's an awfully important horse, sire. I'm sure you would insist that it would take us both to walk her properly."

Evard gave a thin smile of amusement. "You are quite correct, Friend Garvin. I now recall being quite clear that the order explicitly included your brother."

The two guards quickly moved away with the horse. Evard smiled to himself as he bounded up the few short steps to the open doorway and stepped inside.

The dimly lit interiors made it difficult to see, but Evard did not mind. He had been in many darker places than this. His eyes quickly adjusted to the torchlight of the long hallway that lay before him. A series of columns supported the arched ceiling twenty feet overhead. Between each of the columns, the walls held framed carvings depicting various battles and conquests of the Obsidian Army. The floor itself was polished marble, finished to a fine shine that reflected the light of the torches mounted on each of the columns and lit the way toward the warm bronze doors at the end of the hall.

Evard knew that it was all a facade. Torches were a terrible source of light, burning only for about twenty minutes at a time before having to be replaced. No doubt, some hapless warrior was being punished with the never-ending task of replacing and lighting these torches. The hallway itself was a fraud: beautiful stonework that hid the rough original cavern walls just beyond. Before he had left the cabal in Desolis, he had gone to the archives to familiarize himself with Hilt before he departed. He, therefore, knew the history of its construction and, by inference, its true purposes. He drew his shoulders back and strode down the hall, pausing a moment at the doors.

The sorcerer glanced down at his own attire. He wore the black, hooded tunic of a sorcerer of his order. The long, more formal robes of the cabal looked nice in paintings or when depicted in statues, but were not terribly practical for purposes of craft. This costume suited his purposes far better; the hooded tunic had been embroidered with infinite care from metallic threads of gold and silver into very specific filigree patterns that wound around from his chest to the back, and ultimately up over the truss of his head. They served a number of purposes in Obsidian magic, some of which had to do with spell mnemonics and remembering the construction of incantations. There were many who believed that the tunic itself had magical properties, a deception and misdirection that the Obsidian sorcerers never corrected. Evard also still wore a riding cape of similar design, which had kept him reasonably warm on the road and occasionally had offered him shelter from the rains. Beyond these absolute symbols of his sorcery, his dress was rather commonplace, with cloth leggings and high boots to the top of his thighs.

However, he frowned not so much at the thought of what he wore, but the state of his clothing. The intervening rains of the previous week, and mud that followed, had left both him and his clothes in a dreadful mess. He would have preferred to appear before the general in more pristine, and therefore intimidating, attire.

Well, he thought, *I'll just have to depend on the force of my personality.*

Evard pushed open the enormous double doors with both hands and stepped into the general's reception hall.

As Evard expected, this room was a rotunda with a raised platform opposite the doors. To one side of the rotunda, a wooden scaffold reached up from the floor to the domed ceiling thirty feet overhead. The sorcerer glanced up at the dome, which had been plastered over in white with the faint lines of charcoal sketching over its surface. A number of lanterns were fixed at the top of the scaffolding, where a pair of figures had begun work on the fresco that would someday adorn the ceiling.

On this platform sat four thrones representing each of the four generals who commanded the Obsidian Army. Only the third of these thrones was currently in use, its occupant surrounded by nearly two dozen members of his staff. Each of these was hovering like a moth about a flame, trying desperately not to get too close while simultaneously terrified of being too far away. The general's voice echoed throughout the hall, thundering about the nervous chatter of the sycophants.

Evard turned and drew within himself, calling with surety on the power he knew was there. He felt the sudden connection with nothing and with everything that was so familiar to him, and stole from the universal part of that chaos that threatened to consume him every time he approached it. He was a successful thief, for no sorcerer survived being caught by the chaos. With the fragment of chaos now taking form within him, he reached out with his hand and released it into reality with a flick of his wrist. As he did so, he felt, rather than saw, a lock of his own hair turn white.

The enormous bronze doors slammed shut with such violence that their sound shocked everyone else in the room into silence.

Evard turned back to the platform, striding across the rotunda as he spoke in loud, clipped tones. "I am Evard Dirae, Craftmaster of the Obsidians, and your obedience is required."

The wide-eyed general pushed himself to his feet. "This is a closed council of war! I gave no permission—"

"My businesses is with General Karpasic," the sorcerer continued in a booming voice, his booted footfalls across the polished floor never hesitating in their relentless beat. "It is a confidential matter between the general and the cabal. Anyone else who wishes to be party to that conversation will do so at their peril."

The staff and warriors in the room shifted their glances quickly to the general. General Karpasic considered the approaching sorcerer, watching him until he stopped at the foot of the platform. Evard gazed back at Karpasic, waiting.

"I believe our conference is concluded," the general said to the courtiers after a few moments. "Why don't all you make an inspection of your commands while I consult with this Obsidian?"

The staff members and warriors moved quickly out of the hall. Even the artisans scurried down through the scaffolding and hastily exited, closing the bronze doors behind them as quietly as possible. All the while, both Evard and the general stood in silence, considering each other. Neither of them moved or spoke until the sound of the last door closing died in the hall.

Evard was not, by nature, a happy or outgoing man under the best of circumstances. His calm, placid features generally displayed a disdainful indifference to events around him. He had a narrow face that came down to a chin that was almost feminine in its softness. His pale-green eyes, however, were hard and cold. Everything about him was carefully ordered with the singular exception of his hair, which was a dark, wavy mane with something of a will of its own.

Except, of course, when the magic marked it with a streak of white. The mark it left would fade back into its natural color over the course of the week, but for Evard, it symbolized his giving something back to the magic. He had never believed in getting something for nothing.

"My apologies for not having received you personally," the general spoke first. "We knew, of course, of your arrival, but as you can see, we are very busy with plans for the coming campaign and—"

"The Obsidians are certainly most acutely aware of the plans for our warriors, and more particularly, the plans of the generals that command them," Evard interrupted, his voice cool with disdain. "It seems you have been busy indeed here at Hilt."

"Hilt is certainly the most important strategic position in all the Blackblade range," Karpasic said, caution in his voice.

"It is certainly strategic, I will give you that," the sorcerer said, his eyes shifting about the rotunda. "You and your fellow generals have achieved a great deal here at Hilt. You have created a fortress—a monument, if you will—that has all the appearance of the great empires of the past, without having to bother with any of its substance."

"Master sorcerer, you go too f-far," Karpasic sputtered.

"Indeed?" Evard reached up and undid the clasp of his cape as he stepped up onto the throne platform. "The Cabal of the Obsidians would undoubtedly agree that I have *not* gone far *enough*. I must admit, it is a remarkable achievement. You have managed to divert the labor of campaign slaves entirely toward an installation that benefits only the military. I deal in sorcery, but I must admit, you generals have performed a rather phenomenal magic trick of your own. While no one was looking, to have transformed an open rock quarry into a monument to your own might and, it seems, this enormous lava cave into what passes for an underground palace."

"It is truly a magnificent achievement . . . an achievement to the greater glory of the Obsidian Cause," Karpasic added quickly. "It is, as you say, a demonstration of the unassailable might of both the strength of arms and the arcane power of the cabal. We have even begun construction on the Tombs of Eternity, where the memory of our achievements together shall stand for all time—"

"Tell me, General, just how deep are these caverns and lava tubes that are accommodating this installation?"

"We . . . We do not know," the general answered, his eyes studying the floor as he spoke.

"You don't know?" Evard's eyes narrowed. "How deep have you extended your construction?"

"We have constructed ten levels so far," the general continued. "The lowest are where we have set those magnificent tombs to the honor of the Obsidian Cause. Those are constructed in a winding maze of lava tubes, but the workmen have not reported finding an end to them. It is, perhaps, another reason why we call them the Tombs of Eternity, as they seem to go on—"

"And so, as I understand it," Evard said as he folded his arms across his chest, "you sent Captain Bennis into the Hellfire Rift searching for a path that almost certainly does not exist when you have unknown underground passages in the foundations of your fortress."

"Captain Bennis is performing his duty," the general asserted. "Besides, he is carrying a cursed sword. I thought it best that he remove it from our encampment . . . For the safety of our other warriors."

"Ah, very noble of you," Evard spoke in more of a hiss through his clenched jaw. "Unfortunately, the Cabal of the Obsidians have a considerable curiosity about such cursed swords."

"Oh," the general said quietly. "That is unfortunate."

"General Karpasic," the sorcerer said with emphatic fidelity. "You will recall Captain Bennis at once, and you would do well to remember that—"

"I am sorry, Master Sorcerer," the general said, shaking his head. "That is not possible."

"Not possible?"

"The captain and his guide were due back two days ago," the general said, licking his lips. "I myself sent runners to retrieve them. They're missing."

Evard clenched his teeth, screwing tight his eyes in frustration. "You have lost the captain *and* the sword?"

"Captain Bennis was performing his duty," the general reiterated as though, if he said it often enough, it would somehow save him. "It is a dangerous place. Things happen."

"Yes, General," Evard said, casting a cold and calculating look at Karpasic. "And sometimes even to generals."

† † †

Evard stood atop a partially completed watchtower. All of Hilt, and its partially completed glory, lay beneath him.

Only the peaks of the Blackblade range were above him, each shining in the light of a brilliant sunset.

Evard began to whistle. It was a strange, simple tune. Its notes were not entirely precise nor was the sound so loud that it might attract attention of the many warriors or artisans moving in the courts below.

But it was heard.

A dark shape flitted among the peaks. It suddenly rose, bounced, and plunged in the unpredictable winds across the mountain face against which it struggled. With great effort, it crossed over the tower wall and landed without grace at the foot of the sorcerer.

Evard reached down as he leaned over, extending his arm.

"There you are, Monk!" Evard smiled.

The homunculus scampered up the sorcerer's arm and quickly came to perch on his right shoulder. Evard reached up, stroking under the monster's chin. "Well, my friend, it looks as though your master has gotten himself lost. There is no need to worry. I've known Aren since he wasn't much bigger than you. He's too stubborn to die. But now it seems he stumbled onto something that's a matter of prophecy, and I fear he's in over his head."

Evard reached back and lifted the homunculus. He set the creature on a section of the battlement wall in front of him. He consulted one last time the embroidered markings on his tunic, then reached deeper within himself than he had for a long time. Both satisfied and shaken, he raised both hands above his head, weaving them down in front of him in precise patterns, then focusing his palms toward where the homunculus shifted nervously on the wall.

Expanding spheres of light erupted all around the homunculus. The creature screeched, then two screeched, then four screeched . . . Eight . . . Sixteen . . . Within moments, more than five dozen of the small winged creatures were flitting about the top of the tower, each one identical to the first, and each answering to the name of Monk.

Evard collapsed to one knee, a wide swath of his hair suddenly gone brilliant white. He staggered to his feet and reached up with both hands toward the cloud of homunculi circling above him.

"We've got to bring him home before any more damage is done," Evard commanded of the creatures. "Find him and tell me where he is."

Sixty-four homunculi exploded across the evening sky.

Chapter 11

Mistral

Where am I?" Aren moaned.

"So the sleeping warrior awakens," came a familiar voice from somewhere beyond the overwhelming pain that encompassed his head. Aren screwed his eyes shut tightly against the light that threatened to explode if he allowed it into his throbbing skull. He could feel that he was sitting with his back against something uncomfortably hard. Some protrusion was digging into his back, next to his spine.

"Why won't the ground hold still?" he asked, his mouth dry.

"Because you're on a boat," Syenna said.

Aren's eyes flew open despite his better judgment. The brightness of the day nearly overwhelmed him, but he had to get some sense of his surroundings. After an agonizingly long moment, the glare resolved itself into shapes and colors.

That they were on a ship he had to accept largely on the

evidence that, so far as he could tell from where he sat, they were surrounded by water. He had seen ships before, but he had never been this close to one, let alone on the deck of one.

He tried to take it all in. While everything looked extraordinarily well ordered, he could not make sense of his surroundings. It seemed to him an extraordinarily complex conglomeration of various sized pegs, pulleys, beams, masts, and enormous canvas sheets all held together by metal bands and an incomprehensible web of ropes. Above his head, there were men—sailors, he supposed—moving like spiders about this web of ropes, listening to the barked orders of their master at the back of the ship and answering back with tugs on various ropes or shifting the beams from which the masts hung. Everything seemed to be connected to everything else.

"A boat . . . of course," Aren answered with a calm he did not feel. He carefully and deliberately got to his feet but was suddenly unsure as to what he could safely touch without upsetting the balance of the entire, incomprehensible system. He concluded that the railing appeared both solid enough to support him and not critical to the operation of the vessel. He gripped it as though it were the only stable object in his life.

"A ship named the *Mistral*," Syenna said, her eyes fixed on him, watching him carefully as he regained his senses. "She is a *bark*, to be precise."

Aren swung his head with deliberation away from Syenna, still gripping the railing hard to help him remain upright. As he did, he could see a dark, mountainous shoreline that appeared not more than half a league in the distance, filling the horizon.

"Where are we?" Aren asked, peering at the coast.

"It's not important for you to know that right now," Syenna said in flat tones.

Aren turned to look at her as though she were joking with him. "Do we have to play this game? You know I cannot swim."

"Even if you could, you would never make that shore." Syenna shrugged. "Those are the Sawtooth Mountains. Treacherous, rocky shoals and heavy breakers all along their coast. Even if you managed to make it ashore, the mountains themselves are only passable if you know the routes."

"You seem to be familiar enough with them," Aren countered. "Indeed, it occurs to me now that you've been holding back on quite a number of things from your good friend, Captain Bennis."

Syenna only gazed back at him.

Aren decided to try a different tack. "So, how long was I out?"

"Out?"

"Yes, unconscious," Aren continued. "I don't remember ever booking passage on a boat, and I certainly don't remember boarding one."

"It's been about four days," Syenna replied.

"Four *days*?" Aren chuckled and then winced at the resurging pain in his head. "You must have hit me harder than I thought."

"Well, to be honest—"

"That should be different," Aren scoffed.

"We have an apothecary who has been keeping you in a cooperative, very still, and gratefully silent condition since then," Syenna continued, ignoring his remark. "We will be arriving in another day or so at our destination, so I thought it best to get you awake and clear minded before we make landfall."

Aren's head was still spinning, but at least he was able to see through the pain. He was unreasonably thirsty, although the thought of drinking anything—let alone eating—still revolted him. "I don't suppose you would be interested in telling just where we are landing?"

"You'll know when we arrive . . . in the morning or perhaps midday," Syenna said, "if the offshore winds hold through the night."

"Then if you're not interested in telling where we are going," Aren offered, trying to appear more casual than his head would allow. Whatever they had given him, he decided, was still playing havoc with his head and his stomach at the same time. "Then perhaps we could talk about how we got here. Last thing I remember was my standing in front of you, boldly prepared to defend your honor against the enemy when you hit me from behind with something that felt rather like a war hammer."

"As if I needed you to defend me!" Syenna's nostrils flared.

"Well, all I'm saying is," Aren said, pursing his lips into a slight pout as he spoke, "that I was trying to behave in a courteous and honorable manner when you betrayed me."

"Betrayed you!" Syenna's face reflected her contemptuous disbelief.

"You must admit"—Aren smiled at his own joke—"it was hardly honorable to clout me from behind."

"How dare you speak of honor?" Syenna seethed. "When have the Obsidians *ever* acted with honor?"

"Actually, I think on reflection you will see that the Obsidian Empire has *always* acted with absolute honor," Aren countered.

"*Their* honor!"

"Of course it's *their* honor!" The argument was tiring Aren, but he certainly did not want to show any weakness before Syenna now. "What other kind of honor is there?"

"An honor that does not destroy!" Syenna said, anger rising in her face. "Honor that does not kill . . . does not oppress!"

"Do you remember what the world was like before the rise of the Obsidian Empire—what it is like *still* in places where the empire has yet to extend its rule?" Aren shook his head in derision. "Squabbling, petty kingdoms barely worthy of their name pounding one another back into the dirt before anyone could accomplish any real progress toward order. Everyone was too busy making sure their neighbor was dragged back down into the mud that no one could stand up. The world was in chaos, Syenna. The old civilizations of legend were gone in the Fall, wiped out from the face of the world. It was a chance for us to start again, and all we've done since is beat one another up over crumbs. The Obsidian Empire brings order to the chaos, honorable honor, if you like. And I'd like to point out that it wasn't *me* who struck a friend from behind!"

"I didn't kill you," Syenna offered.

"Well, that's a comfort," Aren said with a dark laugh.

"That's the difference between what we serve," Syenna continued, more earnestly. "Men and women should act out of their desire to do what is right and just for one another. That comes from the heart, not the point of a sword. The Obsidian Order wants to enforce change with pain and death. That's not order, and it certainly isn't justice."

"You want to talk about justice? My father was a just man," Aren said, his fist balled up at his side as he spoke, his head pounding. "A good man and a kind man. He was a metalsmith with a small forge. He loved my mother. He was strict with me. We lived in what was barely a village at the junction of a couple of nameless roads. But there were several local groups of brigands who fancied themselves as the masters of all they could see. Unfortunately, each of them thought that my father's little piece of ground was theirs by some divine right. Each in turn washed back and forth over my father's patch of ground until there was nothing left of it or my father. No one bothered about me or that patch of blood-soaked ground until the Obsidians came and put an end to the chaos. Their law was justice."

"Whose justice?" Syenna shot back. "Whose law? Yes, the Obsidians brought order to your frenzied and confusing life, but at what cost? You know where you've been, Bennis, but you don't know where they are taking you . . . taking all us."

"I thought you didn't want to tell me our destination," Aren groused.

"I won't tell you where this ship is taking us, but I can tell you where the Obsidian Empire will drag us all," Syenna said. "The empire is corrupt. The Central Cabal cares only for its own status and power. They only see their growing reach and grip on the land and its people. They speak of high ideals, but all they do is pour the blood and cries of those same people back into the land. You've seen it in the cities you've taken . . . the lives you've cut short."

"That was different," Aren said. He was having trouble following her reasoning. "That was war."

"It's so easy for you to put that in a little box as though it had no connection to anything else," Syenna snapped. "As though the order imposed by the Obsidians was justification enough for a future of enslavement, torture, and despair."

"I've heard all this before," Aren said, shaking his head. "Those words fell from the lips of every petty ruler and self-proclaimed king or priestess who saw the Obsidians coming to knock them off their little thrones and bring their misguided mobs under one law, one justice, and one empire. It may surprise you to know that I don't approve of everything the Obsidians do. I've seen things . . . done things . . . that were not particularly pleasant for me, but I've told myself every time that for all its faults and for all its mistakes and cruelties, it's still better than what I've seen of the rest of the world."

"I think that's enough air for you," Syenna said, though Aren could see the muscles in her cheeks working to control her response. "You want more control and order, I'll oblige you by putting you back in your chains."

"So, we're not that different after all." Aren smiled sadly. "Show me something better, Syenna! Convince me! The Obsidian Empire gave me purpose and a solid place to stand in a world that was all shifting sands. They saved me."

The throbbing in his head reminded him that he had gotten too loud.

"So, tell me, Syenna," Aren demanded. "What did the Obsidians ever do to you?"

Syenna gripped his arm to escort him belowdecks . . . but said nothing more.

CHAPTER 12

Amanda

Amanda sat, as she did each day, in the seat of the bay window of the small cottage, and looked down the street. Through the small squares of wavy glass fixed into the lead latticework, she could look over the top of the harbor town of Etceter to the docks beyond. Each day she would watch as the ships came down the coast from the northwest, or along the eastern shores as they navigated the fringes of the tempestuous Bay of Storms. On a good day, she might catch the dark outline of Siren Isle sitting on the horizon to the north, but far more often, the perpetual squalls that gave the bay its name would veil it from her sight.

Somewhere beyond the darkness, beyond the lightning and the fury, Amanda knew each day that Syenna would be coming.

Amanda shifted her legs painfully beneath her. Although

they always ached to one degree or another, and sometimes with excruciating pain, she had been determined since her sister had last departed, to surprise her by standing on her own when she greeted her at the door.

It had now been more than ten months to the day since Amanda had watched Syenna walk down the length of the dirt road and sail away. Every day since, she had begged and wheedled Sarah, the woman who took care of her, to help her to stand and try to once more walk. Sarah had been appalled and, at first, refused. But Amanda was determined, and would not be distracted from her purpose by tapestries, needlework, or tatting. In the battle between their wills, Sarah at last succumbed to Amanda's unrelenting and stubborn assault and surrendered, on the condition that Amanda continue her tatting and to never, ever let the baroness know that Sarah had ever been a party to such dangerous nonsense.

Amanda winced again, and she pushed her legs free of the blanket that covered them. She looked down at her legs, her brow furling. She tried to convince herself that they looked healthier, that they were not the same emaciated, twisted horrors that they were when last Syenna had left. Had she not seen some improvement? Had she not managed to stand on her own and nearly counted to fifty before she collapsed? And had she not, just three weeks ago, when Sarah had gone to the marketplace as she did every morning after breakfast, stood all on her own in the same bay window and taken two steps into the small room? Amanda was certain she had accomplished it before she had fainted, and she refused to believe Sarah's assertions that she had dreamed the whole thing.

No, Amanda thought, as she covered up her shriveled and

misshapen legs once more, she was certain that things were getting better.

As she patted down the blanket, her eyes fixed on her hands. Her fingers were extraordinarily long and delicate, matched by her thumbs. Both were incredibly strong and capable of doing the most intricate work. Amanda's tatting lace, embroidery, and tapestries were in great demand in Etceter, and the baroness herself purchased all her work. Indeed, the baroness had required that she alone was to purchase the work. Amanda saw this as a great honor, although she had begun to wonder of late why the baroness was so adamant about keeping her work to herself.

Without a thought, Amanda reached up with her perfect hands to push back her long hair behind her ears. Her locks were so light in hue as to be nearly white. As she reached back, her nearly perfect hands caught against the long tips of her pointed ears.

Her hands, it seemed, were the one thing that the Obsidian sorcerers got right that day.

Amanda closed her eyes, determined once again by a sheer effort of will to remember what had happened. The fragments of her memories spun through her mind like shards of glass that had been shattered against stone, shards she was trying desperately to put back in their original places.

She was sitting next to her father as he held the reins. The wagon swayed beneath them as her father sang a silly song for her at the top of his lungs. Mother and sister were in the back of the wagon, watching the rest of the trade caravan as it wound across the prairie, so Amanda had her father all to herself. She laughed at his nonsense song beneath the bright, sunlit sky.

Another splinter. *Black night under a canopy of stars. Cries* and screams tearing apart the stillness. *Mother with her hand over Amanda's mouth, over Syenna's mouth. Whispering desperate words she could no longer remember nor understand.*

Smaller shards. *Running into the tall grass. Don't look back. Syenna is before her . . . Syenna is gone. Father? Dark sounds, wet sounds. Sounds of slaughter. Turn around, Amanda. Turn around for Father. . . .*

Fragments. *Bright skies and dark robes. Your obedience is required. The sunshine is a patch that gets smaller and smaller as they lead her deeper beneath their fortress. In the service of the Obsidian Cause.*

We will make you better. . . .

We will make it useful. . . .

Again . . . That did not work. . . . Try it again. . . .

Amanda opened her eyes. The peaceful light shining down on Etceter almost surprised her. She shivered despite the warmth of the sunlight through the glass. She knew that the memories were there and that they held secrets about her past. But the effort to remember them exhausted her and, as she had done for uncounted days before, she set them aside with a sigh and hoped that tomorrow, perhaps, she would remember them.

Etceter, she thought, was a very pleasant place to live, even if coming by that life was difficult. It was the sole deepwater port on the southern shore of the Bay of Storms, and as such, had become the gateway to the Southern Straits, the only access for the overland trade routes from Midmaer through Quel, or from the small harbor at the mouth of the River Fang. In days long past, Etceter had been a pirate haven, and the town had grown up as a wild and lawless place. Its name was even taken in those days, the word meaning "and so forth," which seemed to perfectly fit a village that had grown up as something of an afterthought. Over time, however, the pirate barons discovered that trade was more profitable—and certainly better for one's health—than was piracy. The original barons transformed their trade from cutlass to commerce and tried to bury their past under as much respectability as they could purchase. While all this gave Etceter a certain element of prosperity, the town itself was far removed from the rest of civilization, and kept at this distance due in large part to the inhospitable terrain of the entire region. Even around Etceter, which was built adjacent to the mouth of the River Barren, the surrounding ground was rocky and difficult to till. Farming was largely an exercise in frustration, with sheep ranching being only marginally more successful. And so, the living breath of Etceter was the constant inhale and exhale of commerce and shipping.

The result of all this was a town of moderate size sprawling out from the base of the Baron's Keep, which was kept safe largely due to the fact that it was too far across the barren countryside to be worth the trouble to attack it from the land, and too dangerous to cross the Bay of Storms to be worth the trouble to attack from the water.

Perhaps, Amanda reflected, that was why Syenna decided that they should both settle here. It was a place where everyone preferred not to have too many questions asked about their past and, in their turn, offered the same accepting courtesy to others. Here, perhaps, was the only place Amanda could be settled on the steps leading into the cottage, her tatting pillow in her lap and the ever-attentive Sarah sitting on a stool nearby, and not draw unwanted attention. Roselyn, the town gossip, could stop by and, leaning across the low stone fence surrounding their yard, tell her the tales of people inside the town and all their secrets, true or otherwise. Chaox, the dockmaster, was considered by all the town to be a gruff, unpleasant man of enormous strength and temper, but he always took off his hat whenever he saw Amanda and spoke to her only in the kindest of tones. He would often stop by to sit with her and gently tell her tales that he had heard off the ships that had docked at the port. Once, when Sarah had discovered two young boys from the town stealing vegetables from their small garden, Amanda managed to calm her down, and had so charmed the boys that they returned the next day to pull her weeds. She then repaid them with some of the tales she had heard from Chaox the day before. Ever since then, the boys returned each week to do chores for her in return for the sound of her voice and her laughter.

All that changed, however, the week before. Marissa, the emissary of the baroness, had come up the road to Amanda's cottage and, to Sarah's surprise, stepped inside at once. She explained to the two astonished women that the council of leaders had been called from many of the adjacent lands, and that they would all be converging here in Etceter for the conference. It was the specific request of the baroness that Amanda remain in her home until the conference was concluded, and to take care not to be seen until Marissa returned.

From that day to this, Amanda had remained in her home, and visits from her neighbors had stopped. Yet, as she had done each noonday since her sister had left, she returned to the seat in her window and gazed down the long street that passed the homes, shops, and the keep that made up Etceter, to the docks and the waters beyond.

Something down the coastline to the east caught her eye. There were already a number of large ships at the docks, each square rigged and flying different flags, but the approaching ship was smaller, with a triangular sail.

"Perhaps today," Amanda murmured. "Perhaps today."

† † †

Syenna stood on the docks, paying off the captain of the bark they had hired. The gold had only been acquired from the baroness after Syenna had secured the prisoner in the stockade and made certain he would stay there. The bark captain now satisfied, and her duties fulfilled for the time being, Syenna turned and looked up the main road of Etceter to face the cottage near the crest of the hill.

She gnawed for a moment on her lower lip. The cottage was the one place in the world that, for months, she had longed to go . . . and the one place she now dreaded more than any other.

Her infiltration of the Obsidian command had succeeded far beyond anyone's expectations. Syenna's knowledge of the land throughout the Midmaer and the Grunvald regions had proven to be too valuable an asset for the Obsidians to ignore. She was soon attached to General Karpasic's command, giving her advice and her guidance, while at the same time relaying, when she could, their plans back to the baroness through intermediary messengers.

And then fate had delivered into her hands an opportunity too good to pass up: an ancient relic from before the Fall. Aren's discovery of an obscure sword in a lost tomb was, in and of itself, relatively unimportant. A single sword, regardless of its magical properties, would not likely turn the tide of the Obsidian expansion. But as a *symbol* of their cause, Syenna knew that the blade of an Avatar could inspire swords in the hands of thousands more. If she could deliver the sword into the hands of the baroness, then she, in turn, could bring it to the Council of Might—the coalition of warlords and city-states that opposed the Obsidians—and use it to raise a proper army against the Obsidian Cause.

And, of course, if the sword *did* have magical properties, then it was vital that such a weapon be denied the Obsidians before they could determine how to use it.

The problem was Captain Aren Bennis.

That the relic sword might actually be magically cursed struck a deep and fearful chord in Syenna. General Karpasic's reaction to the sword, the news of which had run through the camp like wildfire, had only deepened her concerns. It appeared that this ancient icon of ultimate good could only be handled by a commander in the service of everything the icon stood against.

Syenna had already sent word to gather the Council of Might, and feared that the Obsidians might discover the importance of the sword at any time.

The solution was unfortunately obvious: to steal the sword she had no choice but to steal the captain as well. General Karpasic had been unwittingly cooperative in providing an opportunity. She and her associates had moved against Aren deep in the Blackblade range and then used an old pass through the eastern peaks to cross back into the Midmaer. They stayed off the trade routes, following smaller trails along the foothills of the Blackblade, southward to the River Fang. This they followed west, to where the river emptied into the Bay of Storms.

There they camped for two days until, on the morning of the third, she saw the sails of the bark *Mistral* approaching up the coast from the south.

Everything had gone according to plan, but she found herself increasingly annoyed by their prisoner during the journey. Other than expressing a certain amount of chagrin on allowing himself to be captured, Captain Bennis seemed remarkably nonchalant about the situation. Syenna had been braced for recriminations, anger, and disdain; she was prepared to stand against him on her moral high ground with righteous indignation. That Aren seemed only bemused was frustrating her beyond endurance. She had wanted to shout at him from her own pain, to scream into his face all her reasons for what she did and for who she was.

Now, at the bottom of the dirt street that ran through the center of Etceter, Syenna swung her kit back over her shoulder, hung her head, and started her climb. The short walk between the shops and homes that she had known in her youth seemed to be the longest journey she had ever taken.

Syenna paused before the house. The bay window was empty. She pushed through the gate in the stone wall and had barely placed her foot on the first step up when the door to the cottage was suddenly flung open.

Amanda stood in the doorway. Her twisted, misshapen legs were shaking with the effort as her long, delicate hands clung to the framework of the door. Her hair was resplendent in the sunshine, and her large, astonishing eyes were overflowing with tears.

"Oh, sister!" Amanda exclaimed, her voice quavering as she spoke.

Syenna dropped her bag and rushed forward, catching her sister as Amanda's strength gave out and she fell. She held her sister close to her in her arms.

You are my pain, she thought. *You are all my reasons. You are who I am.*

Amanda sobbed out her joy and relief. "I wanted to give you something when you came home again!"

"You have," Syenna replied as tears welled up in her eyes. "You have given me everything."

CHAPTER 13

Councils

Baroness Gianna Baden-Fox closed her eyes in frustration. This effectively blocked the sight of the arguing factions but, unfortunately, did nothing to alleviate the assault on her ears from the increasingly vitriolic arguments being flung in attack and counterattack from all sides of the hall. The baroness opened her eyes once more and tried to take in the turmoil at the center of her keep.

It was too much, and her anger, that beast within her over which she had always held tight control, could be restrained no longer. The baroness stood suddenly from her chair at the end of the audience hall, raised her ornate staff of office, and jabbed its metallic tip violently against the stones at her feet.

The sound shot through the rhetoric, cutting a brief silence in the space of which her words could be heard.

"There will be order in my hall!" The words of the baroness

were a statement of fact whose very tone dared anyone to challenge their absolute reality. "The sovereigns and ambassadors who have come to council will conduct themselves with courtesy within my hall. Those who cannot will find their accommodations moved to my stockade. There you may shout at one another all you like; I will not hear you and will sleep all the sounder for it. So, my most honored and esteemed guests, you will all sit down, or by the Storm Gods, I will have you removed from my hall."

The baroness had been beautiful in her youth, and there were still the remains of a fine woman about her, but time and the sedentary nature of her office had softened her lines and added some girth. Her face was round and looked slightly puffy. But that, her courtiers would say, was where the softness ended. She had outlived her husband, who had set sail on another of his trade missions across the Bay of Storms and never returned, but not before she had borne him five sons. Each of those she raised with an iron will, and each of whom were at sea learning their father's profession. Although she preferred to wear elegant dresses and measured barely over five feet tall, everyone in Etceter, and in many courts beyond, knew her as the Bonesteel Baroness whom anyone would be well advised not to cross.

Slowly, everyone in the hall sat back into their chairs. The terrible tension and animosity could still be felt palpably in the room, but at least now there was silence into which reason might be spoken.

The baroness waited until everyone had settled before sitting down herself.

What a terrible mess, she thought.

As soon as she had gotten word of the related messages from Syenna, the baroness had acted at once, sending word to all the courts of the Council of Might of an urgent need to convene.

The Council of Might was a rather grand misnomer. There were a number of city-states, kingdoms, warlord strongholds, and at least one shogunate that had risen out of the ruins of the Fall, each one struggling to establish order and law out of the chaos. Each looked to the ruins of the past and aspired to their greatness, but none of them had come close to achieving it. At best, each was a shadow of past glory, a flickering ember of the fire that had once lit the world. But with the rise of the Obsidians, these embers were being snuffed out one by one. None of the fledgling kingdoms could stand alone. So the call went out from Tsuneo, the shogun of Ardoris, asking that representatives from the largest of the existing kingdoms form a pact of strength and defense. Seven answered that call, and by mutual acclamation, formed the Council of Might.

It was, in all substantive ways, the last thing they had agreed on.

She had offered the hospitality of Etceter as the most convenient—or, at least, equally inconvenient—location where counsel might be held on such short notice. Gianna was initially pleased that all the members of the Council of Might had responded, including Norgard, who, despite being a member, had declined every invitation to council for the last eighteen months.

The first respondents had given her considerable cause for hope. Ardoris, the city-state beyond the Brightbone Mountains to the east, had sent word that Shogun Tsuneo himself would be attending. Count Ekard, Master of the Council of Aerie, would make the journey from his port city to the west at the tip of the Longfall Peninsula. Everyone expected Opalis to be represented by Ambassador Miriam Heath, as the Titans seldom consented to an audience and never traveled from the city.

That pleasure, however, was quickly tempered when she discovered who would be representing the remaining member city-states. The mountain stronghold city known as Resolute, situated among the peaks of the range known as the Pillars of Night, dispatched Minister Arthur Falcone to represent Marshal Nimbus, as the marshal declined, saying he was too busy with military matters to attend. Ambassador Miles Shepherd, who had been in Etceter when Midras fell, had declared himself the Midras government in exile and, as no word had come regarding the fate of the priestess of Midras, or any of the rest of the government of that city-state, there was no one remaining to contradict the ambassador's assertions.

Most troublesome of all was the appointment of Tribune Marcus Tercius to represent Norgard. No one had expected the emperor himself to attend, nor did anyone know anything about the tribune or had any past dealings with him. What *was* known was that the armies of Norgard had crossed the Nayad Channel from their large island homeland the year before, and had been expanding eastward from the Verdantis Coast ever since.

Now, as the baroness looked around the room, she wondered how the Council of Might had ever managed to agree on a name for themselves, let alone agree to work for the common good.

"Are you all right, Baroness?"

Bending over from where he stood next to her, Gerad Zhal whispered into Gianna's ear.

The baroness turned her head toward her counselor and whispered in return. "Decidedly not. The cawing of these crows has brought a thunderous aching to my head. You are my loremaster; do you know of anything that will rid me of this pain?"

"Short of emptying the hall?" the loremaster responded quietly. "I have an elixir that could provide you with some relief, but I would not advise you drinking it within view of this council."

"A drink is perhaps exactly what I need," the baroness murmured in response. She glanced at the loremaster. "Won't our guests think you and I are plotting something if we keep whispering to each other?"

"Yes, Baroness," the loremaster replied. "But it has also afforded everyone a little time for hot tempers to cool and reflective thought to replace rhetoric. Besides, everyone here is expecting intrigue. It would be bad manners as a hostess not to at least provide them with the suspicion of some."

Gianna tried with only moderate success to suppress a smile playing at the corners of her lips. "You are wise indeed, Loremaster."

"That is, of course, my job," Gerad replied with a nod as he straightened once more to stand next to her chair.

Gianna considered him for a moment. Gerad Zhal had been the loremaster to the Etceter courts for as long as she could recall. He was not much taller than Gianna, with a stocky build and broad shoulders. The baroness had insisted today that he wear the deep blue mantle of his office with its matching flat hat and dangling tassel, but she knew he much preferred his comfortable shirt with the wide sleeves, and his leather vest. The bald top of his head was rimmed with white hair, and his face reminded Gianna of a hedgehog she had seen once when she was a little girl, all at once bemused and mischievous.

The baroness turned her attention back to the audience hall and the problem at hand. The six other representatives in the room were seated to her left and right, three on each side of the room, facing one another. The seating arrangements alone had taken careful consideration.

Ambassador Shepherd turned his angry gaze back toward the baroness. The ambassador from the fallen city-state of Midras had been situated in the seat farthest on Gianna's left. His bushy mustache and long, swept back hair were both iron gray. He wore a crimson red tunic with a long black mantle, the colors of mourning in the culture of his city. He had the broad chest of an old warrior, although his abdomen demonstrated a slight paunch. He had his arms folded across his chest and was fuming over having his speech interrupted. "May I continue?"

Gianna braced herself but nodded graciously. "Pray, do so."

"The point is," Shepherd said as he stood up, "that this ancient relic of the Avatars was discovered in Midras and, by right, is part of my city. Does this not demonstrate the vital and ancient importance of that place to the Avatars themselves? This sword is evidence—a sign if you will—that Midras's fall must be avenged, the city retaken—"

"Your city is *lost!*" bellowed the enormous warrior seated farthest from Gianna on her right. Sir Arthur Falcone, who had come in place of the marshal of Resolute. He was a large, robust man with a voice that was too loud and a temper that was too quick. His broad face and lantern jaw featured a long thin mustache and an even longer scar that ran from the bridge of his nose, across his cheek, and to nearly the base of his ear. His clothing and boots seem to have been chosen entirely out of dull, earthy colors, with the exception of a bright blue tabard featuring the symbol of a dragon, its wings spread wide, embroidered entirely out of silvery threads. "We did not come all this way to listen to your sobbing over a city you could not properly defend and hold."

"None of us could defend or hold our lands against the Obsidians' might," said Miriam Heath from the middle of the three chairs at Gianna's left. The ambassador from Opalis was a slender woman with prominent cheekbones and violet eyes. Her dark, curly hair she always wore pulled back and bound at the nape of her neck at official functions, although Gianna had occasionally seen her informally when Miriam would release her hair into a glorious mane. As ambassador, Miriam was a person of few words, but when she spoke, it was with the full confidence and authority of the Titans who ruled Opalis and, for today, the perfect buffer sitting between Tsuneo and Shepherd. "That was and remains the point of the Council of Might. No one of us alone has the strength to stop the Obsidians. Their magic is powerful, but with this discovery of the Avatar's weapon, we may be able to recover the magic that was lost from before the Fall."

"The Avatars?" Count Ekard chortled, shaking his head.

Closest to her right sat Tribune Marcus. He wore the uniform of the Norgard elite, an ornate breastplate over his tunic and a belted apron of leather straps around his waist. His dark hair was so closely cropped as to be difficult to see at all. He was clean shaven with a prominent, hawkish nose and a slightly receding chin. Marcus slouched casually in his chair, viewing everyone else in the room with thinly veiled distain. "Stories told by children to impress other children!"

"The Avatars existed," Miriam asserted. "The power of their magic shaped worlds and brought us the Virtues."

"It is a pleasant enough fiction, I suppose." Count Ekard, a tall, skeletal man of advancing years, sat leaning forward in his chair just beyond the tribune. Ekard wore the deep purple cassock and matching shoulder cape that signified him as head of the guild council ruling the port of Aerie. Gianna suspected that the guild council was working in league with Norgard and had hopes of profiting from their expansion. Count Ekard had a soothing way with words, and Gianna often had to remind herself not to believe any of them. "These myths about Avatars were brought into existence out of the ancient Virtues, not the other way around. Such bedtime stories about returning champions keep the peasants in line, I'll grant you that, and gives them some sort of false hope to which they can cling."

"False hope?" Shepherd's voice shook. He gestured toward the main doors at the far end of the hall. "The proof is here!"

"A proof that serves Midras," Marcus observed with a casual wave of his hand. "You could not defend your own city against the Obsidians, and now you want us to take it back for you because of some old sword that was found there."

"And how were we to defend Midras when her friends would not come to our aid?" Shepherd demanded. "Where were the Virtues espoused by Ardoris when their armies slept in their beds while children died in the streets of Midras?"

All eyes turned to Tsuneo, Shogun of Ardoris. He was seated closest to Gianna on her left, his arms folded across his chest over his brightly colored robes. He was a dark-complexioned man with a carefully trimmed goatee beard, and he was demonstrably unhappy. He looked as though he expected to be personally under siege. On either side of his chair stood his two "advisers," although everyone in the room knew that their function was to guard the shogun more than give their advice. He always thought before he spoke in his deep, rumbling voice. "Ardoris seeks to discover the Virtues in its heart and live them in its actions. The priestess of Midras sought the Virtues in her own path and by her own counsel. Her plea for aid came too late to have mattered. The children of Midras would not have been served by more deaths sacrificed on the path to the same destiny. There is Virtue in sacrifice for the greater good. There is no Virtue in sacrifice without purpose."

"If so, then Ardoris chooses for its own convenience which Virtues it will uphold!" Shepherd snapped. "The Avatars brought us the true Virtues in ancient days before the Fall—"

"All this talk about the Avatars when it's the Obsidians that are the problem!" Falcone growled. "As much a problem as the Avatars, if you ask me. Behind all them legends and them Virtues they spouted were a bunch of thieving brigands who did nothing but ruin the world with their meddling. Were there a single calamity of the ancient world's myths that weren't caused by some Avatar come stomping about the world and kicking over carts? Damned if I don't believe they *caused* the Fall in the first place. Good riddance to them, says I, and no rusty sword of their make is gonna make a sliver's difference when it come down to battling the Obsidians."

"You are quite right, Sir Falcone," Gianna said with a gracious nod.

"I am?" Falcone was genuinely surprised. No one ever agreed with him.

"The issue is, indeed, the Obsidians and what we are to do about them," the baroness said. "However, something has occurred to me that I think we should consider."

Ambassador Shepherd, still standing, was about to interrupt her.

"Sit down, Miles!" the baroness spoke in her most commanding tone. Shepherd slowly sat back down into his chair. "Everyone here has had a great deal to say this morning, but there is one testimony we have not yet heard."

Sir Falcone glanced about the room. "Who, Baroness?"

"Why, the sword, of course," Gianna replied. "Bring in the sword."

CHAPTER
14

The Bearer

You cannot possibly be serious," Syenna said, shaking her head in disapproval.

"What, this old thing?" Aren stood in the center of his stockade cell, pivoting around once completely in front of her. Although a number of blade strikes still marred the finish and a number of pieces were bent out of shape or missing entirely, there was no mistaking its infamous form. The captain stood before her clad completely in his Obsidian armor. "It was just something I had lying around."

"Take that off at once," Syenna fumed. "You cannot appear at court in that abomination."

"Quite the contrary. It is precisely because I am appearing at court that I must wear my uniform, or at least something that passes for one." Aren flashed a bright smile of mock tolerance. "You would not want me to misrepresent myself. After all, I suspect I am the first representative of the Obsidians to ever grace this court."

"You are the first we haven't killed before getting this close to court," Syenna snapped. "And if you wear that, you may be the first to be killed *at* court."

"You are hardly one to be complaining," Aren answered, gesturing at Syenna with his right hand. "Especially given your own attire."

Syenna drew in a breath between her teeth. "This is the traditional uniform of the Baron's Guard."

"The breastplate is functional enough, I'll give you that," Aren observed as he folded his arms across his own armor and looked her over with a critical eye. "But that enormous red plume on the top of a morion helmet? Your enemy would see you five weeks before you got within striking distance. And those bloused pantaloons with the multicolored stripes? Obviously those will provide you with the perfect camouflage for— oh, let me think—nowhere. Are there many of you dressed like this, or is this some sort of cruel joke being played on you?"

Syenna, not for the first time, ignored Aren's remarks and continued. "I will not have you present the sword in court donning that armor."

"Oh, I see." Aren furrowed his brow in consideration, pouting slightly. Then he shrugged, gesturing toward the long object wrapped in oilskin that lay on his cot. "Very well. I suppose you will want to present the blade at court yourself?"

Aren saw the color drain from Syenna's face as she took a single, involuntary step back, away from him.

"Well"—Aren smiled knowingly—"perhaps not."

Aren turned back to the oilskin wrappings laid on his cot.

He carefully unfolded them, smiling as he uncovered the familiar gleam and shape of the sword. He quickly reached down for the grip, closing his fingers around it.

The odd sensation that came to him every time he picked up the blade again returned. It was a familiar sensation, like shaking the hand of an old friend with whom you had a falling out years before and had long since forgotten what the argument was about. He gazed intently for a moment at the runes on the blade, which seemed forever to be changing before his eyes into new shapes at whose meanings he could only guess.

"You stop whistling that tune," Syenna demanded behind him.

Aren had not even realized he had been whistling. "Really? But it is such a catchy little tune."

"And I have been *catching* it for far too long," Syenna said. "You have been humming or whistling that same tune ever since we left the Blackblade Mountains."

"But it's the only song I know," Aren replied, still gazing at the blade and wondering at the shifting writing.

"I like a song as well as anyone, but couldn't you at least learn something different?" Syenna asked. "And put that blade away!"

Aren chuckled to himself. It was one thing to enter the hall of the baroness in the armor of her enemy but quite another, he realized, to do so with his blade drawn. Being brave was one thing, but being stupid was another thing altogether. He slid the sword into his scabbard and turned again to face Syenna.

"Well, if the court of the baroness needs a fool, here I am," Aren said, spreading his hands wide and bowing slightly.

"Although, given your costume, I rather think you fit the part much better."

"What do you know?" Syenna quipped. "You spent nearly ten days at sea with your head over the side of the boat."

"I was in contemplation!"

"You, great captain, were seasick."

† † †

Miles Shepherd experienced a glacial stillness as he sat nearest the great doors leading to the audience hall. He was surprised at how calm he felt and at the acuteness of his senses. It was as though time itself were slowing down all around him.

As they waited, Shepherd glanced around the audience hall, once more gauging everyone in the room. Directly across from him sat Sir Arthur of Resolute, a warrior whose battles were firmly lodged in his past and now beneath about thirty pounds too much weight. Count Ekard, who sat next to Sir Arthur, would run from any conflict, especially if he thought doing so would profit him. Tsuneo and his so-called advisers, who sat beyond Miriam Heath on his left, would not intervene in his purpose. The shogun's warrior guards would be primarily interested in defending Tsuneo. Miriam herself was strictly an ambassador with no skill with a blade. Gianna and her gray-haired councilor could easily be discounted, as both of them were as inept at weaponry as they were adept at politics. That left the Etceter guards, who might respond, but the baroness had situated them specifically at the very farthest edges of the room so as not to impede the conference. Even that Syenna woman had been relegated to a spot near the door—which was far away enough for Shepherd's purpose.

Shepherd folded his arms low across his lap, his right hand crossing beneath his black mantle. There, out of sight, he touched once more the hilt of his sword. It was a familiar friend whom in days past he had called upon often to defend his priestess and his city. Indeed, he was proud to have been counted among the Guardians of Midras in his younger days, and still secretly carried the skills and craft of that calling.

And, he reminded himself, his oath to uphold.

Everything had been taken from him. All that was left for him was his pain and his oath.

Now he could fulfill his oath.

And he had to stop the pain.

† † †

Aren stood outside the audience hall, bemused at the ten guards flanking him. *What do they think I'll do? Escape?*

The truth was that he could not be more pleased with his current state. Admittedly, he had been rather embarrassed at having so badly misjudged Syenna and for allowing himself to be captured, but it had quickly become very apparent to him that he was really very much in control of the situation. Syenna was loath to touch his relic sword and had warned all the other members of her kidnapping party not to do so. Since they wanted the sword brought here, they had to keep him alive in order to do so. With no fear of being killed, he felt safer here than he had in his own command. His captors had to keep him alive—which meant so far as Aren was concerned, he had his own personal guard. When he discovered that Syenna intended to bring him before the Council of Might, he could not have been more overjoyed. This was a chance to acquire knowledge of his enemy that he had never hoped to achieve. His only real danger was in startling one of his nervous guards and being run through in a moment of panic. His greatest safety, therefore, was in making no sudden moves and being as calm as possible.

No, he had absolutely no intention of escaping . . . at least, not yet.

"Stop whistling that tune!" Syenna demanded under her breath.

"Sorry," Aren agreed.

"You are to walk directly toward the baroness," Syenna instructed. "Avert your eyes to the ground but remain facing her as you approach. Do not look to either side. The floor has an inlaid pattern. Stop on the circular stone in the center of the hall and then wait in silence. Speak only when you are spoken to, and only to answer questions. Is all that clear?"

"It was clear last night when you told me," Aren replied. "It was even clearer this morning when you repeated it before we came up the hill to the keep."

"And while you're at it, get rid of that smile on your face!"

"Quite right." Aren cleared his throat and gave his most serious expression. "Solemn occasion—understood."

Syenna stood in front of Aren, and tapped the base of her ceremonial spear against the great double doors that were the main entrance to the audience hall. The doors opened outward, pushed by two Etceter guards clad in the same odd formal guard uniforms as Syenna.

Aren lifted his chin and strode past Syenna into the audience hall.

An audible gasp greeted him.

Tall pillars on either side of the room supported the beautiful arched ceiling twenty feet overhead. In front of the pillars were set six enormous chairs—three on each side—where an unusual collection of people were sitting. Two were in some sort of military uniforms, while others seemed to be in more ceremonial dress. He assumed they represented various organizations, nations, or states, although he did not recognize any of them by nationality let alone by name. The dark, stern-looking man in the bright robes farthest from him on the right was flanked by two large men who were obviously his personal guards. Aren noted in his mind to be particularly wary of them.

There was a seventh chair situated at the far end of the hall opposite the doors he had entered. There sat a woman in a gown. Aren assumed she was the baroness. Standing at her side was an oddly dressed older man—possibly an adviser but certainly no threat to him. There were guards in the room but those were situated at the perimeter of the room, well back from the chairs. The guards were listless and, undoubtedly, bored with the machinations and debates that had recently filled the room.

Aren continued to stride into the room, his gaze fixed on the eyes of the baroness. They were intent embers looking back at him in outrage. His uniform, he thought with an inward smile, was having the desired effect.

In a moment, the eyes of the baroness shifted suddenly, fixing to Aren's right. The look on her face suddenly softened from its outrage, and her jaw began to drop.

Whether he saw it from the corner of his eye or sensed it in the air, Aren became aware of movement behind him to his right.

Aren spun around, turning his head and raising his arms in front of him.

The older man in the black mantle and the crimson tunic lunged at him with a saber. Aren instinctively shifted his left arm, sweeping it downward. The metal vambrace of his Obsidian armor swung against his opponent's blade, deflecting it outward and away from the captain.

Aren was vaguely aware of shouts and cries rising around him. He stepped into his attacker, turning to his left and trying to arrest the man's sword arm under his own.

His opponent anticipated the move, leaping backward and using the deflection of the blade to swing it back to a ready position. Aren reached down as he turned, the fingers of his right hand wrapping around his sword's grip. He pulled the blade free just as the older man lunged again. Aren shifted the sword in front of him again to deflect the thrusting blade. Steel shivered against steel as the edges of their blades slid down each other until they clanged to a stop at the sword's guards.

In that instant, their blades locked, Aren looked into the eyes of the hatred looking back at him.

Aren's own eyes went suddenly wide.

Aren *knew* this man.

The captain felt his attacker pressing all his weight against the locked blades. Aren responded by suddenly stepping to the side, turning out of the direction of the man's push. The attacker, suddenly with nothing to push against, fell forward. Aren kicked out with his leg, tripping the man as he tried to regain his balance and sending him sprawling face forward to the floor.

Aren quickly stepped over him as the man tried to roll to his feet. The captain kicked away the man's sword at once, bringing the tip of his blade down to his opponent's throat.

The tip of the Avatar blade hung unmoving, less than a finger's width from the man's neck.

The silence in the room felt as though it were charged with lightning. No one moved as time itself seemed to hold its breath.

"Miles Shepherd," Aren murmured.

The ambassador lying on the floor had been staring with hatred up at Aren, but now he blinked, his features softening. "What? What did you say?"

"You are Miles Shepherd," Aren continued, his voice quavering slightly as he spoke. "You loved the spring and the fall in Midras as your favorite times of the year. The city seemed to be the most alive to you then. You saw them as times of renewal and harvest. There was not a day gone by when you looked upon the old ruins of the city and saw them not as they were, but as what they might become through the love and work of the people."

Syenna, her own sword drawn, walked carefully toward her prisoner. The other guards in the hall, awakened abruptly from their stupor, were closing in on him as well.

"You loved the priestess and were honored to serve her as a Guardian of Midras." Aren sighed. "That's why you accepted when she asked you to call for aid. That's why you left the city."

On the ground, Miles gazed up at the Obsidian captain in wonder. "How . . . how can you know these things?"

"Your beloved family was there when the attack came," Aren continued, a sadness coming into his voice. "Your children and your grandchildren . . . and here you were, too far away to help or protect them."

A tear fell from the corner of Shepherd's eye.

Syenna was nearly ready to strike.

"Wait!" The old man who had stood next to the baroness suddenly appeared next to Aren, his arms raised against the approaching blades of the Etceter guards. "I am Gerad Zhal! In the name of the baroness, stand back, I say! Stand back!"

"You're wondering if I know what happened to them." Aren sighed as he looked down at Shepherd. "I am sorry, Ambassador, I do not. The siege was a difficult one, and there were many dead on both sides. But many in the city survived, and your family may well be among them. Yes, there are Guardians who still live, although I cannot tell you the fate of your priestess. We never found her."

Aren pulled the blade slowly away from the throat of the ambassador. It hung in his hand, loose at his side.

"Most remarkable," Gerad Zhal said breathlessly as he gazed down at Aren's sword.

Aren turned slowly, gazing about the room. He at last faced the baroness. His breathing was heavy as he bowed slightly to Gianna. "My apologies, madam, for disturbing your court and your deliberations."

"Captain Bennis!" Gianna spoke suddenly, as though her breath had just come back to her. "You are a servant of the Obsidian Cause, whose grievous crimes against our allies are unspeakable and whose conduct in my own court merits—"

"He must take the sword at once to Opalis," Gerad Zhal exclaimed.

The hall was suddenly filled with half a dozen voices.

"Loremaster Zhal!" Gianna sputtered. "That is out of the question!"

"Hear me! Hear me now!" Zhal shouted, his hands raised over his head, demanding attention. "This may, indeed, be a blade of the ancient Avatars. From what I have seen of it, it has all the legendary markings befitting such a find. These artifacts were powerful, and their powers specific to each blade. The question in my mind is not *if* this blade is of Avatar origin—for I certainly believe that it is—but rather *which* of the ancient blades has been uncovered. So many of the books and writings of the past were lost to us in the horrible chaos that followed the Fall. My own collection here, even as loremaster, is so slight that I cannot possibly make a determination about this weapon. However, Opalis is ruled by the Titans—beings whom, by their very nature, know more of the past than any mortal human—and who have been working tirelessly to recover the knowledge of the past. They will know about this sword and what it portends for us."

"It is only a blade!" Sir Arthur protested.

"It is not only a blade, but a symbol of our glorious past!" Zhad countered. "By itself it may not be terribly significant; how much can one warrior do? But in the hands of the right leader, it could inspire armies to do what no single warrior ever could."

"Then take the thing from this Obsidian whelp and be done with it!" Tribune Marcus demanded.

"But this blade *is* cursed," Zhal said, his hands open wide before him. "It has chosen this man—this vile man—to be its bearer. What if the blade itself is evil and must be destroyed? We cannot know this until the loremasters in Opalis have made a learned and proper examination of the matter."

"So he nearly kills an ambassador to my court"—Gianna glared at her loremaster—"and you want to send him to Opalis?"

"But he *didn't* kill him. Don't you see?" Zhal replied with a smile. "Syenna has brought to us—to all of us—a tremendous enigma and an equally tremendous opportunity. If we could regain the powers of the ancient world, the magic that once was, then we would no longer have to fear these Obsidians. I dare say that having brought her prisoner this far, she could get him safely to Opalis. Wouldn't that suit everyone's best interests?"

† † †

I thought that went well," Aren remarked to Syenna as she shoved him back into his stockade cell.

Syenna slammed closed the ironbound door behind him and locked it without a word.

Aren turned and gazed out the small, barred opening in the door. He could see the stockade wall and the keep just up the hillside beyond. Syenna was stomping off in that direction, most likely to let her baroness know how badly she hated the decision of the Council of Might. Aren suspected it would make her feel better but not change a thing. The council had spoken and, it seemed, in two days' time, they would be leaving Etceter.

The bearer, Aren thought smugly to himself, *is to bring the sword to Opalis.*

Aren carefully removed his armor and, once rid of its burden, sat back on his cot. He relished a moment or two before he once again began whistling his familiar, odd tune, the same tune he had been whistling since they had left the Blackblade Mountains.

He paused, thinking he had heard something.

He whistled the tune once more.

A shadowy head peered at him from beneath the edge of the cot.

"Well, my dear Monk." Aren smiled broadly. "It's about time you found me."

The homunculus flapped its leathery wings joyfully and came to perch at once on the extended arm of the captain.

"I'm afraid you cannot stay," Aren said, and nodded, rubbing his finger under the small monster's chin. "I have a message for you to deliver, and it cannot wait."

Aren gazed into the eyes of the homunculus.

"Personal message to Obsidian Evard Dirae," Aren said. "Captured by enemy force and taken to Etceter. Am being taken to Opalis in South Paladis northeast of Jaanaford on West Jaana River. Arriving in eighteen days. Come and get me there."

Aren thought for a moment and then continued, frowning.

"I've met the leaders of the Council of Might—and I now absolutely know how to defeat them."

CHAPTER
15

*Bay
of
Storms*

The *Cypher* set sail from Etceter the day after the council had pronounced their decision. Given the size of the ship—she was a rather large ship with three masts—it was remarkable to Aren that they had managed to provision her in so short a period of time.

Aren was not by any definition of the word a "man of the sea." He didn't know a belay from a barnacle, though he did recall hearing both terms while aboard the *Mistral*; especially the last, as it had often been applied to him. Even so, he could read a map and knew enough about the world as to make reasonable estimates about distance. They had come aboard the *Mistral* along the coastline somewhere south of the Blackblade range, and it had taken the ship eight days to arrive at Etceter. He had seen the port in Quel on a chart in the captain's cabin once, as well as the position of Opalis in South Paladis. If they sailed eastward from Etceter and back along the same coast they had stayed with while coming here, it would take those same eight days to get back to the mouth of the Fang River and, given the distances involved, another five or six days to reach where the Jaana River emptied into the Bay of Storms. Then, given the overland distance into Opalis, another four days before they arrived.

As the ship slowly drew away from the dock at Etceter, Aren leaned against the rail and congratulated himself on a brilliant plan. Eighteen days more or less, at sea and in transit, to learn all he could from his captors. Eighteen days and his friend Evard Dirae would come for him. Eighteen days and then he would be free to return to his service in the Obsidian Empire, deal at last with General Karpasic, and figure out the most profitable way to be rid of this ridiculous sword.

Aren looked around the deck of the ship. Syenna was gratefully back in the more familiar garb of trousers, high boots, and tunic and was gazing back over the opposite railing at the port town receding in their wake. She seemed particularly melancholy today, and nothing Aren had said seemed to raise her spirits.

Standing near her was that strange old man he now knew as Gerad Zhal. He had a round, jovial face rimmed in white whiskers that extended up over his ears to form a ring around his shiny, bald head. Aren remembered him as the broad-shouldered man who had stood next to the baroness Gianna when he was brought into court. He had apparently packed away his blue mantle and cap for a leather vest worn over his simple, linen shirt and cloth pantaloons. Others in the crew had referred to him as Loremaster, which Aren assumed was his title. Aren was most curious about this man, as he had been the one who had suggested this little journey in the first place, and was now apparently coming along for the ride as well. Aren had thought the suggestion of taking the sword to Opalis was one that would have instigated another near-riot among the delegates of the Council of Might but, to the captain's astonishment, all parties quickly came to agreement.

Well, I've got nearly two weeks on this boat to find out why, he thought to himself.

The *Cypher* was, according to the loremaster, a barque-class vessel and significantly larger than the *Mistral*. Zhal had also gone into a rather lengthy explanation as to just how this barque differed from the caravel on which he had arrived—whose crew had apparently amused themselves by convincing him it was actually a brigantine "brig"—and why the barque was a superior choice for travel. Zhal had continued speaking long after Aren had lost interest in the subject, but the captain did learn one thing from their conversation: the loremaster loved to talk.

Aren's stomach lurched slightly. He frowned. The ship's motion across the waves was not nearly as abrupt as that of the caravel but was nevertheless disquieting.

I am a warrior of the Obsidian Cause, Aren reminded himself. *My will conquers mere physical discomfort. I will corner this loremaster Zhal and make him spill his guts before this voyage is over!*

He drew in a deep breath, his fingers gripping the railing a little tighter.

We are far enough away from the coast, he thought. *They will be turning the ship to the east any moment now.*

But the ship continued its northward course toward the dark, lightning-streaked horizon beyond the Siren Isle.

† † †

Evard Dirae, Craftmaster of the Cabal of the Obsidians, stood once again before the four thrones of the generals at Hilt. General Karpasic was intentionally keeping him waiting. It was a vain display of authority on the part of the general, which was at the moment, of considerable inconvenience to Evard.

Just another knot in your noose, dear general, Evard thought, trying to keep his impatience in check.

At last the general arrived, striding into the room from one of the numerous doors situated behind the thrones. He was, as usual, clanking about in his full armor.

Does he have more than one set of armor, or do they just peel the general out of it every night? Evard mused. He would hardly have been surprised if the vain commander claimed to sleep in the monstrous thing.

"My apologies, Master Sorcerer," the general began speaking even as he stomped toward his throne. "I'm certain you understand that the pressing duties of my command—"

"What I understand is that you are a general, I represent the Cabal of the Obsidians, and that your obedience is required," Evard spoke in loud, clear tones that echoed through the otherwise empty enormity of the hall. "Not requested. Not asked. Not hoped for nor begged, but *required.*"

"You have no right to talk to me that way!" the general sputtered.

"I apparently have every right, as I have obviously just done so and no one has done, or will do, anything to prevent me from doing so again." Evard spoke as though stating a fact of nature.

The sorcerer calmly mounted the three steps leading up to the throne platform, then turned and sat down on General Karpasic's throne.

The general glared at the sorcerer but did not move.

"I have orders for you, General, from the Cabal of the Obsidians," Evard stated as he looked back at the general with cold distain. "You are to organize your armies with the reinforcements we have provided you this week and prepare to march within three days' time. You will then proceed west through the pass into South Paladis and turn your force north. That would be on your right—"

"I understand which way is north!" Karpasic fumed.

"Then your ability to astonish me continues, General. Your objective is to find and secure a five-league-wide region around the junction of the Sanctus and Fortus Rivers at all cost."

"May I ask what is there?"

"You may not," Evard replied.

"Well, is it a city or stronghold or—"

"It's where the Sanctus and Fortus rivers meet, General," the sorcerer said. "It is vital to the success of the Obsidian Cause, and you will carry out your orders as instructed. Is that clear?"

"A river junction?" General Karpasic sputtered. "Where is the glory in conquering some piece of farmland?"

"I assume you'll know its value when you see it." Evard smiled darkly at the general. "Have no fear, General. I'll be back soon enough to help you do the right thing."

"You're leaving, then?" There was more hope in the general's voice than he would have probably liked to have shown.

"Yes, I have an errand for the cabal that cannot wait," Evard said.

"Where are you going?" the general asked.

"That is of no concern of yours, General," Evard sneered as he stood abruptly from the throne. "You have your orders. I suggest that you follow them. The cabal has been debating of late whether some magical 'reshaping' of our generals might produce a better, more trustworthy command of our armies. What do you think of the idea, General? Has it any merit?"

The general blanched as Evard stepped past him.

Evard was in a hurry. The search for Aren had taken up much of his time and too much of his powers in sorcery. He had received his friend's message from the homunculus three days before, and it had taken those days to prepare before he could leave. Now it would be all he could do to reach Opalis by the eighteenth day.

† † †

The ship rolled heavily to starboard, the hull groaning as the waves crashed against it. The shrill whistle of the wind through the rigging, heard even through the four decks above Aren, sounded in his ears like the keening of angry spirits. The single lantern, suspended from the ceiling, swung wildly on its hook, causing the shadows in the room to shift and sway. Water sloshed back and forth across the floor of his cell with every bounding movement of the ship, carrying with it the bucket into which, it seemed to Captain Bennis, the contents of everything he had eaten in the last two days was destined to be deposited. The greatest challenge was to hit the bucket as it slid about the floor, carried by the ever-moving puddle of water that had somehow made its way from the torrent drenching the top deck, down to his brig cell near the bottom of the ship.

"It was really quite a simple matter of knowing where everyone's own interest lay," Gerad Zhal said cheerfully, his back pressed against the larboard bulkhead of the ship, his right leg pushing against the frame of the starboard bunk fixed to the hull opposite him. The stance effectively wedged him in place. "If you know what they want and can show them how they can have it by agreeing with you, then consensus is easy to achieve."

Aren lay sprawled across the bunk, gripping its frame with colorless hands as his head lolled over the edge.

Death, Aren thought miserably, *would have been preferable.*

"Take Aerie, for example," the loremaster continued. "The guildmasters there care more about profit and keeping their trade lines open than for the ancient past. They could care less about this Avatar blade of yours, but they *do* care about keeping Norgard trade in their pocket. So by convincing Norgard that having your relic sword in Opalis made it far more likely that they would be part of the warrior-magic it represented, well, that in turn allowed Norgard to convince Aerie to vote with them in favor of our expedition. Do you see?"

Aren tried to raise his head to speak but could only manage to blurt out the two things he had actually heard: "Warrior . . . magic?"

"Well, *warrior-magic* may have been a carefully selected phrase on my part, I'll grant you," the loremaster admitted, but then dismissed it with a wave of his hand. "But I do believe that some form of ancient magic is evidenced by your sword. Whether that can be put to any practical use by Norgard, or any of the other factions of the Council of Might, is purely a matter of conjecture. However, so long as each of them at least believed in the *possibility*, then they were willing to allow the sword to be brought to Opalis for examination. Alas, it also brings the sword near the borders of Norgard's own conquests, but I believe that is a risk worth taking."

The bucket had slid to rest beneath Aren's face. The smell of his previous meals rose up to greet him. He tried to add to its contents once more, but despite his spasms, there seemed nothing left inside him to contribute.

"The lady Miriam could easily be counted, as she is the representative of Opalis, so long as she could also be convinced that Norgard would remain behind their borders and not simply take the sword from them once it was in reach of their city," the loremaster continued, completely at ease with the lurching of the ship about them. "That essentially left the problem of the two warlords: the paladins of Resolute and the shogun of . . . Is this making any sense to you?"

The ship suddenly heeled over hard to larboard just as it pitched upward at the bow. The bucket was swept across the floor and backward along with the water, both splashing against the back wall of the brig.

Aren was hearing the sound of the loremaster's voice, but little else. At least listening to someone speaking to him, even if he was too sick to register the meaning of the words, was better than suffering the ship's motion alone. Aren let out a loud belch then managed to mumble. "Keep . . . talking."

"Oh, very well then." Gerad Zhal smiled, shifting his boot slightly to strengthen his hold against the heaving wall at his back. "As I was saying . . ."

The room reeled as the bow plunged downward. The bucket

tipping over at last, spilling its contents to mix with the seawater rushing forward. Aren belched loudly once again and then rolled over onto his back. His hands gripped the sides of the bunk, and he closed his eyes, trying to will the universe to hold still around him. *At least I won't have to aim for the bucket anymore,* he thought.

"Are you all right?" Gerad asked.

"No! I mean . . . is it always like this?"

"Oh no!" Gerad chuckled. "It is usually much worse! We hardly ever attempt this kind of crossing anymore. Even the best of our mariners consider it entirely too dangerous to risk. But the weather was particularly favorable, and the baroness felt the need for urgency."

"This . . . is favorable?" Aren muttered through quivering lips. With his eyes closed, he could barely manage to concentrate on the loremaster's voice, even if his words did not make sense to him.

"For the Baden-Fox clan? Certainly!" The loremaster smiled, and the room shuddered under the side impact of a wave. "The original Baden-Fox founded Etceter as a haven for his . . . well, pirate vessels. They became particularly adept at sailing just inside the edge of the storm and raiding the trade ships that passed along the coastlines between the Longfall Peninsula, Elysium, and the Perennial Coast. Even so, no one has actually navigated across the storm this way in my lifetime. It's all rather thrilling to be part of it, don't you agree?"

Aren swallowed hard, keeping his eyes tightly shut as he managed a single, exhausted word. "Thrilling."

"You know, I think you could use some fresh air," the loremaster decided.

Aren opened his eyes to stare at Gerad in disbelief.

The loremaster slid his boot from the opposing bench to stand on the still-careening deck, his feet set wide and his knees slightly bent. To Aren, it seemed that the room was moving around Gerad.

"Let's go up to the top deck," Gerad urged. "We must be somewhere near the middle of the bay by now. We might even see the citadel!"

"Citadel?" Aren blinked hard, struggling to rise up on one elbow while trying to concentrate on what Gerad was saying. "What citadel?"

"Oh, it's a legend passed down by the pirates and mariners of the bay." Gerad smiled back at Aren. "They say that those who sail through the center of the Great Storm will see a great gathering of lights beneath the waves. They tell of a great citadel beneath the waves where the souls of all the dead mariners who have been taken by the storm gather in a place of quiet, peace, and perpetual tranquility. Other legends talk of the citadel, but not as a peaceful place, but a place of constant war between the souls of pirates forced to eternally fight one another. Either way, it would be something to see the lights deep below the storm of the bay, would it not?"

"You . . . You go." Aren waved feebly as he sank back into the bunk. "I can't leave the brig."

"What are you talking about?" Gerad laughed. "The bars are not locked. You're free to come up on deck with me. I'll even help you with your safety line."

"No! Thank you!" Aren said with exhausting vehemence. "When I say I cannot leave the brig . . . I mean . . . I mean, I *cannot* leave the brig."

"You would feel a great deal better if you would just—"

"Go away," Aren said feebly.

"But I was going to tell you all about Opalis, its splendor and the benevolence of the Titans who rule there!"

"Just go away," Aren said, closing his eyes once more and gripping tighter the sides of his bunk.

† † †

The *Cypher* found its way out of the tempest on the evening of the fourth day in the storm. The seas gradually calmed as they sailed on toward the north, and with them, Aren's stomach began to calm as well. By that time, they had been at sea five days.

On the morning of the sixth day, Aren managed to struggle up the ladders from the *Cypher*'s brig through the intervening decks to again see the open sky. He was surprised to see land to the northeast, but Syenna explained that it was not the Ash Coast of South Paladis but Spindrift Island—a place where the barons of Etceter had forever decreed no one should make landfall. No reason had ever been given, and legends had filled the void, but no mariner would challenge a cursed place. Aren did not remember much of what the loremaster had said to him but, much to his surprise, he realized that being on the open deck did help him feel a little better.

By the time the *Cypher* made anchor off the Ash Coast that afternoon, none was more pleased to leave the ship than the Obsidian captain. Opalis was still a four days' journey ahead of them, but at least, Aren reflected, he could keep his meals down along the way.

However, he knew it meant that he would arrive in Opalis in ten days rather than the eighteen he had estimated in his message to Evard. He was unconcerned, though, at having to wait for his friend's arrival.

After all, he thought, *what could happen in eight days?*

PART III

THE
SIEGE

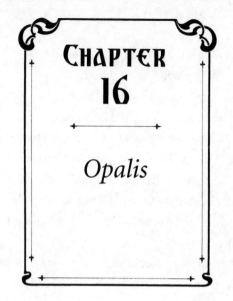

CHAPTER
16

Opalis

The city of Opalis lay at the horizon like a beckoning mirage.

Syenna, Aren, and Zhal, along with six of the baroness' guards, stopped their horses in wonder on the road that crossed the plain. They had followed the Jaana River from the Ash Coast up to the crossroads village of Jaanaford, then continued up the road that paralleled West Jaana for several days. Now, in an instant, the weariness of their journey was momentarily forgotten.

"It's incredible," Aren said, shaking his head. Sitting on the back of the chestnut horse they had placed him on, the vision that had caught his eyes across the plain had made him forget that his hands were tied and bound to the horn of the saddle beneath him. "Why didn't you tell me?"

Syenna smiled in wistful awe. "I didn't know."

"You haven't been here before?" Aren asked.

"If I had only known," she replied.

"It is a most common reaction among those whose eyes first gaze upon the beauty of Opalis," Gerad Zhal said, chuckling, as he urged his horse forward just enough to come alongside the captain. "I would have thought, Captain Bennis, that a warrior in the service of the Obsidian Cause would have seen many such places in the course of his conquests."

"No, Loremaster," Aren said through a lopsided grin. "Never anything like this."

The city proper was encompassed by an impressive curtain wall over thirty feet in height. While there were numerous smaller buildings and tents situated outside of these walls—which the loremaster had informed them was called Brambletown—there appeared to be a great clear space maintained around its base. At several points in the angular twisting wall, stone turrets were fixed, rising into beautiful, slender towers both magnificent and practical. Beyond the wall, Aren could see the rooftops of buildings, many of the spires and domes gleaming brightly in polished brass.

But it was the citadel of Opalis that was a true wonder. Its magnificent dome dwarfed all others around it, shining brilliantly beneath the sky. Yet it was not the morning sun alone that gave it light, for there was a compelling, purple aura streaked with lightning that danced on its surface. The dome was, in turn, cradled in the curved lines of the tower whose form Aren could only describe as resembling a frozen, opalescent flame that swept upward to a peak high above the right side of the dome. From this distance, it was a stunning achievement, the likes of which, Aren was certain, had not existed since before the Fall. He was suddenly filled with a wary dread; this was something that was unknown among the Obsidians. Aren knew that the downfall of every perfect plan lay waiting in the shadows of the unknown.

"Is there something wrong?" Syenna looked at him more carefully.

At least, Aren thought, *she's gone back to wearing the breeches and jacket.* "No, not at all."

"For a moment I thought you looked as though you were going to be sick again," Syenna chided.

"For the last time, I was not sick," Aren said with a haughty grin. "I was merely employing an unusual interrogation technique on Loremaster Zhal."

A loud guffaw exploded from the loremaster.

"Four days in your bunk with your head in a slop bucket and as weak as a newborn kitten?" Syenna considered with a raised eyebrow and as straight a face as she could manage. "I say, that *is* an unusual technique."

"Indeed and dedicated, too," agreed Zhal through his laughter. "He had to torture himself nearly to death before I talked!"

Syenna barely managed to stifle her own laughter.

"Well, it worked, didn't it?" Aren interrupted loudly. "It wasn't my fault that the loremaster didn't know anything worth learning."

"Or I didn't tell you anything worth learning," Zhal corrected through his smile.

"All this over a worthless sword," Aren groused.

"Worthless?" Syenna asked skeptically.

"Yes, worthless," Aren replied.

"Now what are you talking about?" Syenna sighed.

"Look, ever since I found this sword, I haven't been able to attack anyone with it." Aren shrugged as best he could with his hands tied. "What good is a sword that won't kill?"

"Quite so." Zhal nodded. "One of many questions I would like to have answered about your most remarkable weapon."

"And you will share those enlightened answers, Loremaster, when the time comes?" Aren said, turning toward Zhal.

"Absolutely, although sometimes finding the answer isn't nearly as difficult as discovering what question one should be asking. Whatever the questions, all our answers lie in that city on the horizon." Zhal beamed as he urged his horse forward.

"Yes." Syenna nodded. "All our answers."

"And I promise to tell you everything I learn," Zhal said to Aren, "while we're on the ship back to Etceter."

Aren's stomach turned over at the thought.

† † †

Aren Bennis was a captain in the Obsidian Cause.

As such, he did not concern himself with the increasingly heavy foot traffic as the inhabitants of Opalis moved around him. He examined the city they were approaching as he had examined so many towns and strongholds over the past few years, with a military eye toward defense and conquest. The structures and tents of Brambletown outside the city wall were separated from the wall by what turned out to be large depressions with steep embankments. They were rather like oversize moats without the water, although Aren suspected that they might be made to fill with water. It would be easy enough to divert the West Jaana River with a sluice gate for that purpose. Even dry, those deep depressions would make for a formidable crossing. Warriors attacking the wall would have to first charge down the embankment, crowding into the depression before they could climb up the steep embankment opposite them. Only after all that would they have even reached the base of the wall itself. Formations would tend to bunch up in the limited space of the depression, making defensive fire from the walls far more deadly. The only level access into the city appeared to be along the causeways—essentially, ground that had been removed to create the depressions that led to the city gates.

They approached the gate at the southeastern edge of the encircling wall. Here the crowds were thick on the causeway. The gate was recessed somewhat, with a section of wall looking down on the approaches from the left and a turret from the right. Aren noted that there were armed guards walking the battlements above, but not nearly as many as the captain would have posted for the city's defense. Perhaps they were not expecting an imminent attack and were, therefore, maintaining a minimal defense. There were two sets of double gates, each two feet thick and steel-bound, each set separated by a narrow stone tunnel that penetrated through the twenty-foot thickness of the wall. Both gates were open, allowing the people, their carts, and occasional wagons to move in and out without being challenged.

Loremaster Zhal—helpful as ever—had informed Aren that this was called the Storm Gate, since it represented the beginning of the road to the Bay of Storms. The city had three such gates; the two others, known as the Fields Gate on the west side, which accessed the farmland to the southwest, and North Gate, which was, well, on the north. The North Gate was the largest of the three, as its roads connected Opalis with Resolute, situated in the mountains far to the north, and also Willowvale, across the Pillars of Night Range to the northwest.

Aren had heard of Resolute, but Willowvale meant nothing to him. The Obsidian captain was at the very boundaries of his knowledge of the world and felt somewhat concerned that he might fall off if he were not careful.

They passed through the Storm Gate and into the city beyond. After the wide sky beneath the open prairie, the small square just inside the city gates seemed uncomfortably close. A broad avenue curved around the sheer curtain wall of the citadel that towered above them. Buildings were uncomfortably close to one another, and the people on the avenue milled, shifted, and moved around one another like a slow river.

"Hail, Etceter!" cried out a guard who appeared before them from out of the crowd. He was a tall man with a stocky build. His wide face was made even wider by the carefully trimmed, dark beard and broad smile. His hair was a tight thatch of curls about his tanned face. He was clad in a padded cerulean doublet with the image of a falcon, its wings spread wide, emblazoned across the front. He wore no armor, so far as Aren could tell, but rested his left hand casually on the hilt of a rapier strapped to his side. He raised his right hand, palm open toward them, in salute.

"Hail, Opalis!" Zhal called back, returning the open-palm salute from the back of his horse. "It is good to see you again, Captain Trevan."

"You as well, Loremaster Zhal!" The captain of Opalis smiled even more broadly than before. "We had word of your approach two days ago. I was nearly of a mind to come and get you, fearing you might get lost along the way."

"Now what kind of a loremaster would I be if I couldn't remember my way home?" Zhal chuckled.

"Exactly my point." Trevan smiled. "I see you have brought a rather large contingent with you. Perhaps you would be so good as to introduce them to me?"

Aren gnawed at his lip. The citizens who were thronging the streets were drawing back toward the edges of the square, stopping to watch the unusual events unfolding before them. He had assumed that Syenna and Zhal wanted to keep their journey and its purpose a secret, but now they were on horseback in the public square of the city being introduced to a guardian of the city as though they were paying a social call. Aren was uncomfortable with the attention it would draw to him.

"Of course. Mikas Trevan, Captain of the Opalis Legion," Zhal announced with a slight bow from his saddle. Zhal smiled and gestured toward Syenna. "May I present the Lady Syenna, Shieldmaiden to Baroness Baden-Fox."

Shieldmaiden? Aren thought. *What's a shieldmaiden?*

"A great pleasure," Mikas responded, bowing in Syenna's direction. "Opalis welcomes you."

"And Aren Bennis, Captain of the Westreach Army of the Obsidian Empire, conqueror of Midras, and adviser to General Milos Karpasic," Zhal said easily.

The murmur of voices from the citizens crowding the edges of the square suddenly diminished to an uncomfortable, shocked silence.

Trevan looked askance at the loremaster, as though he were expecting Zhal to break out into laughter over his own joke.

Aren watched as the knowledge quickly dawned on the commander of the Opalis Legion's face that his old friend was in earnest.

"Captain . . . Aren Bennis," Trevan said in somewhat icier tones than before. His smile fell slightly at the corners, and the commander's eyes shifted sharply toward Aren. He took him in all at once, and his eyes narrowed under furrowed brows when he saw that Aren was allowed to wear his sword, but yet his hands were bound. "Opalis . . . welcomes you as well. I am most curious about you, sir. I am keen for a most earnest discussion between us. May I offer you the hospitality of the Opalis barracks?"

"Captain Trevan." Aren nodded toward the commander, his ears filled with the silence of the square. "I look forward to such an opportunity, if it does not put you out."

"Oh, I insist," Trevan said emphatically. He then turned to the loremaster. "What brings you back to Opalis the Beautiful, old friend?"

"Consultation with our loremistress," Zhal replied. "Is she in residence?"

"I believe you will find her in the Athenaeum, as usual," Trevan replied, pointing down the wide avenue to the left as they entered the gate. "May I accompany you?"

"I can see it from here," Zhal said, laughing. "I hardly need a guide!"

"Even so," Trevan said, his eyes fixed on Aren. "I believe I shall insist."

† † †

Lanilan Stranthas, Loremistress of the Athenaeum of Opalis, sat with her elbows on the desk in the center of the

Athenaeum, both hands cradling her chin. Her thick, curly hair was tucked up into her flat cap, its annoying tassel pushed out of the way at the back of her head. Her large, dark eyes took in the manuscript pages in front of her with such devout interest that she had completely forgotten the rest of the world.

The manuscript had recently been brought in from ruins discovered far to the east of Jaanaford in the Blackblade foothills. The parchment, discovered in a stone box, was badly deteriorating but could still be separated and was remarkably legible. She had been carefully transcribing the text to new papyrus sheets when the contents had distracted her. She became so absorbed in the story they told that she forgot that she was supposed to be writing it down.

It was the tale of ancient royalty—a lord—who had once walked the face of the world in the days before the Fall. His deeds were mighty and miraculous. It was not the first time that Lanilan had encountered stories about this lord, for he appeared in tales told in diverse and distant cultures. There were great differences between the details of the stories, but each one had several common elements, the most unifying of which was the belief that this lord—regardless of which name he chose—would return to the world after the Fall and bring with him its final judgment: doom or redemption depending on the culture's need.

This particular text dealt with the shattering of the moon. It told the story of the lord—named Brinist in this version—fighting the Dragon of Chaos. Lord Brinist's sword swept across the sky to deal the final blow to the dragon, but the dragon was too quick, and dove beneath the arc of the blade. The sword of Brinist, missing its mark, cleaved the moon instead, dragging it across the sky and causing the remains to bleed white blood. . . .

The loremistress shook her head and smiled to herself. This was actually an Avatar story in most of the renditions of the tale, but for some reason the author of this text had mistakenly combined the Avatar and the lord figures into one character. She wondered if whoever had originally written the text had purposefully left the Avatar out of the story for some reason of their own.

Lanilan returned to examining the text.

The wound it caused in the heavens broke the bones of creation, which fell as sharp blades from the sky and wounded the world. In rage, the lord turned upon the Dragon of Chaos and . . .

"Mistress Lanilan?"

She became aware of people standing in front of her.

Lanilan looked up. She could not be entirely certain that they had not spoken her name several times.

"Oh, my apologies," she said, standing up. She straightened her deep blue mantle, the silver chevron of her office extending down from her shoulders to a point in the front, and reached back to place the tassel in its proper position over her right ear. There were a number of people standing expectantly before her. "Greetings, Loremaster Zhal!"

"Greetings, Loremistress." Zhal bowed his head toward her. "Did you not get word of our coming?"

"I did." Lanilan nodded, still trying to extricate her mind from the story on the desk before her. "I did . . . but I was not expecting you quite this soon. But, no matter. I am prepared to assist you as I can. What have you brought me?"

Zhal turned, gesturing toward the man with bound wrists who was standing behind him. "This man—"

"He is of Drachvald, judging by his complexion and the shape of his ears," the loremistress said at once. "The clothing would indicate that it originated somewhere near Rhun . . . most likely part of those commonly issued to the ranks of the armies operating in the Midmaer. This means he is either a mercenary or a regular warrior, most likely in the service of the Obsidian Cause, which—"

"Loremistress!" Zhal interrupted. "We know all that. His name is Captain Aren Bennis—he's a warrior of the Westreach Army of the Obsidian Empire."

"Really?" the loremistress asked. "He seems . . . shorter than I would expect."

"Well, be that as it may, he is," Zhal continued to press on. "This is Syenna, a shieldmaiden of Baroness Baden-Fox. . . ."

"How do you do?" Lanilan nodded. "I've never met a shield-maiden either. Tell me, the Rite of the Shieldmaidens—do they still involve the four tests of—"

"Loremistress," Zhal continued insistently. He was apparently intent on keeping Lanilan's curiosity limited to one subject at a time. "You already know Commander Trevan."

"Well, yes, of course! But then why did you bother to bring him to me?" Lanilan blinked at the loremaster.

"It is not Trevan, but Captain Bennis who we have brought to you, and it is because he is the bearer of something that is a mystery to us," the loremaster said. Zhal turned again toward Aren. "Show the loremistress your sword, Captain."

Aren raised his eyebrows, holding his bound hands forward.

Zhal sighed and then reached out, unbinding the captain's hands.

Aren rubbed his wrists, then reached across to his scabbard, pulling out a sword. It gleamed even in the dim light of the Athenaeum.

Lanilan's eyes widened with wonder.

"Do not touch it, Loremistress," Zhal warned. "There appears to be some sort of curse associated with the artifact."

Syenna spoke up. "We believe it to be an Avatar blade."

"As indeed you should," Lanilan said, nodding. "Do you think it would be possible for us to get a rubbing of the blade on papyrus? I would dearly like to study the writing on the blade more closely."

"That may not be of much help," Zhal commented. "The engraved writing on the blade appears to change from time to time."

"That, itself, is significant," the loremistress said, leaning closer to the weapon.

Commander Trevan, who was standing behind them, stepped forward, frowning as he, too, looked at the blade. "Is this why you've come?"

"What do you know about this blade, Loremistress?" Zhal asked.

Lanilan considered for a moment before answering. "I believe it may very well be a blade of the ancient Avatars. Its shape is in the pattern found in several of the Scrolls of Libris. The question may be not whether it is an Avatar's weapon, but rather *which* Avatar's sword."

"What do you mean?" Syenna asked.

Lanilan took a step back from her desk as though it would give her a better perspective on the artifact. "There were many Avatars before the Fall, and many Avatar blades. Many of them were named and had specific qualities. You see the symbol on the pommel at the end of the hilt? One curved sword is showing there when there should be three."

Aren lifted up the hilt to look at the pommel more closely. "That's odd. I'd never noticed that before."

"The chamber where we found it was filled with symbols of three interlocking blades," Syenna said.

"And so it would be." Lanilan nodded. "It's a classic symbol of the Avatars and found in a number of different places. What we need to determine is which sword you have found."

"An Avatar blade?" Trevan spoke up. "The Avatars were the embodiment of the ancient Virtues! How is it that a sword of the Virtues can be held by this servant of death and darkness?"

"That may depend on *which* servant of death and darkness you're dealing with," Aren said with some irritation in his voice. "Can I put this away now? Please?"

"Yes." Lanilan nodded again. "I've got to research some texts from the vaults. Once you have found lodgings, Loremaster, perhaps you could return and assist me?"

"Certainly," Zhal responded. "I would be delighted."

"Commander Trevan?" Syenna said suddenly.

"Yes, Lady Syenna?"

"Would you be so good as to find appropriate accommodations for Captain Bennis?" she said. "I think he would be most comfortable surrounded by other warriors."

"At once, Lady Syenna," Trevan said. His grip on Aren's arm made the captain wince. "Will you be joining us?"

"Presently," Syenna said. "I've a question for the loremistress."

Trevan drew Aren with him out of the Athenaeum, Loremaster Zhal at their heels. Presently, the great doors shut in the distance. Only then did Syenna turn back to face the loremistress.

"What is your question, child?" Lanilan said.

"My . . . my sister," Syenna whispered, her voice quavering.

"Yes, child," the loremistress asked, leaning across her desk. "What do you want to know about your sister?"

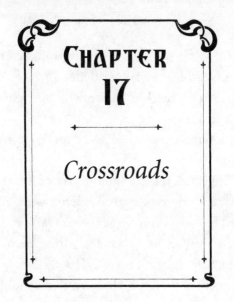

CHAPTER
17

Crossroads

Commander Trevan dragged Aren awkwardly into the antechamber of the Athenaeum as Loremaster Zhal closed the doors behind them. They had passed through this room before on their way into the Athenaeum. The narrow windows of leaded glass on either side gave gentle illumination to the room. The opposing set of double doors, Aren remembered, led back out of the building and to the crowded street.

"I'm afraid I must insist on your handing me your sword, Captain Bennis," the commander said from behind Aren.

Aren turned his head toward Commander Trevan. The man's left hand had a grip like iron. "You might want to reconsider that, Commander."

Trevan's eyes narrowed. "Which part of *insist* was not clear to you?"

"Probably the part where you try to take a cursed sword from the only man, so far, who has been able to touch it," Aren replied. "Trust me; this is a really bad idea."

Trevan grimaced, reaching down with his right hand to the grip of the sword.

"No!" the loremaster cried out as he turned from closing the doors.

Trevan's fingers closed around the grip of Aren's sword.

The commander's eyes went suddenly wide. They shifted in an instant to focus on Aren's face. Trevan's mouth opened as though he wanted to speak, but all he managed was to draw in a long shuddering breath. His right hand started to shake so violently that the blade rattled loudly inside the scabbard.

Aren gazed back into the eyes of the commander as he held as still as possible.

Suddenly Trevan released his grip on both the sword and Aren's arm. The commander staggered backward several steps before he regained his footing. He stood there for a moment, considering Aren before, at last, he blew out a long breath and then nodded to himself as though he had just answered his own question.

"Commander!" said Zhal as he rushed toward Trevan. "Are you all right?"

"Yes, I . . . I am quite myself," Trevan answered, although his words were more confident than the sound of his voice.

"What happened to you, Commander?" Zhal asked, his words coming in a rush. "Please, tell me: what did you experience when you—"

"Not now, Zhal," Trevan said to the loremaster, though his eyes remained fixed on Aren. "We will talk about this later."

"I did try to warn you," said Aren as he held both his hands up, his palms open as a sign of submission.

Trevan drew in another breath and then nodded. "Yes, you did, Captain. May I ask you, what were your intentions in coming to Opalis?"

Aren shook his head, and gave a wry smile. "Believe me, Commander, I had no intentions whatsoever in coming to Opalis. The loremaster and Syenna, however, both seem to have had a large number of intentions in bringing the sword here. I believe that if they did not need me to be the pack animal for this prize, they would have been just as happy to have tossed me into the Bay of Storms."

"Will you give me your word that you will do no harm to my city?" Trevan asked.

"Trevan, what are you thinking?" the loremaster spoke quietly to the commander. "Can you seriously trust a warrior of the Obsidians cause?"

"He will honor his word," Trevan responded, and then turned back toward Aren. "Well, Captain? Will you promise not to harm Opalis or its citizens?"

Aren considered the question for a moment before answering. "Commander, you know that is a promise I cannot keep forever. The Obsidian Cause is a force of order and destiny that will not be denied. There may come a time when its armies may be at your gates, and I may be among its ranks. However, there may be an oath I can take that will satisfy both of our honors. Loremaster, how long do you expect your investigations will take into this apparently useless weapon?"

"It is difficult to say," Zhal replied, stroking his mustache in thought. "There's getting access to the texts in the Titans' library, the research itself and, perhaps, some experimentation with the blade. We could, of course, stumble upon the answer in a matter of days, but it is more likely that the answer—if there is one—will be known in three to five weeks. That is also assuming your cooperation."

Aren nodded and turned back toward Trevan. "Then I may offer my word that I will do no intentional harm to Opalis or its citizens for a period of, say—"

"Three months," Trevan said.

"One," Aren countered.

"Two," Trevan offered. "I need at least two months."

Aren smiled and shrugged. "Two months, then. You have my word."

"Two months?" The loremaster looked at Trevan in disbelief. "And just what are you going to do with those two months?"

"Well, to begin with," Trevan said as he moved to the outer doors and threw them open wide. "I believe I will introduce this Obsidian captain to our city—since he will enjoy our hospitality from inside the city walls for quite some time."

"You're inviting me to stay?"

"Oh, I absolutely insist." Trevan bowed slightly as he spoke. "As will every guard of the Legion on every wall and at every gate."

† † †

Aren stepped out of the main doors of the Athenaeum and onto the colonnade that made up the front porch, and stopped at the top of the broad stairs.

The avenue curved before him, bending on his right around the wide base of the citadel's outer wall. Its battlements were sheer and smooth, standing straight up out of the ground and rising thirty feet up to an overhang. The masonwork of the stones that made up the outer wall was so expertly set that, even with Aren's keen eyes, it was nearly impossible to distinguish the seams between the stones. The citadel rose another sixty feet above the top of the outer wall, the curve of its tower sweeping around a central dome that gleamed in the morning light.

Aren turned and looked to his left. There, the avenue continued its gentle curve to the right, between an amazing variety of small, independent buildings, crammed uncomfortably close to one another. The majority of the buildings were of wattle and daub construction: dark, wooden frameworks filled in with a combination of wood strips, mud, clay, and straw. The others were of wood or stone construction. Most had flat walls and squared corners, but there were a number of others whose curved lines were far more organic and that tried, in their small way, to emulate the citadel that towered above them. Of those that were set at the edge of the street, however, they all appeared to have one feature in common: the main floor represented a shop, craft room, or other place of business, with the living quarters situated on the floors above it. Above the doors of each of these establishments, Aren could easily see the ornate signs depicting the various services or goods being offered at each shop. He realized at once why each sign was situated high above the street: for the avenue was so filled with people, they would easily block the view of any advertisement situated any lower.

The ebb and flow of the people in the street seemed to be at its greatest, however, directly across from the Athenaeum. There, the citizens of Opalis moved like a river into the opening between the walls of the citadel to the right and the end of the line of shops on the left. Beyond them lay their great open market. Aren could see the stalls and small tents set up in a sprawling hodgepodge. Toward the leftmost edge of the market, Aren could make out the great fountain that formed the central supply of water into the city.

Opalis was indeed a city far more opulent and beautiful than Aren had ever seen. He remembered that there had been a number of discussions among the command staff of General Karpasic regarding this mysterious city located at the farthest reaches of their maps. Stories from some of the trade caravans coming out of South Paladis told of a city filled with unspeakable wealth and treasure. Given the extraordinary and magnificent citadel of the Titans, it was obvious to him that the city lived up to the legends told about it. Yet, the city was defended by an inadequate number of warriors along a single wall of defense. Once that single wall was breached at any point, there was only the outer wall of the citadel remaining, with the surrounding city lost. To the captain's trained eye, this was indeed a juicy and incomparable fruit, ripe for the picking.

Aren had given his word that he would not act against the city for two months. However long he had in the city, he could occupy himself with learning more about this place, its so-called Titans, and, more important for him, more about this strange, cursed sword that seemed to be more trouble for him with every passing day.

"Do you know where you will be staying, Loremaster?" The commander was speaking to Zhal as they, too, stepped onto the porch.

"The last time I was here," the loremaster said, a slight wistfulness in his voice, "there was a charming little inn under the

Westwall near Elders Hall. I thought I might try there. Then I believe we should begin our investigations in earnest later this afternoon. Will the captain be in your charge?"

"He will be with me," Trevan replied.

"Then perhaps you might bring him back here to the Athenaeum about the second hour after noon," the loremaster said.

"We shall both be here," Trevan replied as he stepped forward to stand next to Aren. The commander gestured toward the street with his left hand. "May I show you to your quarters, Captain?"

"I would be grateful to you, Commander," Aren replied with a slight nod.

Aren followed Trevan down the steps and into the teeming street, a smile on his lips. He had promised to do no intentional harm to Opalis or its citizens for two months, but he had not promised to remain here. Evard would find him and free him of the city in eight days' time, and he could then proceed northward and deal with the ridiculous command of General Karpasic.

Evard's last communication through the homunculus had been most illuminating. General Karpasic had been ordered to move his replenished army out of Hilt and march northward up the broken road into North Paladis. There was something in the region that was vital to the Obsidians. Although Evard was not clear as to what the objective was, nevertheless it was good news so far as Aren was concerned. It meant that the general and his army would be marching as far from Opalis as possible.

The last thing he needed was for an invading army to complicate his escape.

†††

General Milos Karpasic sat astride his heavy destrier war-horse, contemplating the crossroads directly before him.

To either side of him sat the captains of his staff, each one astride their own courser war-horses and, as per his orders, resplendent in their battle armor despite the vast plain before them being completely devoid of any enemy. Each of these captains held with dogged determination to a strained silence as they waited upon the general.

Behind the general and his captains, the mighty Westreach Army of the Obsidian Empire stretched backward along the ancient road toward the pass through the Blackblade Mountains from which they had marched only the day before. They had broken the encampment early, formed into their ranks and files, and ordered into their columns along the road. The army had been less than an hour into their planned march when the scouts had returned with news of the crossroads just ahead. This discovery had brought all progress to a complete halt as the general had ridden forward with his captains to contemplate the crossroads.

Now the archers, foot soldiers, sappers, mounted knights, wagon teamsters, cooks, coopers, weaponsmiths, armorers, pikemen, lancers, and a train of assorted siege engines all waited anxiously in the rising heat of the morning to learn if the column would be turning right or left at the crossroads. The special units—elves, satyrs, fauns, and the newly delivered trolls—felt little interest in which direction was chosen, as they were a vast minority in the army. The humans of the Westreach Army, however, were invested very keenly in the decision.

So everyone looked to the captains.

And the captains looked to the general.

"My lord general," Captain Halik said quietly, although in the silence, his voice sounded like thunder.

"Captain Halik," the general said. "You are disturbing my deliberations."

"I beg your pardon, my lord," Halik said, clearing his throat but determined to press on. "I do not understand the need for deliberation."

"Captain Halik seems to forget himself," offered Captain Gorn.

"May I remind Captain Gorn that our orders from the Cabal of the Obsidians was specific and explicit," Halik said, frustration creeping into his voice. "We were directed to march from Hilt, follow the old road north through the Dragonspur, and follow the Sanctus River into North Paladis to the place where it joins the Fortus River."

"Yes, Halik, and once there, we are to encamp and hold that location until we receive further instructions from the cabal," sneered Captain Odman. "We are all perfectly aware of our orders."

General Karpasic was barely listening to the argument raging around him from his captains. He was aware that they were talking about orders and plans and duty, but he was concentrating on his own problem and how he might deal with an unfortunately messy mistake.

The general believed he was magnanimous enough to admit he did have some faults. However, he would never admit that to anyone *else*; doing so, he convinced himself, would be a terrible blow to the troops who so adored him. To himself, however, he would from time to time revel in the humility of admitting he was not perfect. Oh yes, he had faults.

Yet if there was one thing he was good at, it was self-preservation.

Captain Aren Bennis had served him well but, on reflection, perhaps too well. The captain was always overstepping his authority, showing off by appearing more competent than his superiors, and consistently calling attention to himself through public displays of victory, conquest, and achievement without sharing credit with those who had supported him in spirit.

After all, thought the general, *if it had not been for Milos Karpasic, Captain Bennis would never have had the opportunity to lead his warriors in the first place.*

So the time had come to be rid of the ambitious Captain Bennis, and the scout Syenna had provided him the perfect opportunity to do so without incurring the ire of the captain's deadly and powerful friend among the Obsidian sorcerers.

But something had gone wrong with the plan.

Karpasic had his own sources among the Obsidians. It was through them that he had learned that the ever disobedient Aren Bennis had refused to disappear quietly, which would have so easily cleaned up the whole mess. Now he was on his own, it seemed, which was certainly far worse. But fate had provided the general with an unexpected opportunity, as the troublesome captain was even now being moved to a place that was just barely within the reach of the general's forces.

A lot of unfortunate things can happen in the confusion of battle, the general thought, *especially when you're on the wrong side of the battle line.*

"In the field of battle, situations often become fluid," General

Karpasic said at last. "A commander's prerogative is an important asset."

"But we're not *in* battle," Halik said. "We're stopped on a road in the middle of nowhere, debating a junction!"

"No, Captain Halik, we are not debating a junction." The general smiled. "We are considering an opportunity."

"Opportunity?" Halik was stunned.

"Yes, Captain, an opportunity!" General Karpasic urged his horse forward and then turned it to face his captains. "An opportunity that comes seldom to any true warrior. An opportunity to take the initiative, to obtain a prize before it can be claimed by anyone else and all in the name of the Obsidian Cause. In one move—one bold move—we will be able to pay our army in inestimable plunder, secure our flank, and resupply our forces. What greater service can we do on behalf of the Obsidian Cause?"

"Where are you taking us, General?" Halik asked with dread.

"Why, north to the Sanctus River"—the general grinned—"as we have been ordered."

Halik let out the breath he had been holding.

"And we will get there," the general finished, "by way of Opalis."

CHAPTER 18

Innocents

"Six days I've been here." Aren frowned. "Six of the most miserable days of my life."

The late afternoon sun had just dropped below the western horizon, casting beautiful, soft shadows among the buildings of Opalis under its afterglow. Laughter sparkled through the air as groups of shop owners and craftsmen, some with the lamps already lit in the windows of their homes above, went about the work of closing for the day. Vendors, whose business time was only just beginning, were wheeling their carts to and fro along the great curve of the Muse Way—that great circular avenue that carried the carts and citizens around the outer ring of the city—each looking for their favorite place from which to sell their prepared foods and art.

"The most miserable days of your life?" Syenna rolled her eyes as she popped another small, steamed dumpling into her mouth from the greenleaf basket in her hand. She managed to talk around it as they strolled past the Fields Gate in the direction of Elders Hall. "I've watched you march through the mud in the rain, try to set up your tent in the midst of a blizzard so strong that it might have blown your horse away, and even watched you make your way across parched land where the only standing water would kill you from the smell alone. Now you're trying to tell me that you're miserable here?"

Aren looked balefully about at the gentle evening settling over the streets of Opalis.

"Very well then, Captain Bennis," Syenna said, turning angrily toward her charge. "What is so terrible about your life here in Opalis?"

"Why don't you call me Aren anymore?" The captain folded his arms across his chest, considering her thoughtfully. "You used to call me Aren."

"I've called you a great many things in my time," Syenna continued to press her argument. "And don't try changing the subject. Tell me what is so terrible about spending an evening under pleasant skies in a peaceful city filled with art, music, and good company—yours exempted, of course."

"Don't you see it?"

"No! I don't!"

Aren placed his fists on his hips in frustration, gazing down and to the right as he considered how he might explain what he was feeling.

"It's all that Trevan's fault," Aren exclaimed.

"The commander of the Opalis Legion?" Syenna laughed in disbelief. "He's the one who gave you permission to wander the city streets on your own, over my rather strenuous objections, might I add."

"All part of his nefarious, diabolical plan," Aren insisted.

"Letting you out of your prison cell during the days and evenings . . ." Syenna was so far nonplussed by the captain's arguments. "How is that nefariously diabolical?"

"He didn't just let me out of my cell. He lent me these clothes so I might move about the town without upsetting anybody," Aren said insistently. He was dressed in a clean tunic with a fitted leather vest. "Then he rather adamantly insisted I wear this . . . this . . . thing, this . . ."

He gestured toward the scabbard at his hip.

"The blade of the Avatar?" Syenna urged.

"Yes, thank you . . . This blade of the Avatar on my hip every time I leave the barracks." Aren huffed. "That Trevan would allow a prisoner as dangerous as me to walk about the city without an escort in my view, is recklessly irresponsible. To allow me to do so armed, I believe is evidence of some serious mental deficiency."

"So, tell me how you proved him wrong." Syenna said as she reached into her small leaf basket for another dumpling. "Tell me which farmer you murdered in his bed or what blind beggar you have robbed here in Opalis on behalf of the great Obsidian Cause."

"*None of them!*" Aren railed.

"None of them?" Syenna smiled.

"Because . . . Because . . ." Aren struggled to speak the words. "Because I . . . *I care about them.*"

"You?" Syenna looked at him skeptically. "Oh please!"

"I know! It's terrible!" Aren said. He pointed toward a clean little shop on the west side of the street and then beckoned her to follow him toward it. "Here, for instance."

Syenna looked up at the sign over the front of the shop. "The Brothers Tassilo and Toschlog?"

"That's right. Tassilo is a flax merchant originally from Port Crucible while Toschlog was a tailor originally trained in Aerie. Each of them came to Opalis on business—one from the east and one from the southwest—and by absolute coincidence arrived in Opalis on exactly the same day. Both of them walked into a shop called Petersons Linens, one hoping to sell flax to manufacture cloth, and the other one hoping to buy cloth to manufacture clothes. And it turned out, to their absolute amazement, that the shop was run by twin sisters, one named Alice and the other named Alex. Well, one convenience led to another, and in time each of the men married one of the sisters, and they all decided to rename the shop. As you see, it is something of a private joke."

"Really?" Syenna said. She looked into the warmly lit storefront nearly twenty feet away. Within, she saw a tall, thin man with curly dark hair who was fitting a new coat on one of the legion warriors of the city. Near him, a lithe woman with long ginger hair was refolding linens and setting them back on the shelf. "That's a charming story, but I don't see what it has to do with your being miserable."

"Well, it's not all charming," Aren said as he, too, gazed into the shop. "Tassilo occasionally gets very jealous of his wife, who enjoys working with customers in the shop, and Toschlog has never been able to figure out a way to reliably tell one sister from the other. And the truth is that Alice has trouble defending herself in loud arguments, while her sister can hold her own. So when Tassilo occasionally confronts his wife with his jealous fears, it is often Alex who switches places with Alice to endure the argument, which is exactly the kind of confusion Toschlog dreads the most."

"I see you know these people very well," Syenna observed.

"That's the point."

"What's the point?"

"I have *never met* these people!" Aren complained. "I walked into their shop two days ago. I asked Alex Toschlog about a new pair of trousers. She asked me to return later when her husband returned. That's all that was said, and that's the only time I've been in the shop. And now, every time I walk past, I wonder if Alice is all right, whether Tassilo has found a way to express his love to his wife, and whether Toschlog has figured out a way to know which wife is which. I *care* about these people. I *know* these people, and they have absolutely no idea who I am."

Syenna's eyes narrowed. "And me? What do you know about me?"

"Nothing! That's one of the most frustrating things about all this," Aren griped. "It's like I'll walk up to compete strangers, know all about them in an instant, and yet with you, who has been practically standing next to me since I picked up this cursed, oversize cheese knife, it won't tell me a thing about you. It's like the curse is some sort of game, and the sword wants to torment me by not telling me the rules. I've certainly thought about just tossing the thing as hard as I can into the nearest trash heap and walking away, but the thought always comes to me that it would have beaten me if I did—and I just cannot let this thing win."

Syenna tried to keep a smile from her face.

"Sure, laugh at my problems; but it isn't just with Tassilo and Toschlog," Aren remonstrated. He began walking northward along Muse Way, indicating the different shops and stalls along the way. "Over there ... That huge, bald man with biceps the size of my thighs? That's Ozen the armorer. He makes the most amazing greaves, but he also makes a point of visiting his mother every fortnight and still regrets not asking the Weber girl to dance with him at the spring dance ten years ago. And dance? How about Felicia, the girl over there, selling the meat skewers at her father's cart? She used to love to dance until a horse was spooked in the marketplace and trampled her legs. It was painful for her to learn to stand again, and now she walks with an awkward gait, but still she dances in her room where no one can see, just so she can feel the music again."

"So, what is your problem?" Syenna demanded. "These are people—good people—living their lives as best they know how. Why should their joy make you miserable?"

"Can't you understand?" Aren pleaded. "I know what's coming!"

"What do you know?" Syenna demanded. "What is coming?"

"What always comes. What I always bring," Aren said, his gaze shifting into the distance of his memory. "I have stepped over the bodies of a thousand people just like them. Every conquest, every siege, and every occupation. Their faces were there, and I never saw them. I knew that they had died, but I never gave any thought to what might have died with them. I never thought about their hopes for the next day that would never come, the children who they would never see grow into their own lives, or the comfort that they would never give or receive again.

That's why I am miserable. The city is too great a prize to be left alone. Whether it is the Obsidians or the Norgard or some other city-state, it does not matter. One day and soon, Opalis will be taken by someone like me, and these people will suffer."

Syenna drew in a breath to speak but thought better of it.

"You see? I've hardly lifted a finger, and I've already made a ruin of your evening." Aren shrugged and then allowed a wistful smile to play across his face. "Let me make it up to you. There is this woman who always sets her trade just a little farther down the street. She goes by the name of Marissa Coals, although her last name is actually different. She does the most amazing charcoal sketches of people's faces. Her life has not been the easiest. I think you will like her."

As Aren and Syenna moved down the curve of Muse Way, they could see that the evening crowd had pulled back from the side of the street, the sound of gruff shouts rising as they approached. Aren pushed his way to the front of the crowd, Syenna at his heels.

It was Marissa Coals. She was surrounded by a group of large, coarse men. They were generally filthy—caravan drivers by the looks of them, Aren thought—and quite obviously drunk. Normally these rowdies, as they were referred to in Opalis, kept to the taverns outside the walls where society and entertainment were generally more to their liking. But occasionally, a group of rowdies would find their way in through the gates. Usually, there was no trouble, as the townsfolk dealt with them with kindness and respect, and the rowdies most often responded in kind.

But now and then, things could go wrong.

"Has someone called for the Legion?" Syenna asked a bystander in the crowd.

"They have been sent for," the man responded, concern and fear in his eyes. "But we don't know how long before they arrive. . . ."

Marissa, tears streaming from her eyes, was being pushed back and forth among the six men. One of them was holding her money purse high above her head, taunting her.

"Come on, Syenna," Aren said. "We need to break this up."

"You promised the Legion commander," Syenna growled at him. "No trouble!"

"I promised not to act against the city or its citizens," Aren said, trying his sword. "This is *for* the city."

Aren stepped forward, his sword swinging loosely in front of him. He called out to the men, using the voice that could reach soldiers in the heat of battle. "The fun is over, lads. Drop the bag. Walk away."

Most of the rowdies stopped at the sound of his voice and took a step back from the weeping Marissa. The largest of them, however, still held the coin purse and turned slowly to face the approaching Aren.

"Drop the bag." Aren continued to approach. "Walk away."

The man had broad shoulders, a thick neck, and a sloping forehead. His nose was wide and appeared to have been broken at least twice.

Aren continue to advance, the sword in his hand. In his mind, he knew he was bluffing. As he got close, he was certain that the sword would tell him some deep secret about his opponent's childhood, or that he had been unloved, that some trauma in his past had robbed him of his humanity and forced him to be a bully and a thief. Every time Aren had drawn this cursed sword, it had told him something about his enemy that had stayed his hand.

The man looked into Aren's eyes.

Aren looked into the man's soul.

All he saw was darkness.

This man is a thief.

This man is lazy.

This man is cruel.

This man will kill.

A vicious smile dawned on Aaron's face.

This man had earned the edge of the blade in his hand.

The man saw the change in Aren's face. In a flash, the brute turned and plunged headlong into the crowd, bowling a number of them over as he fled from the street between the buildings, Marissa's purse still gripped in his hand.

Aren rushed after him. At once, he found himself running in desperate pursuit through the maze of narrow alleys between the closely situated buildings. The man ahead of him was fleeing with desperation, weaving between the homes and shops, trying to shake his pursuit. Frantic, he dropped the purse, but Aren managed to pick it up without missing a step.

The man turned again, his breathing becoming labored. Aren heard the sound and smiled to himself, for he was running his prey to ground and knew it was only a matter of time.

The man ducked into a narrow alleyway between two large buildings.

Aren followed him and was halfway to the end when something appeared that made him slide to a stop.

The end of the alleyway was filled with a strange bluish-purple light. Lightninglike tendrils reached across it from its edges.

Aren could see nothing beyond it. He took a step back.

The wall of roiling blue light suddenly rushed in his direction. Aren turned and started to run back down the alleyway, but the wall of light came toward him with a speed he could not have imagined. In a moment it swept over him.

And then it vanished, leaving the alleyway completely empty.

CHAPTER 19

Dispossessed

Aren was quite suddenly not where he had been.

He was still running, but his surroundings had changed in an instant. The dark alleyway had been replaced by a brilliantly lit hall of white marble, polished floors, and alabaster walls rising to an arched ceiling overhead. The wall of blue light that had overtaken him in the alley was now in front of him. It had washed over Aren and was rushing away from him down the hallway. Confused and disoriented, Aren tried to stop, but his boots slipped on the gleaming surface underfoot. He tried to recover, but it was too late. He lost his footing, stumbled, and then came crashing to a rolling and sliding stop in the middle of the hall.

Painfully, he picked himself up and, per his training, looked around him. The wall of blue light had come to a stop at the end of the hall about thirty feet from where he stood. Aren watched it warily for a few moments. With some trepidation, he turned around, suspicious that it might chase him once more, but it remained where it had come to rest.

Aren slipped his sword back into his scabbard. The hall down which he had just run had two enormous doors set on either side. Beyond those, the hall opened up into a rotunda. At three equally spaced points around the circular room, statues stood against the walls, each one bowing slightly inward as though the overhead dome were supported on their backs and its apex were too low for them to stand. One of the statues was of muscular man, his hand raised in a defiant fist. The second was of a different man, this one with his hand raised palm open as though swearing an oath. The third was a remarkable woman, her hand placed over her heart. In the center of the room, on a raised pedestal, stood eight smaller statues that appeared to be facing outward in a ring, but each of these was covered in black cloth.

Aren stepped up to one of the draped figures. He reached a tentative hand upward toward the shroud.

"Aren Bennis."

Aren had heard the voice. It was a deep tone, so quiet that he might have questioned hearing it if it had not penetrated his bones. It seemed to come from every direction at once.

"Welcome, Son of Ruin."

The voice was somewhat louder now and undeniable. Aren stepped cautiously into the rotunda. Beyond the great central statue, he could see a curving hallway between two of the eight statues at the edges of the circular floor. To his left was another hallway, this one wider than the others, with great columns on either side. It was also considerably shorter, ending in polished bronze doors as wide as the hall was long and reaching to the full forty-foot height of the ceiling.

"Welcome, Son of Hope."

The voice was coming from beyond the bronze doors. Aren stepped carefully down the square hall. The handles were set into the door nearly fifteen feet above his head. Aren considered them for a moment as he stood at the base of the double doors.

"Let us hear you."

Titans, Aren thought. He had searched around the base of the citadel and, as Trevan had told him, there were no openings in the wall and no apparent way to gain their audience. It was obvious to him that one did not speak to the Titans until they wished to be spoken to. And now that time had come.

Aren pressed a hand against each of the doors and pushed.

The doors swung inward in silence and with surprising ease.

Three Titans sat upon their thrones opposite the door at the end of the great hall. They were colossal beings, dwarfing the captain as he entered, and looking down at him as he stepped into the room before them. Two of them were male in form, muscular and powerful, while the third was a female of exquisite beauty and perfection. Each of them was dressed in beautiful flowing robes, but it was the first of them who held in his hand a towering ornate staff. The filigree ornate carvings along the shaft appeared to move and change on their own. The head of the staff branched into three prongs between which eight spheres of different-colored light revolved around one another in constant motion. The base of the staff, pressed against the floor, pulsed with a bluish-purple light similar to that which encompassed Aren and brought him here.

Aren stood before them in silence. They had brought him here. Given the circumstances, he thought it wise to let them ask him questions before he ventured any of his own.

"Captain Aren Bennis." It was the voice of the first of the Titans, the male to his left. "You have brought an artifact of the past. . . ."

"Of despair . . ." continued the second male Titan.

"Of promise," finished the female Titan.

"Why have you brought this destiny to Opalis?" asked the first Titan, the staff turning in his right hand.

Aren spoke to the faces looking down on him. His voice sounded small and insignificant in the expanse of the room. "To learn of the sword, its origins and powers."

"That is why the loremaster of Etceter has brought you here," said the female Titan. "That is why the shieldmaiden Syenna brought you here. It does not answer our question."

Aren licked his dry lips, considering for a moment. "I did not choose to come here; I was forced to come here against my will."

"You are a skilled warrior," said the second Titan. "You are both cunning and resourceful. Had you wished it, you could have found some means of escape."

"Even now," said the female Titan, "during the time you have been in Opalis, you have been given your freedom during the day, and yet you remain in the city. You have not come to Opalis for the loremaster's reasons, nor for the shieldmaiden's reasons. Nor have you truly come against your will. Tell us, Aren Bennis; why have you come?"

Aren furrowed his brow. "Because I needed to know."

"What did you need to know?" asked the first Titan.

"Why this blade chose someone like me," Aren said in a voice barely above a whisper, as though he'd rather not have anyone in the room, including himself, hear the words.

"Answers come only to those who are capable of comprehending them," said the second Titan. "Asking the question is not the same as understanding its underlying truth."

"However, our need is desperate and requires your immediate enlightenment," said the third Titan.

The first Titan nodded in agreement as he moved the towering staff into his massive left hand. "Then we are in agreement. Aren Bennis, if you would be so good as to show us this sword that troubles you so, I believe we can help you down the path of enlightenment."

Aren drew in a breath and turned to look down on the scabbard at his side. He reached across his body to take the hilt of the ancient sword in his right hand. The blade rang slightly as it slipped from the scabbard.

Aren lifted his face to look back at the Titans.

His face immediately fell to the picture of chagrined disbelief.

"Oh, you have *got* to be joking!" he blurted out.

The outrageously huge hall around them now appeared to be of the more common size. The thrones remained before him, as did the Titans, but all three of them were now only slightly taller than Aren himself. For a moment, Aren could not decide whether they had shrunk or he had grown to their size.

The first two Titans still looked much as they had a few moments before, but what had previously appeared as godlike physiques were now more naturally strong rather than exaggerated. The third Titan's beauty was still evident, but no longer of the unworldly quality that had impressed Aren a few moments before.

The staff of the first Titan had also changed somewhat, in its appearance as much as its size. What had looked like ornate filigree down the shaft, Aren could now see were intricate mechanisms that shifted and turned in constant motion. The base of the staff still contained the orb of bluish-purple light, but Aren could now see streaks of purple lightning dancing across its surface, much like he had seen on the citadel dome as they approached the city.

Aren had the look of someone who had just discovered he had been cheated at cards. "*You're* the Titans?"

The first of them stepped forward, the mechanical staff still in his left hand. "We are what remains of the Titans. My name is Grannus. This is my brother, Boreus, and our sister, Sequana."

"But you're just . . . people," Aren said, shaking his head. "Humans, just like anybody else."

"That is not true," Boreus said with a severe look. "Our origins are not found among the circles of this world. Our ancestors walked different sands on different shores."

"You mean, across the oceans." Aren blinked, trying to comprehend.

"Much farther still," Sequana gently corrected him. "We lived in a place far beyond your shattered moon, beyond your stars and sky."

"The civilization of our world was great and produced many marvelous and powerful devices," Grannus said, "but in the end, even those marvels could not save us from the Fall."

"The Fall?" Aren shook his head, trying to understand. "I thought you said your lands were far away. The Fall was here."

"The Fall was not in your world alone; it came to many places and many worlds . . . in some far worse than others," said Sequana, her face troubled.

Sequana walked over to the polished bronze doors—now appearing to be a more reasonable size—and pulled them open. A much shorter hall opened into the rotunda, which, to Aren's surprise, had remained the same size as he remembered it.

"Nowhere was it worse than in our world beyond your sky," Sequana continued as they stepped into the rotunda. "A darkness fell with no hope of dawn; a noise with no hope of music. The Avatars were known among us, too. Our people had come to know of their means of walking between the worlds and had managed even to duplicate the technique with our inventions. In the end, perhaps, we brought the Fall upon ourselves."

"That was our parents' guilt talking," Boreus argued. "They were farmers whose knowledge was limited, far removed from those who might truly know."

Aren saw now that the central statue was that of a woman. She was reaching into the dome above. The captain looked up and saw that the dome was filled with a fresco of stars around a central circle whose edges depicted a portal to a pastoral scene of farmland and peace. The other eight statues were reaching upward as well.

"Our plantation was remote, far from our cities. We had many devices for our convenience and protection, but none of us fully understood the principles behind their functions. We could operate them, even repair them on some level, but we never *understood* them. As chaos descended upon our world and the fabric of its being was unraveling, our parents attempted to use these devices to save our family."

"What happened?" Aren asked.

"Something went wrong," Sequana said.

"Perhaps it had something to do with the world coming apart at an elemental level, or maybe the devices simply were broken," Boreus said. "We can't know. What we do know is that we escaped through a gateway from our world into this one. We had hoped that the Fall was like a storm that we could wait out here and then return to our home. Our ancestors never expected that the calamity in our own world would be mirrored in this one. We arrived only to find the gate back to our world was shut. We do not know if our world survived."

"That's what we have been doing here," Grannus said, cradling the staff now in his crossed arms. "The devices of our forebearers are failing. We do not understand entirely how they work, and the technology of this world is unlike our own. For centuries we have been gathering all the knowledge of your world that we can so we might adapt its devices to our own, struggling ever since to find the means to return home."

"Centuries?" Aren turned a skeptical look toward Grannus.

"Travel between the worlds changes time," Grannus said. "The Avatars spoke of it as well, how time in this world passed differently than time in our own or in theirs."

"Avatars!" Aren said at last. "Back again to these Avatars! This is all a very charming—if entirely bizarre and unbelievable—tale, but what has any of this to do with me?"

"You hold the sword of an Avatar," Sequana stated as though the thought alone were sufficient.

"Yes, and so?"

"Each of the ancient blades reflected the Virtues in some degree or another," Grannus said. "This particular blade was

known as Eye of the Scales. From what we have learned, it reflected three of the principle Virtues espoused by the Avatars
from before the Fall. One of them was 'true sight.'"

"It gives you better vision?"

"No, better perspective," Sequana said. "It strips away the facade of pretense to see the underlying truth: a viewpoint beyond personal bias or prejudice. The references we have found
to the sword are incomplete and in some places contradictory.
Some say it was wielded by Lord Brinist in ancient times, while
others assign it to other Avatars of legend."

"It has two other aspects as well," Boreus added. "Although
so far the texts have only agreed on 'true sight.' Perhaps further
research may be of help in this matter, and we have granted permission to both Loremaster Zhal and Loremistress Lanilan to
access those texts we have that refer to your blade."

"Again, interesting," Aren insisted. "But why did the sword
of some long-dead Avatar choose me?"

"Because the sword does not empower you." Sequana bowed
slightly as she spoke. "You empower the sword. It is your honesty that opened this aspect of the sword, not the other way
around."

"And it is that honesty to which we are appealing. We need
you to save the treasure of Opalis," Grannus said. "If we are ever
to find our way back to our home, the treasure must be kept
safe, and we believe the sword chose you for that purpose. Our
powers are failing, our devices weakening—"

"Look, you have the wrong man," Aren said, shaking his
head as he stepped backward, away from them. "I'm not the guy
who saves the treasure; I'm the guy that plunders it!"

"But they are coming!" Sequana pleaded. "They will be here

in a matter of days, and we do not have the strength to stop them!"

"Coming?" Aren asked. "Who's coming?"

"The Westreach Army of the Obsidian Empire," Grannus said. "Couriers from the caravans have brought word that the army is marching down the broken road and may reach Jaanaford as soon as three days from now."

Aren was dumbstruck. "The Westreach . . . General Karpasic's army?"

"You must find a way to stop them from finding our treasure," Boreus insisted.

"Are you out of your Titan minds?" Aren shouted. "Karpasic is *my* commander! I'm an *officer* in the Westreach Army! I'm supposed to *help* them conquer and plunder any city under their siege!"

Grannus cocked his head to one side. "Then perhaps in that case you would like to see the treasure?"

Aren gaped.

"Would you?"

Aren felt the fire go out of him. He was truly baffled. "Of course."

Grannus motioned Aren to follow him down the long hall where he had originally arrived in the citadel. He approached one of the side double doors in the hall and threw them open.

The room held ranks of shelves, each of which was filled with books, scrolls, and inscribed plates.

Grannus walked across the hall and opened the other set of doors. That revealed another room filled with bound papers, maps, and scrolls.

"The accumulated knowledge of the last three centuries,"

Grannus said. "We have spent the wealth of Opalis to gather as much of the wisdom and learning of your known world as possible."

"What do you see, Aren?" Sequana asked.

Aren rested his left hand on the pommel of his sword.

He saw the truth.

He drew in a long, shuddering breath.

"Karpasic believes the city to be a treasure house," Aren said quietly.

"And when he finds that the treasure is the written word on parchment?" Boreus pressed for an answer.

"He will do what he always does," Aren answered simply. "He will burn it."

CHAPTER
20

Unwilling Help

ackals!" Trevan roared, slamming his fist down on the wide table, causing the various maps scattered across its surface to jump. "Worse than jackals . . . carrion birds at the heels of jackals!"

Syenna picked up the scroll before it had stopped rocking back and forth on the top of the table. They stood in the map room of the Legion barracks.

"This missive," Syenna said as she unrolled it. "They cannot possibly mean what you say."

"Oh, they mean it, all right!" Trevan pushed himself away from the table and began pacing once more behind it. "Read it! It's all there in the fifth paragraph from the top!"

Syenna's eyes moved down the page. In moments, she found the section and began to read aloud. "It says, 'The Warlords of Resolute sympathize with the concerns of their fellow noble warriors of South Paladis, but reports of military activities throughout the region have caused the council in Resolute to reevaluate their strategic position against these insurgents of unknown strength and location.'"

"Keep reading!" Trevan seethed.

"'The council is resolved to abide by their agreements with the Elders of Opalis, their rightful representation of the Titans who rule them, and the people whom they protect, and shall, in due course and at the proper time, support the cause of their defense with.'" Syenna paused, glancing over the top of the scroll at Trevan. "What does this mean, 'in due course and at the proper time'?"

"It means they are not coming," Trevan snarled. "They are worried that the force marching in our direction is either a feint, or part of a greater strategy on the part of the Obsidians to strike against Resolute while her armies are engaged with us far south of their city. Maybe they are right. I don't know. But what I *do* know is that they're leaving us on our own. They won't risk leaving their own city defenseless just to defend ours."

"What about Norgard?" Syenna asked.

"What about them?" Trevan huffed.

"Their armies recently completed a campaign of conquest just beyond the Pillars of Night," Syenna said. She pushed a number of maps out of the way before finding the one she sought and then pointed at the spot to the west. "They have two armies encamped right now, here in Willowvale. I understand that they are only of partial strength, but they could be here in a matter of no more than two days if—"

"The armies of the Norgard Empire crossed the Pillars of Night last night"—Trevan nodded as he gazed at the map—

"down Superstition Canyon at the western edge of the South Paladis Plain. . . ."

"Excellent." Syenna smiled with relief.

"And then immediately encamped at the mouth of that same Superstition Canyon," Trevan concluded.

"They . . . stopped?" Syenna was having trouble believing what she had heard.

"Yes, they are at the western edge of our prairie, simply waiting until the Obsidian Army has done most of the work for them," Trevan said, gritting his teeth as he spoke. "They are more than happy to let both the defenders of Opalis and the attackers of the Obsidians bleed each other white on each other's swords before they arrive to fulfill their agreements with the Council of Might. In this particular case, being late is, for them, far better than never arriving at all."

"You mean they'll wait until Opalis has fallen?" Syenna gaped.

"Yes, they will wait." Trevan spoke the words as though he were spitting them. "Then once we have fallen, the city has been plundered, and the Obsidian Army has been weakened, then the glorious legions of the Norgard Empire will show up at our gates as liberators. How grateful will whatever remains of our citizenry be to accept their dictatorial rule!"

"But the others," Syenna said, her voice rising both in pitch and volume. "The rest of the Council of Might, surely they would not allow—"

"You know as well as I do that Etceter depends more upon the sea for its defense than any standing army." Trevan sighed. His eyes continued to be fixed on the map as though if he looked at it long enough or hard enough, it might reveal a miracle to him that he had somehow overlooked. "But even so, there are not enough merchant ships to properly convey the army you do have across the Bay of Storms, and if you tried to march them overland, you would have to pass through Midmaer *and* the Blackblade Mountains . . . both of which are now part of the Obsidian Empire. Ardoris is even farther from us than Etceter, and on the wrong side of Midmaer even if they could get here in time. The only remaining member of the vaunted Council of Might that might come to our aid are the Guildmasters of Aerie—and they *won't* because they stand to profit more from having Opalis in the hands of Norgard than to remain independent."

"Then we need to hold out against the siege," Syenna insisted. "Give the baroness and the shogun Tsuneo time to relieve the siege and attack Karpasic's army from the rear. We've sent word; all we need to do is hold out until they arrive."

"That could be a long time," Trevan said.

"Do you have somewhere else to go?" Syenna asked.

"No." Trevan smiled ruefully. "Nowhere in particular."

"Neither do I," Syenna continued. "But that doesn't mean everyone must stay. Shouldn't we evacuate the city—get everyone out who is not needed for the defense—while there is still time?"

"Evacuate them to where?" Trevan asked, pointing back down toward the map. "Should we send them west into the welcoming steel of the Norgard Empire? Or east toward Jaanaford, directly toward the approaching Obsidian Army? North across the open prairie in the direction of Resolute, where just a few elements of the Obsidian Army could hunt them down to extinction . . . or perhaps south, where they could be caught on the shores of the Sea of Storms? There is nowhere I can send the citizens of Opalis that is safer than within these walls, and there is no safety here, either."

"What about Captain Bennis?" Syenna asked as she gnawed at her lip. "Hasn't he been speaking with the Titans directly?"

"From when they first brought him into the citadel until as late as yesterday, yes." Trevan nodded, straightening up. "What's your point?"

"Well, the Titans are supposed to be the font of all wisdom," Syenna urged. "They must have had a purpose in choosing him to have audience with them now."

"I've lived here for all my life," Trevan said, "and I've never once seen the Titans. If they have some plan as to what we might do to defend the city or defeat the Obsidians, they have not communicated it to me nor, so far as I know, to Captain Bennis either. Still, they apparently *did* choose him. If he has a plan, however, I would be very much obliged if he would show up and tell me what it is."

"Where is he?" Syenna asked, glancing about them despite the fact that the room contained only the two of them.

"He's back in the citadel, I suppose." Trevan shrugged, crossing his massive arms over his chest. "Not that I know how Aren gets in or comes out of it. I saw him earlier this morning, but he seemed in too great a hurry to speak with me or answer my questions. One thing he made clear to me, however, is that he no more has the answers to this problem than I do." He then turned toward the door, yelling. "Centurion!"

A warrior of Opalis launched himself in through the door as though he had been waiting outside on a spring. "Yes, sire!"

"I'm worried about the defenses on the Long Wall," Trevan

said. "I want to see the stonemasons in charge here immediately. How is the crop gathering coming?"

"Some of the farmers are complaining about having their crops appropriated," the centurion replied. "They say that they are not yet ripe for picking."

"If the Obsidians burn down the fields," Trevan answered, "they won't ripen any more than they already have—"

"Commander," Syenna interrupted. "How long do we have before General Karpasic arrives with his forces?"

Trevan eyed the centurion, contemplating whether such information should be given in front of the young warrior. In the end, he decided it no longer mattered.

Trevan cleared his throat before he spoke. "The first elements passed through Jaanaford earlier this evening."

"That soon?" Syenna whispered.

"They must have force-marched down the Broken Road." Trevan nodded. "By sunrise we should see the first elements moving toward us from the southeast."

"Then war is come to Opalis." Syenna nodded.

"There may still be time for you to escape," Trevan continued, a softness coming into his eyes that Syenna found unexpected in the warrior. "You might take your loremaster and guard contingent at once south to the Ash Coast; Karpasic will be too intent on the city to be looking for a small group on the prairie—especially if you leave the captain here with us. From there, it may be possible for you to find a ship back home."

"I very much appreciate what you are saying, Mikas." Syenna nodded with a wistful smile. "I have already dispatched the guards to the coast earlier. I've tried to get the loremaster to go with them, but he is obsessed with learning the nature of the

Avatar's sword and refuses to leave before he gets some answers from the captain."

"And you?" Trevan asked.

"Let's just say that the shieldmaiden is searching for a few answers of her own," Syenna replied.

† † †

Syenna stepped out of the Legion barracks and into the eastern curve of Muse Way. Behind her, just beyond the barracks, was the towering facade of the Long Wall. Directly across from her on the other side of the avenue, the towers of the citadel soared overhead. On the avenue that ran along the base of the citadel foundations, the street was crowded with citizens, but their mood had changed completely from when she had last walked the cobblestones three nights before. The people's eyes were cast downward as they walked, the light in them now dimmed, the spring in their step dulled. There was an undercurrent of resignation spiced with desperation in the air. Some few moved with frantic purpose; most of them shuffled listlessly. War was not yet upon them, but the anticipation of it had already poisoned the city.

Syenna, however, felt frustration more than anything else. She had come to Opalis certainly on the command of the baroness, in whose service she was dutifully sworn, but not just in her service alone. Coming here had afforded her an opportunity she had longed for, and she had taken advantage of it as soon as said opportunity presented itself. But so far, the loremistress had been unable to provide her satisfactory answers, either to the question of the sword or Syenna's own dilemma.

One problem at a time, she thought to herself.

The problem most immediately at hand was finding Captain Bennis. According to Aren, the gate into the citadel moved from place to place in the city, and you did not so much find the gate as the gate found you. This was all well and good so far as getting into the citadel, but leaving it was another matter. The gate would deposit those leaving at some random location in the city—always in a hidden place out of sight of others—and, according to Aren, had a tendency to leave the person disoriented for a time. Syenna did not trust the captain; the explanation sounded like a story Aren might invent to cover his escape.

With Karpasic's army so close, Syenna was not about to let Aren out of her sight any longer than necessary. So, each evening after Aren visited the Titans—where he had spent the day reading, according to the captain—Syenna took it upon herself to find him as quickly as possible before he had the chance to make a fool out of her.

She decided to walk northward this time, and try the narrow alleyways between the buildings just east of the North Gate first. She would then make her way over toward Elders Hall and try the alleys there while working her way around the inside of the city wall. She knew from the last couple of days' experience that the citadel exit portal could be anywhere within the limits of the city wall, so one section was as good a place to start as another.

Syenna moved quickly through the sparse evening crowd, circling past the northeast entrance to the central market, then ducked between the buildings to weave her way down the narrow passages closer to the wall. The homes here were taller and housed several families within the same structure. An open sewer ran down one of the wider alleys. She stepped over it and turned another corner.

It was darker here than the passage she had just left. A man in silhouette was a shadow leaning against the side of a building, waiting for her.

"There you are," she muttered as she quickly stepped toward him. "It's about time you gave me some answers to my questions!"

She reached out for the man's shoulder, turning him toward her.

The man turned, raising his right hand. He had been slouching, but now he straightened to his six-foot height. A dim spark flashed at his fingertips, and an iridescent bubble suddenly floated at the man's shoulder, partially illuminating his face.

She stepped back in sudden shock.

"I quite agree," said the man with the pale-green eyes.

Syenna instinctively reached for her sword, drawing it at once and knowing, somehow as she did, that she was too late. The man standing before her wore a black hooded tunic embroidered in intricate patterns with silver thread. She had long known the meaning of such clothing, and fear closed like a fist around her heart.

The man stood perfectly still as he spoke.

"You are looking for answers, are you not, Shieldmaiden of Etceter?" The man grinned, no humor in his eyes.

"Stay away from me!" Syenna tried to sound strong, but the words tumbled from her quivering lips, weak and resonant with fear.

"What happened to your sister?" the man murmured. "Why

could you not stop it? What can possibly be done . . . to fix her? Restore her? Save her? Are these not the questions that burn to be answered for Syenna of Quel?"

Syenna could only manage a guttural cry that lodged in her throat.

"I have the answers for you here," the man said. He opened both of his hands before her.

A pair of black polished obsidian stones lay, one in the palm of each hand.

"All you have to do is bring Captain Aren Bennis to me," the man said. "Hand one of these to Aren, hold the other in your hand, and then touch him. That is how you will bring him to me. Once he is with me, I will give you all the answers you seek."

"Why . . . why do you want him?" Syenna said, her mouth dry.

"Are you asking another question?" The man grinned viciously as he spoke. "Answers can be expensive . . . and sometimes they cost us more than they are worth."

"What if he doesn't want to come?" Syenna swallowed hard, trying to think.

"But he *sent* for me." The man smiled again. "All you need to do is tell him that Evard Dirae has come for him. Is that not worth your sister's life?"

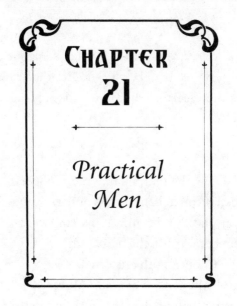

Chapter 21

Practical Men

General Milos Karpasic, Supreme Lord of the Westreach Army, was utterly exhausted. He fancied himself a great warrior, an old campaigner who was tough as steel and tireless as the tide. Yet, as he stood at the flap entering his tent, watching the last shreds of sunset bleed over the horizon, he could feel the creaking ache in his bones and the stiffness of his muscles.

Time, he thought. *I am running out of time.*

For the sake of the guards standing watch on either side of the entrance to his tent, Karpasic straightened up, arching his back as he puffed up his chest. He felt several of the vertebrae crack back into place though not nearly enough of them. The guards were watching him out of the corners of their eyes. He did not dare show weakness to those under his command. He knew, more than anyone, that those who were younger, faster, and stronger could smell it when someone above them was ripening and ready to be plucked from their position. One is always the most fearful of becoming the prey one once hunted in one's youth.

"Sentry!"

"Aye, sire!"

Karpasic knew the man's name was Coopersmith but preferred to keep the man beneath his notice. "You will find Captain Halik at once. Order him to assemble my war staff and present them here within the half hour."

"Aye, sire," Coopersmith answered.

"Do it *now!*" the general barked. "Move!"

The sentry only blinked once before bolting from his post.

Karpasic turned and stepped into his tent. There were several compartments in the large portable dwelling that not only fit his stature as master of the Westreach Army, but did duty as both his residence and place of command. His staff had set it up for him, as they always did, in advance of his arrival. They had chosen this spot according to his instructions, which, in this case, meant that they had settled the encampment at the farthest reach of their days' march. Karpasic realized he should have been more specific in his instructions. The army had crossed the river at Jaanaford, sweeping over the town there like a carpet of locusts as they followed the Broken Road that afternoon, but then by early evening had stopped to encamp. Upon arriving at the encampment, Karpasic realized that the army had stopped just short of their objective and that they needed to press on to Opalis that night. Captain Halik had insisted that the army needed a night's rest before they approached the city, and pointed to his tent already erected and awaiting his plea-

sure. Karpasic's first look at his comfortable retreat now beckoning him against the banks of the West Jaana River nearly
overcame his better judgment.

Now, weary from the prolonged ride and out of sight of his
staff, he was grateful for at least the short respite despite the
urgent thought that kept pushing at him from the back of his
mind.

"Another day," he muttered to himself. "I cannot afford one
more day's march. Tired or not, we have to press on before . . ."

The general stopped his musings, suddenly glaring at the
dark-clad figure that was sitting casually on his throne.

"Get out!" Karpasic snapped.

"Oh, must I?" the man in the Obsidian cloak asked with exaggerated disappointment. "And after coming so *very* far just
to see you again."

"I said get out, Dirae!" Karpasic could feel the heat in his face
as he flushed with anger and embarrassment at once. *How did
he find me? How do I explain this?*

"And here I thought you and I had come to an understanding," Evard said as the words dribbled from his lips in mock
hurt. The playful pout drew tight as his cold eyes fixed on the
general. "But I suppose when one misplaces an entire army of
warriors more than a hundred leagues from where they are expected to be, one might be a bit . . . out of sorts and not prone
to entertain sudden company. Especially if that company happens to represent the Obsidian Cause in whose service that general is *supposed* to be engaged."

Karpasic held very still.

Evard shrugged and pushed himself up from the chair. "I
supposed you are right. I'll just go back to Desolis and report

to the Inner Circle that I have found their missing army for them. It will be up to them to deal with those whose faulty sense of direction and complete inability to read a map has brought them so far from their expected duty."

Evard walked past Karpasic, reaching for the flap covering the tent exit.

Karpasic tilted his head back toward the sorcerer as he spoke. "Master Dirae . . ."

Evard stopped before the exit, turning toward Karpasic as he spoke with impatience. "Yes, General?"

"We are both practical men, are we not?" the general offered.

A slight smile played at the edges of Evard's lips. "I have always considered myself so, General."

"Could we . . . talk for a bit?"

"Why?"

"We might both profit from some conversation."

"I would not mind a little give and take," Evard replied cautiously.

Karpasic nodded and then moved toward his ornate chair. He did not sit in it, despite his aching legs begging the rest of him to do so. Instead he rested his hand on its back for support and then turned to face the sorcerer. "We are on a resupply and forage sortie."

"A . . . forage sortie?" Evard failed to hide the laugh behind the words. "You force-marched an army of conquest for the Obsidian Empire in the opposite direction from your orders for three days just so you can resupply it?"

"There were . . . There are unique objects being held by the city that are critical to the Obsidian Cause," General Karpasic said, although the words sounded unconvincing even in his own head. "We had received knowledge of it, and it required swift action if these objects were to be secured."

"And I suppose that these . . . objects," Evard continued for the general, "are of such a nature that you wish to keep the knowledge of them to yourself until such time as they can be properly secured."

"Just so," Karpasic agreed. It was a convenient lie, of course, but the response of the Obsidian sorcerer told the general that the lie benefited them both in some way. Evard appeared to be supporting Karpasic or, at the very least, not bringing the weight of the full fury of the Inner Circle of the Obsidian Cause down on his neck.

"It is most fortunate for you, General, that I already know about at least one of these 'unique objects' to which you refer," Evard said offhandedly.

Karpasic fixed his eyes on Evard. The story had been a pure fabrication on his part, but now the Obsidian craftmaster appeared to be supporting it. "Indeed?"

"Yes," Evard replied, folding his hands together casually behind his back as he took another step into the tent. "It is an ancient artifact that appears to have been lost while in the possession an officer in your command . . . a Captain Aren Bennis, I believe."

Karpasic could feel the color drain from his broad face. "Captain Bennis is . . . I regret to inform the craftmaster that the captain died some weeks ago."

"Then I am delighted to inform the general that his report is in error," Evard said with quiet calm. "Captain Bennis was taken captive by operatives of the so-called Council of Might and carried away for interrogation regarding the artifact, which is, by the way, still in his possession."

"That is not possible," Karpasic blurted out.

"I assure you it is," Evard said, the tone in his voice cold. "Despite the efforts of some persons to have arranged for it to be otherwise."

"This artifact you mention . . . you mean that sword of his?" Karpasic swallowed and tried to shift the conversation away from the dangerous ground of who ordered Aren's death. The memory of holding that cursed blade sent chills over his flesh, but he knew with the sense of any merchant trader that one never gave away the value of the item being bargained over. "I believe he showed it to me once. It's nothing, Craftmaster—just a rusting old blade."

"Have care, General," Evard cautioned. "This 'rusting old blade' is all that stands between keeping or losing your command. I say it is an ancient artifact of immense power the recovery of which drove your decision to move your army to the south. Do you not agree?"

Karpasic drew in a breath. "My mistake, Craftmaster. It is, indeed, the primary reason I acted with such haste for its recovery."

"I suspected as much." Evard nodded and gave a pleasant smile. "Now, if I may anticipate your plans further, it was most fortunate that I found you here during your march so we could work together to execute your brilliant plan for the recovery of the artifact."

"It is fortunate indeed," Karpasic lied. "And would the craftmaster care to detail what my brilliant plan might be?"

"You will remain encamped here for three days while I

extract the artifact and Captain Bennis from his captivity in Opalis," Evard said casually. "After that, you might consider your objective completed and turn your army back up the Broken Road so it may return to where it is expected to be."

"An excellent plan." Karpasic swallowed. "Even if I say so myself—but with a necessary modification."

"Necessary?"

"Yes, Craftmaster," Karpasic said, stepping toward the sorcerer. "My army was promised spoils from this march. They were promised a prize in Opalis. They are earning their wages, and they must be paid if they are to remain in the service of the Obsidian Cabal."

"It is a waste of your army, General." Evard shook his head. "Even if you were to take it, Opalis will be expensive to hold and a drain on the Obsidian Empire to maintain so far from Desolis."

"I am afraid that my army will insist we take it," Karpasic said with a wistful grin, "but we have no desire to keep it."

"Ah." Evard nodded. "I see."

"We are, indeed, practical men," Karpasic said, walking over to face Evard. "I will issue the order tonight, before I retire, for the army to encamp here for three days' recovery from the march. Will that be agreeable?"

"It is indeed, General." Evard bowed slightly.

The general bowed in return.

Captain Halik ducked into the tent at that moment, his breathing heavy from his exertions in coming so quickly. He was still fastening the buckle of his breastplate as he entered.

"My thanks for your hospitality, General," Evard said as he turned. "I look forward to our next meeting."

Evard passed Halik as he exited the tent. Halik looked in astonishment after the Obsidian sorcerer who had just swept past him.

"General Karpasic! What was an Obsidian—"

The general held up his hand to silence the captain and then quickly stepped over to him. "Follow him. Make sure Craftmaster Dirae leaves the camp. Then return to me."

Halik left at once.

† † †

Evard immediately noticed the captain of the Westreach Army following at his heels. He determined to make it only moderately difficult for the man to keep track of him as he made his way to the edge of the encampment. The exercise was barely a distraction, giving him time to reflect.

Karpasic was as predictable as he was stupid. For Evard, that meant he could be controlled so long as the Obsidian sorcerer could keep the right leverage on the fool. He could only hope that Karpasic would give him the time Evard needed to do what he had come to do.

He doubted it, however, since he was, after all, a practical man.

† † †

He has left the encampment, sire," Halik reported, sweat pouring from his brow despite the chill of the night penetrating the general's tent.

"Well done, Captain," Karpasic said as he sat on his throne-chair. He gestured to a much smaller chair that he had ordered and that was set in front of him. "Please take a seat."

"General," Halik said uneasily. "You have always insisted that your staff stand in your presence. . . ."

"Was my invitation unclear?" Karpasic said, his voice rising despite its tired sound. "Sit!"

Halik hesitated a moment longer before lowering himself onto the chair.

"Now, listen carefully to me, Captain," Karpasic said. "Did you leave standing orders for the army to decamp in the morning and march on Opalis?"

"Aye, sire." Halik nodded. "As per your orders."

"Very well." Karpasic sighed. He desperately wanted to fall onto his cot and let the ache in his body fall away from him in sleep, but he had this one last task to perform. "Now, I am now revoking those orders and issuing new orders that the army remain here in camp for the next three days."

"Very well, General." Halik stood up. "I'll issue those orders to the commanders at once and—"

"Did I give you permission to leave?" Karpasic yelled, his voice carrying beyond the tent.

Halik blinked. "No, sire!"

"Then *sit down*!"

The captain slowly took to the chair once more.

"It will be unfortunate that those orders will somehow not reach their commands until *after* the army had already broken camp and made their march the rest of the distance to Opalis," the general stated with pointed emphasis to his captain. "You may apologize now for that failure, which will take place tomorrow morning."

"I . . . I apologize," Halik said in some confusion, but clearly understanding his commander's intention.

"You are forgiven this understandable failure in the chain of command," Karpasic said. "It will be unfortunate that delivering this message will be so impractical."

"Yes, sire," Halik agreed.

"And we are, after all"—Karpasic sighed as he lifted his bulk off his enormous chair and added—"practical men."

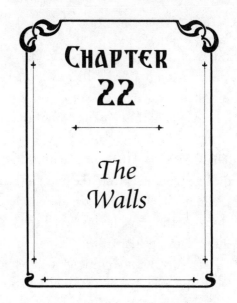

CHAPTER 22

The Walls

The dawn rose bloodred in the east. The high clouds were bathed in the crimson light, coloring the world below. Beneath it, the Westreach Army of the Obsidian Empire marched with purpose in a wide line of advance across the expansive prairie toward the walls of Opalis.

Aren watched their approach from atop the Long Wall near the Storm Gate Tower. He stood next to Commander Trevan as they watched the approaching army from behind the defensive crenellations. All along the top of the Long Wall stood ranks of the city's longbow archers. Their quivers were situated upright at their feet, filled with arrows, but their enemy was still miles away. There was nothing for them to do but watch their approach with the silent apprehension of the dawn.

"Those look like pikemen in the front center of the line," Trevan observed.

"They think you have knights or possibly some sort of mounted cavalry." Aren nodded. "There will be ranks of foot soldiers behind them, and archers arrayed behind them."

Trevan glanced over at the captain. "Anything else you care to tell me?"

"They will have disbursed their special units in block formations down the line separately from the human warriors," Aren said as he turned his back on the horizon and leaned against the upright stones of the crenellation. The towers of the citadel rose before him, shining like frozen flames in the morning light. "A third of their mounted knights will be positioned at the flanks, with the remainder positioned behind the line. Any heavy siege units they might have will be farther back still. They will sweep around the defensive walls of the city—most likely burning the outlying buildings to the ground—and then settle in for the siege."

"Why are you telling me this?" Trevan asked.

Aren looked over at the commander. "Is there anything you're planning to do about it?"

"No," Trevan admitted with a rueful smile. "How do you know what formations they'll take?"

"Because they were my idea." Aren nodded in return. "How long do you believe you can hold out?"

"As long as necessary," Trevan said with grim confidence. "Word has gone out to the baroness, and she will bring the warriors of Ardoris to our aid. Six weeks until they arrive—perhaps eight. By the time they arrive, your Westreach Army may have lost their appetite for the fight."

"I would not count on that, Commander," Aren said. "Karpasic believes Opalis to be a treasure city and, by now, so does every captain, knight, warrior, cook, and ratcatcher in his army."

"You think he's told them that?" Trevan asked.

"No, but I would have if I had them at my command. General Karpasic, on the other hand, would have tried to keep that knowledge to a select few, and there is nothing more difficult to maintain in an army than a secret," Aren replied. He shifted his gaze past the citadel to the rooftops and spires of the beautiful city within the walls. "Every warrior is persistently aware that their life or their death, their comfort or their misery, their deprivation or satiation can depend upon the whim of a decision made by someone in authority over them. The only means a soldier has of influencing this role of the dice is to know something more than the warrior standing next to him. The trafficking in rumor is a currency on the battlefield more valuable than gold. So, from the moment Karpasic even muttered the words *treasure city*, talk of it would have spread among his soldiers with the ferocity and speed of a dry grass fire."

Aren turned back around to face the approaching army. "As long as they believe that this wall beneath us is all that stands between them and relief from their pain, they will do *anything*, endure *anything*, and sacrifice *anything* to obtain it."

"Then we both have everything to gain," Trevan observed.

"And everything to lose," Aren agreed.

"It must be difficult for you to see your comrades approaching," Trevan observed.

"It is, I will admit, a rather unaccustomed perspective." Aren grinned. "I am usually on the outside, trying to force my way in."

Trevan turned from the horizon to face Aren. "So why are

you still here? Syenna went looking for you last night. Somehow you managed to avoid her entirely."

"I was hardly avoiding her." Aren frowned. "I wonder that I haven't seen her at all. Do you think she's avoiding me?"

"I rather doubt it. She seemed almost frantic until I told her you were in your cell." Trevan glanced at the captain. "She was certain you had left Opalis to join your comrades and welcome them to the city."

"Reports of my departure have been greatly exaggerated." Aren sighed as he batted his eyelashes.

"So why are you?" Trevan pressed.

"Why am I what?"

"Still here?"

"I told you I wouldn't do anything to harm the city." Aren shrugged. "I gave you my word and, by my reckoning, you are safe from me for another, what, five weeks? Of course, if the siege lasts longer than that, you may have to kill me . . . just as a matter of principle. But until then, how could I break my word?"

"No, that's not it." Trevan shook his head. "I *know* you, Aren."

Aren looked sharply at the commander.

"That's right," Trevan replied. "The day you came into the city, I tried to take your sword—that blade of the Avatar. It didn't show me much of you, but it was enough. You thought you knew exactly who you were when you were a captain in the service of the Obsidians, but the sword has opened your eyes."

"Well, then let the sword open *your* eyes instead," Aren snapped. "I'm tired of it."

"Really?" Trevan laughed. "Tell me, Captain Bennis of the

Obsidian Cause, why do you still have the sword? Why haven't you just given it away?"

"Haven't you heard?" Aren rolled his eyes. "The thing is cursed. There's not much market for a cursed blade."

Trevan shook his head. "Then why did not just throw it away or toss it over the side of the ship when you crossed the bay?"

"I was doing plenty of tossing on the ship," Aren advised him with a chuckle.

"But you still kept the sword," Trevan persisted. "No one, including the blade, is forcing you to keep it. If you really wanted to, you would long ago be rid of it. So what is it? Why do you keep it?"

"Your eyes are open too," Aren sneered. "You tell me."

"Because now you've seen things, know things," Trevan said, gazing back toward the horizon. "Why do you think I let you wander my city? I knew you would see my city in ways you had never seen any city among all your miserable conquests ever before. And now you can no longer pretend you are blind anymore."

"Well, even a blind man could see that you won't be able to hold anything outside the walls," Aren said, changing the subject. "Did you evacuate Brambletown?"

"The last of the caravans left for the west this morning." Trevan nodded. "Those that didn't leave with them have all come in the gates. We'll be closing those soon. I can only hope we'll be able to open them again not that many days from now."

Aren turned his back again to the horizon, his eyes falling down past the rooftops below him to the long and crowded arc of Muse Way.

All this time you've been at my heels, and now I can no longer feel the breath of your pursuit at my neck, Aren thought. *Where are you, Syenna?*

† † †

I am sorry, Shieldmaiden," Lanilan Stranthas said with an exasperated sigh. "I just can't help you."

"But there has to be something," Syenna urged, her voice in a near panic. "Something you can tell me, someplace you can send me that can give me an answer!"

"There are no answers," the loremistress replied. She spread her hands wide over her research table, gesturing to the stacks of books and jumble of scrolls on its surface. "This is all it . . . every reference I have plus everything from the Titans' own libraries related to transformational magic. I've even researched a number of religious texts and some of the formulas we've been transcribing from the cloaks of the Obsidians we have managed to kill. Look, over here . . ."

Lanilan guided Syenna by the arm to the end of the table. "These are the Scrolls of Merkin, the most complete collection of his reflections on sorcery remaining today. They detail so much about how sorcerers, wizards, and conjurors functioned in the days before the Fall, even though the Fall predated Merkin by over one hundred years. The problem is that the magic he describes no longer works the way it once did. The Fall caused such a fundamental change in the makeup of the world, that magic as it was practiced in that time is practically useless. Oh, here and there may be some principles that are still functional, but the shattering of the moon and the fall of the Shards ended the ways of magic as it was practiced then. New magic sprang from the world, but it was wild, untamed, and

worked completely differently on a fundamental level. This"—
she pushed Syenna farther back down the table and pointed
toward a thick book—"this is the *Codex Sublima*—perhaps the
only one of its kind outside of the vaults of the Obsidian fortress at Desolis—and its spells, incantations, and transformations are so filled with contradictory notes and corrections as
to be nearly useless. The Obsidians, it appears, have only a
marginally better understanding of their magic than we do.
Worse, there is nothing in it describing basic functioning sorcery as practiced by the Obsidians. It is as though everyone
who was to read this book already would and should have a
working knowledge about sorcery before it would even begin
to make sense."

"But the letters," Syenna urged. "You said the correspon-
dence from the woman in Port Crucible—"

"The Epistles of Arabella?" Lanilan sighed. "Yes, I read those
as well. The nature of the magic that was performed on her was
different than that suffered by your sister."

"But she *was* a subject of the transformations," Syenna
said quickly. "You said her account might have given us
some clue as to how the Obsidians went about their magical
experiments. . . ."

"Much of what the woman writes is the random gibberish of
a fevered mind," Lanilan said, shaking her head. "It doesn't tell
us anything that can tell you about what happened to your
sister, let alone how to change it."

"But there must be something," Syenna whimpered. "Something you've overlooked . . ."

"I'm sorry—truly sorry, Shieldmaiden—but I've explored
every avenue available to me," the loremistress said quietly.

"Only the Obsidians know what they did to your sister. They are the only ones who might know how to undo it . . . but from what I've read, I'm not even convinced that they understand their own sorcery that well. Even if they could, how would you ever convince a sorcerer to help you?"

"No!" Syenna screamed in agony, tears of frustration forced from her eyes to streak down her cheeks. "There's got to be another way! You've got to offer me another way!"

The loremistress looked at Syenna, shaking her head sadly. "Another way? Another way to . . . to what? Change the past? Rewrite what has already been written? What other possible way is there?"

But Syenna was already running out of the Athenaeum doors.

† † †

The smoke from the raging fires of what had been Brambletown drifted in heavy patches across the top of the city wall. Aren had followed Trevan over the Storm Gate to the South Wall as they had observed the fires being set in Brambletown. They had moved down the line of defenders on the wall until they were situated between the pair of towers overlooking the Jaana River below.

There, they had spent the day watching the outer town burn to the ground. Now it was evening, judging by the fading light beyond the pall of smoke. The Westreach Army was moving along the opposite side of the river and burning the ramshackle town as they moved. Aren and Trevan could no longer see the army through the smoke, but Aren was certain they had reached the Harvest Bridge southwest of the Fields Gate by now and would have completed the encirclement of the town by joining with the forces that Karpasic had ordered to surround the town on the northern side.

Aren held the corner of his cloak across his mouth, trying to keep the occasional dark cloud from choking his lungs. It was difficult to see through the smoke to the approaches to the base of the wall below, but it was essential for the defense of the city.

The defense of the city. Aren's laughter at his own thoughts was punctuated by coughing. *If I do see Karpasic's warriors charging the wall, am I supposed to raise the alarm or join them?*

It troubled him that he could not answer the question easily. He knew his duty to the empire, and he truly believed that the Obsidians were a force of law in a lawless world. The order the Obsidian Cause was bringing to lands overrun by chaos and contradiction was worth its price in blood. But now, on the walls of the city he had come to know too well, he was wondering whose blood was paying that price and whether the cost was too high after all. Karpasic was an opportunist rather than an idealist; he reveled in spilling other people's blood to pay for his conquests and his spoils of war. Where, in practice, where were the ideals of the Obsidians on which Aren had justified every act he had performed on their behalf?

Aren crouched on the wall, contemplating those forces he served on the outside of Opalis and those fragile ideals that he saw living within the city.

"Do you see anything?" Trevan choked out next to him.

"No," Aren answered. The smoke drifting toward the wall was being whipped by a southern breeze, offering occasional clear views across the approaches to the wall. "The setting sun isn't helping any."

"It's been a long day," Trevan said.

"It's going to be a longer night," Aren observed. "The fires are still burning, but at least they seem to be dying down. What about the West Wall and Long Wall?"

"They report a continuous siege line established beyond the approaches," Trevan replied, wiping his hand over his eyes. "They're setting up a camp to the southeast well out of archery range along the banks of the river. The North Gate road has been cut off."

"It's a siege then." Aren nodded. "They look like they'll be settling in. But I've been thinking, Commander. This doesn't make sense."

"What do you mean?"

"This siege," Aren said, cocking his head out beyond the wall. "I think the Obsidians would be just as surprised to know this army is at your gates as you are at finding them there."

"You think the army is acting on its own?" Trevan squinted at the captain through the smoke.

"I think General Karpasic may not have the luxury of time that a siege requires," Aren said. "There may be a way to save your city after all. If you can manage to hold out here for a week or perhaps two, there may be time enough for the Obsidians to put pressure on the general. Then he might be willing to listen to a more reasonable voice."

"Your voice, I take it," Trevan said dryly.

"I rejoin my army, the army goes back to the campaign it was ordered to pursue, and the city and its people remains intact. I'd say it was worth the price of losing a single prisoner." Aren shrugged as he tried to peer through the smoke. The depression to the south was bordered by the river. Aren could see shadowy figures moving at the farthest edge of his vision. Some of those warriors were men who he most likely knew by name. He wondered how many of them would be glad to see him.

Aren turned around, leaning his back against the crenellation set into the outside top of the wall. He could see the rooftops of Opalis and, occasionally, a glimpse of the towers of the citadel through the swirling ash and smoke. The city was beautiful, but only rich in all the ways that Karpasic either did not understand or despised. The city and its people deserved a better fate than what awaited them, Aren thought, but what could he possibly do about it?

Aren turned. Something caught his eye to the west. The smoke swirled with the breeze over the top of the wall and cleared suddenly, revealing a short set of stairs that joined two sections of the wall that had been built at different heights. At the end of the higher section of wall, he could suddenly see the western tower through the smoke.

There, standing atop the wall was a woman wearing a long, white gown. Her dark hair had been carefully coaxed into tight curls. She stood with confident poise, though there was a deep sadness about her countenance. Her large, watery eyes looked back at Aren with a fixed, pleading gaze.

Aren shook with a start.

He had seen this woman before.

She turned from him, walking west along the top of the wall.

"That woman!" Aren blurted out.

"What woman?" Trevan, who had been watching over the wall, turned toward him.

"That w-woman walking away from us," Aren stammered as he pointed westward down the length of the wall.

Trevan frowned as he peered to the west. "What are you talking about? I don't see anyone."

The top of the western wall had vanished beneath another veil of ash and smoke.

"She was at Midras. I saw her in the ruins there. She was the one who warned me of the Guardians just before they attacked. She was the one who led us to—" Aren suddenly clambered to his feet. "Come on! We've got to find her."

"Find who?" Trevan called after him as Aren hurried westward along the top of the wall.

"Come on!" Aren called back. He came to the stairs leading upward and quickly ran up them. Aren could hear Trevan running behind him, struggling to keep up. He rushed past the rows of archers from the Opalis Legion stationed all along the top of the wall. The western tower was a vague shadow through the smoke, getting darker and more solid as Aren ran.

He saw her moving along the wall behind the sentinels and beyond the western tower. The warriors, each looking outward in anxious anticipation, took no notice of the woman as she passed behind them, the wide skirt of her dress flowing as she ran.

Aren dashed after her, passing around the western tower and continuing along the top of the wall. He caught another glimpse of her as she turned where the wall jogged outward before it continued toward the northwest and the Fields Gate Tower.

Aren's boots slid along the stones as he rushed around the jog in the wall. He could see where the wall ended at the Fields Gate Tower. A guard stood at the closed door that entered the tower.

The woman had vanished.

Aren approached the guard at once. "Where is she?"

"Who, sire?"

"The woman," Aren insisted, frustration rising in his voice. "Dark hair and a white dress . . . She just passed here!"

"Sire?" the guard answered, a puzzled look on his face.

Trevan caught up with the captain. "Did any pass this post just now, Mordan?"

The guard looked back at them with a genuinely puzzled expression. "No, sire! Everyone here has stayed at their posts. We are not due to be relieved for another hour."

"I'm not talking about the guards!" Aren shouted. "It was a woman who . . ."

The guard stared blankly back at Aren.

"You're sure you saw someone?" Trevan asked.

"I tell you, she was the same woman," Aren insisted. "She was wearing different clothing and looked at the time as though she had gone through the siege, but I would remember those eyes . . ."

Aren stopped speaking.

A terrible shouting could be heard in the distance beyond the walls.

"No!" Aren muttered in disbelief. "He wouldn't be that stupid . . . *couldn't* be that stupid!"

Trevan turned toward the sound, a terrible cacophony of noise that grew louder by the moment.

"They're coming." Aren grabbed Trevan's shoulder. "Get your warriors to the wall, Trevan. Do it now!"

"I thought you said he was going to settle into a siege?" Trevan said.

"Karpasic isn't going to wait for a siege and he isn't going to negotiate to spare the citizens or the town," Aren insisted. "He's going to throw his army against the walls of Opalis as hard he has to for as long as it takes to bring it down . . . and he's going to do it right here at Fields Gate!"

The color drained from Trevan's face as he turned toward the guard. "Mordan! Run the wall and tell the captains they have to hold their ground. Prepare weapons and fire on anything that enters the moats outside the wall. Go! Run!"

Mordan ran at once, his cries diminishing as he hurried along the top of the wall. Already the archers were moving, nocking their arrows and preparing for the first volley.

Trevan turned and called down the wall. "Captain Artemis!"

The young captain was a woman clad in her armor, her weapon at her side as she came running toward them. "Hail, Commander!"

"Ring the bell, Artemis," Trevan said without preamble.

Artemis straightened at the command. "The bell, sire?"

"You heard me, Captain," Trevan said. "Do it now."

"Sire!" Captain Artemis said, her right fist rising to her chest in sharp salute. She ducked at once through the door of the tower and disappeared.

"A bell?" Aren asked. "What does the bell . . . ?"

"We may not have told you everything about the defenses of Opalis," Trevan said quickly, and then he turned to one of the knights standing behind the line on the wall. "Sir Llewellyn! Take Captain Bennis here back to the barracks at once and secure him . . . then muster whoever remains and bring them back here at once!"

"Aye, sire!" the knight replied. "You're coming with me, Captain Bennis."

"I am doing no such thing!" Aren snapped. "If you're going to save this city from this lunatic, you're going to need—"

"Here they come!" someone shouted down the wall. The dull, harplike sound of bowstrings being released filled the air. They were in near unison at first but quickly fell into a continuous, ragged volley.

A wuthering sound came in almost instant reply. Aren could see the long streaks rushing over the wall like a sudden, deadly rain. They arched downward, some short of the wall, some rushing down on the wall, and still more falling toward the rooftops and streets behind them.

Aren fell at once and rolled toward the crenellations at the top of the wall. Commander Trevan cried out as he leaped into the doorway of the tower. Captain Llewellyn ducked behind the tower, shielded by its bulk. The archers along the wall ducked behind the crenellations, but not all of them were quick enough to avoid the terrible cascade of arrows.

Blood began to stain the top of the wall. Aren could hear the panic rising from the streets of the city behind the wall.

Aren pulled himself up and looked out. The depression was filling with water from the river, the sluice gate having at last been opened. Ranks of warriors from the Westreach Army had fallen at the volleys from the walls. Some lay unmoving while many more struggled to get back to their feet as the waters rushed toward them. Others, still carrying their ladders to assault the walls, were pressing forward under a renewed withering round of arrow fire from the walls. It was a death pit; the charge there was faltering as the dead and drowning were slowly being covered by the diverted waters of the West Jaana River.

But it was the causeway coming toward the gate that gripped Aren's attention. There, running toward the gate were three monstrous creatures the likes of which he had never seen before. They were human in general shape but gargantuan; each stood nearly fifteen feet in height. They had arms the size of tree trunks, powerful legs that were larger still. They were clad in armor patterned after the Obsidian design, but at an enormous scale. Their eyes glowed red in the failing light, fixed on the closed gates to the north of the tower.

Behind them was a phalanx of warriors, their long shields held up in tortoise formation. Those in the center held their shields over their heads in an overlapping pattern while those at the sides of the formation held them so as to form a wall at their sides. These made their way more slowly along the causeway and toward the gate.

"Captain!" Sir Llewellyn shouted, reaching down to grab Aren. "You're coming with . . ."

Another volley of arrows flew toward the wall from the smoke-laden darkness of the burned town beyond the walls. Aren flattened against the crenellation just as the arrows slammed against the stones. A dozen arrows slammed against Sir Llewellyn, though none found their mark between the plates of the knight's armor. He staggered backward under the hail of blows, losing his footing and falling on his back.

More archers lay still along the wall. Blood began to form in pools, mixing one with another from the fallen on the wall.

Aren then heard the bell ringing frantically from its bell tower over the Fields Gate.

A hand appeared before Aren. He took the hand as it pulled him up and swung him back around the tower.

"Stay here!" Trevan shouted as he released Aren's hand.

"Not likely!" Aren replied.

The wall shook beneath their feet. Both the commander and the captain reeled slightly.

Trevan regained his footing, drawing his sword. "What was that?"

"You've got a problem!" Aren yelled, and pointed down past the tower to the approaches of the gate below.

The gigantic creatures had reached the gate. Arrows stuck out from them like quills. Each of them seemed more enraged than harmed by the wounds.

"They're not attacking the gates!" Trevan shouted in disbelief. "They're attacking the *stone*!"

The monsters gripped the stones around the gate, wrenching them from their places and tossing them aside. The gates, no longer having stone to hold them in place, tore loose with the stone as the wall at the gate began to collapse.

Suddenly a sheet of purple-blue light fell over the city, a dome of lightning and shifting light extending from the citadel tower down over all of Opalis. It fitted itself to the top of the wall, a great shield over the city. The volley of arrows from the Obsidian Army broke against its surface, sliding down to clatter harmlessly on the ground. The arrows of Opalis's own archers, however, passed unhindered from the wall through the shield, continuing their work of death against the undeterred waves of warriors struggling to reach the wall.

"The Titans' Shield," Trevan said as he gazed up in awe-filled relief. "I just hope it lasts long enough."

"How long is that?" Aren asked.

"I don't know," Trevan said. "We've never had to use it before."

The ground beneath them again shook. The monstrous giants were further outraged by the magical shield that had fallen over the city. They began pulling huge handfuls of stone out with both hands. In a moment the gate collapsed entirely, the wall crashing downward.

The great wall began to come apart beneath their feet, the tower behind them shuddering.

"Oh no!" Trevan cried out.

The wall continued to collapse in their direction. Trevan grabbed Aren by the arm, pulling him away from the tower and throwing him back along the top of the wall. The tower came apart behind him, crashing down on top of the commander.

Aren staggered back to his feet.

The tower was gone.

Trevan lay partially buried beneath its stones.

He was not moving.

CHAPTER 23

The Gate

ren rushed toward the fallen commander. He dropped to his hands and knees and pulled fiercely at the debris, shoving the shattered stones aside. He turned his face back down the wall, shouting desperately. "Llewellyn! Help me!"

The knight stood unmoving on what remained standing of the wall, blinking back at him.

"Sir Llewellyn!" Aren barked in his command voice. "Come here! Now!"

The knight shook as he broke the bonds of the stupor that held him. He dropped beside Aren, pulling furiously at the stones that had nearly entombed the commander. In moments, the battered, dust-laden form of Trevan had been uncovered.

A pool of blood was spreading out from beneath Trevan's head.

"Help me get him free," Aren ordered as he squatted down, pressing his boots against the rubble as he positioned himself at the head of the still figure of the commander. He could feel himself slip over the blood beneath where he sat. Aren put both arms beneath the commander's shoulders and pulled, trying to slide the fallen warrior out of the wreckage. Trevan's body remained where it had fallen. "Keep digging!"

Trevan's body came free on the second try.

Aren stopped at once and examined the body before him. It was obvious that both the legs were badly broken. The external bleeding from the head did not concern him nearly as much as the less obvious and far more dangerous internal bleeding at which he could only guess.

"He's still breathing," Aren observed.

"What do we do?"

"What?" Aren looked up.

"Please, sir." It was the knight Llewellyn, gazing up at him from where he knelt next to his commander. "What do we do?"

It was not until that moment that Aren realized just how truly young the knight kneeling next to him was. It was not just the years that were reflected in the large eyes staring back at him, but no amount of training had prepared this man for the reality of what he was facing.

How many more of you are there standing on these walls? Aren thought at once. *How many will die?*

Aren stood, taking in the battle around him. Time slowed in his mind as he turned. Below the wall on which they stood, he could see a group of elves, each of their bodies marked with paint, charging across the flooded approach, running across on the backs of the fallen dead beneath their feet. They were trying to reach the breached gate and fallen wall ahead of the humans, who were still in their tortoise formation and inching their way closer by the moment on the causeway. The warriors on the wall continued to fire their arrows down on the elves, but they moved with such swiftness and erratic course that the archers were having trouble leading them properly. On the other side, where the wall had collapsed and with it the Fields Gate, Aren could see the magical barrier had extended down to the debris and was keeping two of the enormous beasts at bay, but the third had reached into the rubble and pulled a huge slab of stone that had formed the top of the gate. The monster was lifting the stone upward with all its strength against the glowing barrier.

There, as the stone was pressed upward, an opening in the barrier was widening between its colossal legs. Lightning raged at its edges, struggling to close in on itself, but the screaming monster held its ground, pushing harder upward.

Beyond that opening lay defenseless all the city of Opalis.

"Run to the barracks," Aren said, his voice more strong and sure than he felt. "Order everyone there to the Fields Gate. We have to hold the gate or the city is lost. Do you understand?"

The knight nodded.

"Go! Now!"

The knight jumped up and fled eastward down the wall.

Aren took in a deep breath and then knelt down next to the motionless body of the commander. The once bright blue mantle of the commander was now stained with his own blood and caked with dust from the collapsed tower, but the silver crest of the falcon with its spread wings could still clearly be made out. Without hesitation, Aren reached down for the edge of the

mantle and quickly pulled it free over the lolling head of Trevan.

"Please," he muttered to himself. "Don't anyone look too
closely."

The smoke of Brambletown still drifting over the broken
wall, Aren quickly put Trevan's mantle over his head. It settled
heavily on his shoulders even as he turned around back toward
the wall.

"Captain!" he called.

"Hail, Commander!" came the reply through the obscuring
smoke.

"Concentrate your fire on the causeway!" Aren called back.
"Ignore the elves unless they try to scale the wall!"

"Elves?" the captain asked back. "What are elves?"

"Those painted monsters charging the wall," Aren corrected.
"Just . . . just fire on the causeway!"

"Aye, sire!"

Aren looked about the wall. The collapse had left a slope of
debris just beyond where the tower had once stood. Part of the
wreckage had cascaded outside the mystical barrier, but much
of the sloping jumble lay inside the glowing and flashing blue
lights. Aren bound down the rubble, nearly losing his footing
on the slope twice before he found more stable ground at
the level of the city. Several of the buildings nearest the gate
had been heavily damaged as well, causing Aren to cross back
behind them into the alleyways that connected to Muse Way
beyond.

He burst into the street filled with chaos. Citizens were
running in blind panic, desperate to find safety where none
could be found. Aren pushed through them for a few moments

before bursting into the square behind where the Fields Gate had once stood. The square was empty now, the gate smashed to ruins and the walls to either side fallen as well.

There, where the gate had once been, stood the gigantic form of the monster, raising the stone over its head, pushing the glowing shield of the city back.

Between its feet, Aren could already see the elves pouring into the square.

Aren, facing them alone, drew his sword.

"Khianati!" Aren yelled as loudly as he could, directly toward the large elf charging toward him before the others. He knew this would be the chief of the elves, who always preferred to lead them into battle. *"Pengkhianatan dari belakang!"*

The chief of the elves stopped, looking around in confusion, anger, and outrage.

"Peri dikhianati!" Aren shouted. His voice was hoarse and dry. *"Peri terjaga! Hewa meningalkan Peri matikan!"*

The elven chief raised his arms and screamed. His piercing voice made Aren cringe, but he knew it had been shaped that way to carry over the noise of battle.

The elves stopped their charge, their weapons raised in anticipation of death and conquest.

Aren kept his eyes on the chief. He was enormously powerful and terrible to look at. Aren could not remember this particular chief, but he fervently hoped this one would react in the same way as every other chief he had commanded.

In that moment, Aren knew the chief.

He knew there was nothing there.

Nothing, at least, in the sense of what had once been there. This had once been a man, he knew, and that man had been reshaped by the Obsidians into this monster of war and conquest. There was nothing here of his life, his former self, his memories, or his soul. Whatever this man had once been had been stripped from him and replaced with hatred, fear, and power.

"*Kebelakan!*" The chief's voice was a screeching sound like that of a hawk. "*Seranglah kebelakan!*"

The elves turned at once, rushing back between the legs of the gigantic monster still holding the stone aloft to keep the way open.

Aren smiled and followed them toward the opening.

He could see out of the corner of his eye the warriors of the Opalis Legion rushing down Muse Way from both the north and the southwest. Syenna was with them, running before them and toward him.

Beyond the legs of the straining monster lay the Westreach Army of the Obsidian Empire.

His army.

"Aren!" Syenna shouted after him. "Stop! I order you to stop!"

Aren's grin widened. Syenna was the closest to him but not close enough to stop him.

"Archers!" Syenna shouted to the walls. "Stop him! Stop him before he escapes!"

Aren shook his head as he ran. The mantle on his shoulders would confuse them, make them hesitate just long enough.

The sword in his hand flashed in the light of the mystic shield above him.

Aren altered his course and charged directly at the gargantuan leg of the monster straining to hold open the breach in the mystical barrier of Opalis. The creature, he realized with surprise, was not one human enlarged in form, but multiple humans merged into a single form. In the end, the difference did not matter, for he knew that none of those who originally had been reshaped by the Obsidians were there any longer. He swung the sword with both his hands on the grip, cutting with all his might at the back of the enormous creature's ankle just above the heel. The blade sliced with unexpected ease through the tendon before connecting with bone.

Aren pulled the blade free, stepping back from the creature as quickly as he could.

The monster howled in pain, suddenly toppling sideways. The force of the mystical barrier drove down the stone, crushing it on the creature's head and driving it into the rubble of the fallen gate.

Aren drew in a ragged breath, taking a few steps away from the restored city shield and the howling, outraged warriors of the Westreach Army beyond it. The Avatar's sword remained poised in his hand. He watched the gigantic creature warily, but the monster did not move and, in any event, appeared to have fallen outside the Titans' Shield. Aren stood upright and glanced down at the sword with new appreciation.

Something caught his eye.

The symbol on the sword's pommel had changed. Now two of the three curving blades on the symbol were shining brightly rather than the singular one he had noticed before.

"Now that's odd," Aren chortled. "I wonder what *that* is supposed to mean?"

Aren sheathed his sword and turned back to face the square. The warriors of the Legion stood watching him as he walked toward them wearing the mantle of their commander. Aren saw a familiar face standing near Syenna and walked in their direction.

"Sir Llewellyn," Aren said. "You have arrived just in time. Form ranks from a third of your knights to guard this gate, then form watches out of the remaining knights. Have them guard this breach in shifts. Then find Captain Artemis and have her organize the remaining archers and warriors into watches along the remaining walls. Once that's done, find someone who could organize any stoneworkers in town to see if anything can be done about repairing this wall. Do you understand all that?"

"Yes, sire," Llewellyn replied.

"One last thing," Aren said as he removed the filthy and blood-stained mantle from over his head.

"Yes, sire?" Llewellyn said.

"Give this to . . . Give this to Commander Artemis when you see her," Aren said. "I think she'll know what to do with it."

"Yes, sire." Llewellyn nodded, considerable relief in his voice.

Aren turned toward Syenna. "I was being taken back to the barracks, but this ridiculous siege interrupted my escort. I don't suppose you would mind taking me there?"

"You're still here," Syenna said in disbelief. "You could have fled and rejoined your army. Why are you still here?"

"What? And let General Karpasic win?" Aren snorted, and started walking down Muse Way toward the barracks.

Syenna followed him in silence.

CHAPTER 24

Collateral Damage

A ren threw himself down into a chair against the wall in the commander's chamber of the barracks. He cast a baleful eye at the commander's own empty chair, situated behind the massive table still covered with maps of the city and the surrounding region. With a heavy sigh, Aren leaned onto the back of the chair.

Syenna had followed him down the curving length of Muse Way, the entire distance from the shattered Fields Gate past the Storm Gate, and finally to the barracks at the base of the Long Wall. Neither of them had said a word the entire distance. Now she stood in the doorway, leaning against the frame as she looked down at Aren.

Aren pulled out the sword, gazing at it.

"It's an interesting thing to me," Aren muttered at last as he turned the blade in his hand. "Just how deeply swords can cut.

I don't think I really knew it before now, but these sharp edges sever more than skin, muscle, and tendon. I've seen swords separate a body from its life. Surely that is deep enough for any keen edge. But even that is not deep enough—not for true warriors or the empires they serve."

The sword flashed in the warm light of the burning oil lamp as he twisted it. The blood streaking its blade looked nearly black in the dim light.

"No, Syenna," Aren continued, his eyes unexpectedly welling up, his voice shaking. "The swords and knives and every other artifice of death slice down through a person's soul. It separates the living from their past—the leaves, twigs, and branches from their roots. It neatly draws and quarters the conquered from who they were. Their history and their stories, their writings, and what they hoped to be. Then after it has carved out the guts of their civilization, the conqueror promises to make up for this vivisection by transplanting his own pride, legends, and beating drums in their places. Then they hope—hope, mind you—that their prey will be grateful for this new 'life' they never wanted or needed."

Aren looked up at the shieldmaiden. Syenna's breath was coming in shallow gasps.

"You know what I'm talking about, don't you?" Aren said as he gazed at her, the sword gripped tightly in his hand. "Your father was a trade merchant out of Etceter. He worked the long overland routes through Midras to Port Crucible, as well as the eastern routes across the Grunvald up into Rhun."

"What?" Syenna gaped. "No, I—"

"You would often go with him, along with your mother and your sister, on the longer expeditions so that he wouldn't be lonely for you," Aren continued, his eyes fixed on her. "You spent the long hours on the road next to your father at the front of the trade wagon."

"You cannot possibly—"

"What did you talk about?"

"Everything. He taught me, m-mostly," Syenna stammered. "He talked about the signs of the land and the turns in the road. He knew every boulder, every tree, every peak and mound of the route."

"He knew the signs of the weather, too," Aren continued for her. "He knew when to make camp and when to press on to the next well. But he didn't know anything about the Obsidian Empire growing deep in the Grunvald Plain. He didn't know until that night, when a small cadre of Obsidian knights happened on the caravan's encampment. . . ."

"No," Syenna said breathlessly. "Don't do this."

Aren looked away from her, gazing into the surface of the sword, the runes shifting before him. He could not read them, but somehow the images came to his mind.

"Your mother was emphatic when she took you girls aside," Aren said quietly. "She told you to run into the tall grass of the prairie and to hide there until she came for you. That young girl who had sat beside her father for all those leagues on the wagon was obedient at once and ran for the grass. She realized only too late that her younger sister was no longer behind her. So she did the only thing she could think of doing: she obeyed her mother and hid."

Syenna was shaking visibly.

Aren lowered the sword slowly until the tip touched the ground. Then he looked up at Syenna again.

"Your mother never came for you," he said, sighing.

Syenna shook her head once, her jaw clenched, as a single tear ran down her cheek.

Aren stood up slowly. He slid the sword into his scabbard and turned to face Syenna.

"It would have been tragedy enough for a lifetime that those knights killed your parents along with everyone else in the caravan that night," Aren continued. "But taking the stores and trade goods was only part of their instruction. The Obsidian sorcerers had a special request for young humans, those who had not yet grown to maturity, whose flesh and bones were still forming and growing. It was early in the development of their craft in altering the form of living things. They needed young children on whom they could experiment—make mistakes and learn from them."

"They took her," Syenna growled through her clenched teeth. "They took her to that . . . that place—"

"But you couldn't help her," Aren urged in a soft voice.

"I had to survive first." Syenna nodded, the words spilling out of her. "I remembered what my father had taught me. I found the grottoes, and I found food. I found the routes, trails, and towns. Every step along the way, I drew from my father's words and added to them. I entered the camps of the warlords. I learned the ways of the fist, the sword, and the shield."

"But you did find her." Aren nodded, folding his arms across his chest as he leaned back against the heavy table. "You did rescue her."

"I overheard a camp of mercenaries talking about a caravan that had been taken the year before." Syenna nodded again. "They said that the children were never killed but taken as slaves to a place called Shard. There, they said, the sorcerers were reshaping them into monsters that might put the mercenaries out of work."

"So you went to Shard," Aren said, clearing his throat. "How did you . . . ?"

Syenna shuddered violently, her face a mask of pain.

Aren looked down at the ground. "Never mind. It doesn't matter. The point is that you did rescue your sister from Shard. . . . You did bring her home."

"What was left of her." Syenna nodded yet again. "She was one of their 'failures' at shaping elves."

"And now you want to find a way to fix her," Aren said. "That's why you came into the Westreach Army, using the skills your father taught you and those you learned in order to survive. So you could have your revenge on the sorcerers who crippled your sister. . . ."

"Yes."

"And force them to tell you how to undo what they had done."

"Yes!"

"All so that little girl hiding in the tall grass of the plains could stop those knights that took everything from her."

"Yes!"

Aren drew in a long breath.

"Those Obsidian knights *made* you, Syenna," Aren said softly.

Syenna's eye went wide, her face contorted in fury. She lunged toward him from the doorway in blind rage, her hands outstretched like claws wanting to gouge at his flesh. There was no thought of drawing a weapon in her angry charge. Aren caught her as she rushed forward, gripping her outstretched arms and twisting as she plunged toward him. He spun around her, carrying her momentum into the edge of the table, which groaned as it slid suddenly back against the wall. Aren pressed Syenna back over the edge of the table, making it impossible for her to gain her footing. His face was inches away from her snarling countenance.

"They *made* you, Syenna," Aren repeated as he struggled to hold her still. "They robbed you of your family, of your past, of your hopes, and your future just as surely as they are going to do the same to this city and its people. They failed to remake your sister into one of their monsters, but they reshaped that little girl hiding in the tall grass of the plains into—"

"Into a monster?" Syenna shouted as she continued to struggle.

"No," Aren answered. "Into a shieldmaiden of Etceter."

Syenna stopped struggling. Her breath was ragged, but her eyes were suddenly focused on Aren.

"Do you want these people of Opalis to have their life torn from them as it was torn from you?" Aren asked. "Do you want them to lose the better part of who they may become?"

Syenna relaxed beneath Aren's grip. He released her slowly as he straightened back up and took a step away from her.

Syenna's lip was bleeding slightly from where she had bitten it. She licked the wound and then spoke. "My sister . . ."

"Yes." Aren nodded.

"You know she means everything to me," Syenna said, regaining her footing in front of the table.

"Yes, I know," Aren agreed.

"Then I have something for you," Syenna muttered as she

reached into the pouch that hung from her scabbard belt. She pulled out a pair of items and tossed one toward the captain.

Aren caught it and turned it over in his hand.

It was a black obsidian stone.

"Where did you get this?" Aren asked.

"From your friend," Syenna said, stepping suddenly forward and placing her hand on his shoulder.

"Wait!" Aren said suddenly. "That may not be a good—"

A dome of deep blue light erupted around them.

† † †

The dome of light collapsed with a thunderclap.

Aren blinked as his eyes became accustomed to the sudden absence of light. Syenna was still touching his shoulder, but they were no longer in the barracks of Opalis. Above them, the shattered moon, its fragments preceding and trailing it across the sky, shone light down on them, its bluish rays illuminating the gentle rise on the prairie. As Aren turned, he could see a small encampment farther down the rise, to the north, he gauged, judging from the positions of the moon and stars.

"Well, if it isn't the late Captain Aren Bennis," said a figure approaching from the encampment.

"I'm not late." Aren grinned as he recognized the voice. "Let's just say I'm early in a unique way."

The man approaching wore the robes of an Obsidian sorcerer. He held out his arms wide, giving a hearty laugh that was reciprocated by Aren as both men embraced.

"You *do* know this man?" Syenna stepped back from them in wary anticipation.

"Of course I know him!" Aren beamed. He turned his friend toward the shieldmaiden. "May I introduce you to Evard Dirae, Craftmaster of the Obsidian Cabal."

"We've met," Syenna said in a tone as dry as dust.

"Enthusiastic as ever," Evard commented with a slight nod.

"I've brought him to you, as I said I would," Syenna said, stepping forward. "Now you have a bargain to fulfill."

"A bargain?" Aren said, stepping away from the sorcerer and gazing on him with mock respect. "You mean you actually *bribed* a shieldmaiden to bring me here?"

Even in the dim light of the moon, Aren could see that Syenna's face had flushed.

"It seemed much simpler than asking you to walk out through the Opalis guard and Karpasic's army," the sorcerer observed.

"True enough," Aren agreed, standing back as he casually rested his left hand on the hilt of his sword. "It would have been difficult to know who wanted me dead more, the Opalis Legion or General Karpasic."

"Our bargain," Syenna reiterated in a stronger, more insistent tone.

"Oh, go ahead and give her the bribe." Aren grinned. "Whatever it is, I'm sure I'm worth it."

"I sincerely doubt that," the sorcerer said, laughing. "But if you insist . . ."

The sorcerer reached within the folds of his robes. He produced a vial with a stopped cap. A thick, greenish liquid glowed within. He stretched out his hand with the vial toward Syenna.

"As promised," Evard said with a gracious smile. "Have your

sister drink this, and within a day she should be released from the mistakes that were perpetrated on her form."

Syenna's eyes narrowed at the sorcerer.

"Well, if you're not interested." Evard shrugged as his fingers started to close.

Syenna snatched the vial from his hand.

"If you'll wait a moment here," Evard said with a slight bow, "I'll arrange the return to your city."

Evard walked with Aren, moving in silence to a distance of about a hundred yards from where they left the shieldmaiden before Evard stopped, just at the edge of the rise.

Aren turned his gaze to the south. The city of Opalis lay in the distance, its walls and towers lit by the fires of the West-reach Army encircling it.

"I thought Karpasic was supposed to take the army north," Aren observed.

"He was," Evard agreed. "And he didn't."

"Well, I'm sure that as a member of the Obsidian Cabal"— Aren smiled—"you'll be more than happy to explain to the general that he has a mistaken sense of direction, and why he should move himself and his army back to where they are supposed to be."

"No," Evard said. "I think not."

Aren looked sideways at his friend. "You're going to let General Karpasic get away with this? I didn't think the Cabal of the Obsidians was so forgiving."

"We are not forgiving, but we are pragmatic," Evard observed. "The city will need to fall to us eventually; the army is already here, so why not take advantage of it?"

"What advantage is there in having the Westreach Army reduce the city to rubble?" Aren said, his eyes fixed on his friend.

"Order must be structured," Evard said as he gazed over the city in the distance. "When a garden is left too long without the care of the gardener, it grows wild. Weeds infest it, and the symmetry of the planted crops and ordered rows is torn asunder. After a time, when the gardener returns to find his plot of ground overrun and in shambles, it behooves him to burn down the field, rework the ground with a sure plow, and bring order again to the garden."

"Vegetables do not suit you," Aren said. "You always seemed more of a dealer in meat."

"Plant or animal, it doesn't matter," Evard said. "We raise and harvest them both."

"To the greater purpose of the Obsidian Cause," Aren said.

"To the greater purpose of the Obsidian Cause," Evard repeated in affirmation. "Oh, Karpasic will have to pay for his reckless insubordination. I'll find a way to deal with him. But in the meantime, I've come for you as I said I would, and we can leave this butcher's work to those who have a bigger taste for blood than we do."

"And just where are we going?" Aren asked.

"Why, I am going to escort a hero of the Obsidian Cause back to Desolis." Evard smiled, clasping his hand on the captain's shoulder. "You are going to present this famous sword of yours to the cabal so that you may personally receive what I have already been assured to be their very substantial and valuable thanks."

Aren nodded. "And I'm assuming there's something in this for you as well."

"Well, there certainly will be some measurable consideration for the sorcerer who brings you safely home," Evard said with a smug grin.

Aren considered the city in the distance. Campfires fanned out around its walls in all directions as the warriors of his own Westreach Army prepared for another assault. The magical shield fell over the city like a glowing dome. He knew that the Titans could not maintain it for long.

"But why settle for so little?" Aren continued. "Presenting a little sword is nothing compared to a city full of slaves."

"Where is the advantage in surrendering the city to Karpasic?" Evard asked, turning toward his friend.

"None, I quite agree with you," Aren replied. "But there is considerable advantage for us both if the city surrenders to someone else. Say, someone whom we both know and trust."

"I see that you have someone in mind," Evard chided.

"Well, I never thought the title of captain suited me very well." Aren nodded toward his friend. "Imagine the spectacle of the two of us riding at the head of a column of victory, me with the sword of an Avatar, and you with an entire city of prisoners for the Obsidian Cabal to transform into whatever form they wish!"

"What about Karpasic?" Evard asked, folding his arms across his chest as he considered Aren's plan.

"Who do you think they'll follow?" Aren asked with a twisted smile on his face. "The man who is offering them another chance to charge the walls of Opalis, or the man who will end the siege?"

"That would solve a number of problems at once," Evard agreed. "What is your play?"

"Send me back into the city with the woman," Aren said as he reached up, rubbing his chin as he considered. "I'll convince the elders of the town that I'm leading them to safety as refugees. I figure that if Karpasic agrees, it will take three days to empty the city. I'll lead the refugees out while delivering the city to Karpasic intact."

"And how am I supposed to convince Karpasic to do that?" Evard demanded.

"Tell him he can have the city and everything in it once I've left with the 'refugees,'" Aren said. "All he has to do is let us leave the city with enough food for the march to Hilt and enough worthless sentimental junk to convince the people to leave."

"You think Karpasic is fool enough to accept that?" Evard asked.

"He's fool enough to accept a great deal less than that." Aren chuckled. "But tell him we'll leave the weapons behind, as well as all the gold and jewels the city has to offer. Once the city is emptied, that magic shield over it will come down, and the city and everything in it are open for plunder."

"He'll think you're out to cheat him," Evard suggested.

"Tell him he can even inspect everything my prisoners are carrying just to make sure none of them are smuggling out anything of value," Aren said. "In the meantime, you have three days to get to Hilt, muster the army assembling there, and prepare to receive the slaves—I mean, 'refugees'—who I'll deliver to you. Then, as heroes of the Obsidian Cause, we'll be in a position to deal with Karpasic."

"I have to admit, Aren, I am impressed." Evard nodded with a smile. "Are you sure about that Syenna woman? Do you really need her?"

"She has a great deal of pull with the people in Opalis," Aren said with a shrug. "She's come too far not to cooperate, and her word has a great deal of influence with the elders of Opalis. I can guarantee her cooperation."

Evard considered the plan in silence under the stars.

"It's only three days," Aren urged. "Three days and Karpasic gets his city and we will practically own the rest of the world."

Evard looked at him with a thoughtful gaze and then nodded.

They both turned back, walking with long strides down the slope of the hill toward the glowing sphere that had transported Aren and Syenna from the city.

"So, can I see this fabled sword of yours?" Evard asked as they walked.

"I wish you could," Aren said casually. "This one is a reproduction . . . something they made for me to carry around in public."

"A false sword?" Evard frowned. "Where is the real one?"

"In Opalis," Aren said with a dismissive wave of his hand. "It's troublesome, but it's one of the reasons I have to go back. You did want me to bring it with me, didn't you?"

"Without doubt," Evard answered as they stepped up to where Syenna stood, waiting, her eyes downcast. He turned toward Aren and took him by the shoulders with both hands. "Three days to get to Hilt?"

"Three days and I'll be coming to meet you," Aren replied, beaming as he took his friend by both shoulders in return. "You know where to find me."

"Until that day, friend." Evard smiled.

"Until that day," Aren returned. He then took Syenna by the arm and stepped into the blue glowing sphere.

Aren and Syenna vanished.

The sphere collapsed with a thunderclap, disappearing as well, leaving Evard alone on the slope beneath the shattered moon.

† † †

Aren and Syenna stood again in the barracks room of the Legion commander as the glowing sphere imploded out of existence behind them.

The smug look on Aren's face contorted into sudden rage. He leaned back, raising his clenched fists in front of him as he screamed at the ceiling above them.

Startled, Syenna took several steps away from him.

Aren opened his right fist. He had clutched the black obsidian stone so tightly that it had left an impression in the palm of his hand. The captain drew back his arm and hurled the stone with as much force as he possessed toward the wall. It caromed into the corner, rebounding off the walls several times before skittering to a stop beneath a stool by the door to the room.

"Aren?" Syenna asked. "What happened?"

The captain's face turned toward her and was red with fury. "They lied . . . He lied! To *me*! To *you*!"

"Who lied?" Syenna said in confusion. "What do you mean?"

Aren rushed toward her, prying open her hand, stripping the vial from her grasp.

"No!" she screamed, clawing at him.

Aren held her off with his right arm as he threw the vial hard against the wall. The glass shattered, the liquid drawing a stain as it flowed toward the floor. Aren turned back to Syenna, his arms gripping the woman tightly in her panicked frenzy.

"Poison! Poison!" he shouted at her again and again until the word registered through her pain. She suddenly stopped struggling. "What did he promise you? *Exactly* what did he promise you?"

"Answers," she said as she sagged in his arms. "I wanted to know what could be done to save my sister."

"I could have told you that answer," Aren said, his voice hoarse. "Nothing. Nothing can possibly be done except to end her existence. That's the answer he put in your hand. It's the only answer the Obsidians have for their failed abominations."

Aren helped Syenna toward the commander's chair that lay on its back on the floor. He reached down, righted the chair, and set Syenna down onto it. He knelt in front of her, looking into her tear-stained face.

"We can't save the city?" Syenna asked quietly.

"No," Aren said. "But we may be able to save its soul."

Syenna looked into his eyes, uncomprehending. "What?"

"The Obsidians are not interested in studying the blade of the Avatar," Aren said. "They want to *bury* it deep in the tombs beneath Desolis—and they want to bury me there with it. They are afraid of this blade and what it represents—the truth. The truth about them—about me—about all of us and our past. They don't mind Karpasic and his brutes burning all the books, scrolls, and records because they *want* them burned—they want nothing left that would question the lies behind their power, their superiority, and their authority. That's where the real battle is taking place. That's the war we have to fight."

"How?" Syenna sighed. "You said we only have three days."

"We're going to lose the city," Aren said, looking with intensity into her eyes. "But in three days we may still be able to win the war."

PART IV

THE TIDE

Chapter 25

Bargains

Tribune Marcus Tercius leaned back into the chair with a luxuriant stretch. The canvas of the large tent that sheltered him rustled slightly in the evening breeze. Before him the Legate of the Norgard, commander of the Fifth Norgard Army, stood glaring with a mixture of shock and outrage at the large, robe-clad man who had just materialized among them.

Inwardly, Marcus was delighted. He had come to the tent of Legate Planus Argo, anticipating another boring evening of the tales of his military conquests. Legate Argo was an angular man with an expansive forehead and prominent cheekbones above a grim, narrow mouth. His armor often seemed to wear him rather than the other way around, but there was no questioning his strategic savvy on the battlefield and his uncanny ability to navigate the intricacies of Norgard politics. However, his skills as a storyteller were low on his list of accomplishments. Indeed, the evening had begun with the legate precisely meeting the ambassador's low expectations. The unexpected arrival had interrupted the legate's droning narrative with a surge of excitement. This subsided, however, when the stranger had spread his arms wide, showed his hands to be empty even though he spoke softly of bringing a great gift to the legate and his Norgard army.

"What is the meaning of this?" the legate demanded, his right hand fumbling to find the grip of his sword that was leaning casually against his own chair. "How did you get past my guard?"

"I am merely a humble traveler asking the hospitality of your tent," the man answered. "And I come bearing urgent and vital information for the legate regarding the siege being conducted against the city of Opalis."

"I already know all about the place," said the legate as the back of his hand brushed against the sword hilt, causing it to fall, clattering to the ground.

"Oh, I think we should hear the man out," said Marcus through his amused smile. "He might surprise us."

"I doubt that," Argo snarled as he turned back to face the intruder and tried to look casual as he hooked his thumbs into the belt at his waist. "The Army of the Obsidian Cause has surrounded the Treasure City of South Paladis. They think it can be plucked like some ripe fruit hanging low for the taking. The West Jaana River will swell with the blood of both sides before that city falls."

"Which, as I recall, is precisely why we are here," observed Marcus.

"Indeed," interjected the large, robed man standing before them. "There are mighty legions of the Norgard that are encamped about you. Even now they await your command with anticipation. Still, you watch like cunning crows observing a great battle from afar, waiting for the warriors to exhaust themselves upon one another, and once all is laid to ruin, you come to pick clean what remains of the carcass."

Argo's nostrils flared in indignation. "How dare you come into my tent—"

"A fair assessment," interrupted Marcus, tilting his head slightly to the right. "I take it that you have something better to propose?"

"In two days there will be an opportunity for the legions of Norgard to secure for themselves and for your empire not only a great victory, but the prized city itself," the man answered in solemn tones, his eyes shifting from the legate to the tribune.

"An intriguing prospect," the tribune applied, raising his eyebrow. "And just who are you to suggest such an opportunity?"

"My name is Boreus," replied the Titan.

† † †

Marshal Nimbus, supreme ruler of the mountain city-state of Resolute, walked with great and rapid steps from the transept archway toward his elevated throne at the end of the Courts of Valor. Three knights of the Resolute Orders trailed behind him, struggling to buckle on their breastplates while balancing their helmets at the same time. They were the only knights available on such short notice to attend the marshal in the hall with any semblance of decorum.

"Has Falcone gone completely insane?" the marshal seethed as he strode up onto the platform, his voice rising with every step. "I dispatched him to that counsel in Etceter with perfectly clear instructions to keep us out of anything to do with their Council of Might, and now he has the gall to show up with an emissary?"

Marshal Gerhard Nimbus sat hastily on his throne and glared down the length of the magnificent hall. He was usually struck with the awe-inspiring beauty of the Courts of Valor, its vaulted architecture and the slanting columns of sunlight streaming in through the tall windows that gave the space different aspects, depending upon the time of the day. Now, however, the site did not give him any pleasure, for his minister was not only arriving several days earlier than expected but was bringing unexpected trouble with him.

Gerhard was a methodical commander of the knights in Resolute. He ruled their mountainous realm of dedicated warriors with a firm and steady hand. It was said of him that the features of his square face were set as hard as flint and that the scar that ran from his forehead down his right cheek must have been chiseled there. His black, wavy hair was held in place by a simple steel band that passed for his crown. His face was clean shaven although those who had met him occasionally wondered privately what sort of metal could hold an edge that could effectively scrape the marshal's face. It was that very stonelike immovability that now caused him to scowl. If there was anything the marshal hated, it was a surprise.

His attendant knights were rushing to their assigned tasks. Two of them, one male and one female, quickly took their places at the base of either side of the platform, hastening to put their ceremonial armor in order. The third hurried toward the far end of the hall, reaching the great double doors there at a near run. He slid noisily to a stop just short of the doors, struggling to catch his breath.

"Let them enter," Gerhard bellowed, his words bounding through the expansive space.

The knight at the far end of the hall turned toward the doors, his chest still rising and falling rapidly, and stepping aside, pulled one of them open.

Two figures stepped into the hall. One of them was instantly recognizable to the marshal, but it was the second that immediately caught his attention.

She was a tall woman with an exquisite shape and elegant features. There was something exotic and transcendent in the look of her face. Her hair was so light in color as to appear nearly white, and its thick, single braid extended beyond the middle of her back. The elegant robe that she wore only hinted at what the marshal realized was a magnificent figure underneath. The sight of her was so astonishing that the stone-faced marshal was completely robbed of words as she and the marshal's foreign minister walked the length of the hall and came to stand before him.

"Lord Marshal," Minister Falcone began. "May I present . . ."

The stupor that Marshal Nimbus had fallen into suddenly shattered. He turned at once in his throne to face his ambassador. "Minister Falcone! You are not expected to return from your mission for at least another five days. Are we to assume that you failed in your charge to reach Etceter as was your express duty?"

"No, Lord Marshal," the ambassador said firmly. "I completed my charge to Etceter and was returning to your court as per your orders. I had not yet reached the Middle Downs of the South Paladis this very morning when our cadre was approached by this woman."

"The Middle Downs?" The marshal stared at Falcone in disbelief. "And only this morning? Then how did you—"

"She brought us here," Falcone said with a shrug as though that were all the explanation he had.

The marshal's gaze shifted to the woman. "Who are you?"

"Sequana of Opalis," the woman answered, bowing slightly.

The marshal's jaw dropped. "A Titan!"

"Yes, Lord Marshal," Sequana answered quietly.

"By thunder." Gerhard breathed in wonder. "The tales of your kind are legendary among my people. Do your brothers still live? Are the skills of your craft still as powerful and wondrous as in the stories of old?"

"My brothers live for now," Sequana answered with a gentle and beguiling smile. "And how our skills compare to your stories would depend upon how those tales are told."

"Then why, may I ask," said the marshal, "has Sequana come to the Courts of Valor in Resolute?"

"To surrender to you," Sequana answered softly.

† † †

General Karpasic sat on his horse among his warriors on the plain north of Opalis. Captain Halik urged his own horse up next to the general as the warriors shifted aside to make room for him.

Everyone had their eyes on the North Gate of the city.

"Are you certain he will be coming out?" the general asked in a low, irritated voice.

"The sorcerer said he would open these gates as soon as the refugee caravans were organized inside the city," Halik replied. "Captain Bennis . . ."

The general scowled at the mention of the name.

"Captain Bennis sent a message out this morning with one of their legion's squires saying that they would be evacuating the city today," Halik continued. "He said they would leave by this gate."

"You needn't look so worried, Halik," General Karpasic sneered. "I gave that Obsidian sorcerer my word that none of them would be harmed and that your friend the traitor captain could lead them back to Hilt."

"Begging your pardon, General," Halik said, his eyes fixed on his commander. "Are those your intentions?"

The general looked sideways at Halik. "Why do you ask?"

"You have occasionally interpreted your orders from the Obsidians with broad latitude," replied Halik carefully.

"Indeed I have." Karpasic chuckled as he turned to look again upon the North Gate. "However, in this particular case, I am in complete agreement with that sniveling sorcerer Evard. The longer these people believe they are being led to freedom, the easier it will be to deliver them into the hands of the Obsidians, and the sooner they may be reshaped into the creatures that will swell the ranks of my army. I am, as you can readily see, the most obedient servant in the Obsidian Cause, especially on those occasions when their purposes suit my own."

"Then we are to let them pass unhindered," said Halik.

"Hardly," Karpasic said, setting his jaw firmly against the thought. "The arrangement is that the citizens may leave the city with their pitiful personal possessions and nothing more. They are to leave all their weaponry behind and, more important, all their coins, gold, gems, jewels, and riches of the city. That is why your men are here, Halik. I want everyone and everything coming out of the city inspected and searched. Every wagon, every cart, every chest, barrel, and bag. Every man, woman, and child is to have every pocket turned out and every fold cloth examined, prodded, and pinched. Not so much as a garnet or copper piece is to leave the city."

"And what of Captain Bennis?" Halik asked. His voice was low and troubled.

"What of him?"

"What will be his fate?" Halik pressed further for an answer.

"Why, he will deliver his precious refugees into the hands of his conspirator Evard Dirae," said the general, a strange smile playing about his lips. "And what his fate will be then, at their hands, will be something you will tell me."

"I'm not sure I understand. . . ."

"Because, Captain Halik," General Karpasic said as he turned toward the young captain, "it will be your charge to follow the refugees to Hilt and deliver our dear Captain Bennis over to the Cabal of the Obsidians for what I believe will be the last time. I have handpicked a unit of elves to help you do just that."

"You mean, I'm l-leaving?" Halik sputtered. "But, General, I am due a share of this campaign!"

"A share I will personally increase tenfold when you return,"

Karpasic answered. "It will be worth it just to be rid of Bennis once and for all."

The sound of the timber bar shifting against the wood of the far side of the gate was followed by a loud thud. Halik could feel the army tense around him. He turned away from the general to face the wall of the city.

The North Gate was flanked by two towers and the city's wall extending from those in either direction. The magical shield that had protected the city since their arrival, and that had proven to be so costly in their assault on the Fields Gate, could still be seen extending above the wall despite the daylight shining down upon the plain. The elegant and remarkable towers of the citadel within the city rose high up over the walls, taunting the Westreach Army with the promise of plunder beyond the dreams of avarice. The eyes of all Karpasic's army who were within sight of the North Gate were fixed upon it.

The enormous gates shifted. Slowly at first, and then with increasing speed, they swung inward toward the city.

Halik found himself holding his breath along with every warrior around him. The promise of riches without further pain or sacrifice seemed almost within their reach.

CHAPTER 26

The Open Door

"A re you sure this is going to work?" Syenna whispered into the air between them.

"No," Aren answered in hushed tones into that same air. "But who is sure of anything anymore?"

Syenna sat upright, her back stiff as the horse beneath her walked down the tunnel between the two sets of gates. She felt vulnerable without her armor. She especially felt the absence of her sword and scabbard. It had hung so long at her side that it had almost become part of her. Now it lay abandoned among the pile of weapons left in the center of the marketplace along with every other weapon in the city.

She turned slightly in her saddle to look at Aren. She wondered for a moment why it was that his strange weapon would be the only one carried out of this place by anyone whom she was willing to call a friend. Everything had been arranged according to

Aren's will, but now, faced with the helpless reality before her, powerless before their enemies on open ground, she wondered if Aren had some private game that he was playing with all of their lives.

Aren rode on the back of his own horse beside her. He wore what remained of his Obsidian armor; the breastplates and backplates and one of the spike-adorned shoulder guards. *He even looks like one of them,* Syenna thought.

Behind them were arrayed all the citizens of Opalis, prepared to follow them through the gates and, they hoped, to longer life.

"You're sure about the Titans?" Syenna asked, and not for the first time.

"Grannus has remained to maintain the shield," Aren answered. "You can see that for yourself."

"But the others—"

"Each of them has sent word," Aren reassured her once more. "Everything is as ready as it can be made."

"Is that ready enough?" she asked.

"Well, we are about to find out," Aren said as their horses walked through the outer gate of the city.

The Westreach Army continued to maintain its encirclement of the city, but now, facing them across the causeway of the North Gate, they seemed a formidable and continuous wall.

Syenna slowed her horse. Doubt filled her mind.

"Stay with me," Aren growled back at her. "They have to know we believe this!"

Syenna swallowed and urged her horse forward next to Aren. Together they slowly rode the length of the causeway until they were within a dozen strides of their forward pike line. Aren stopped his horse and waited.

A large man in shining black armor stepped forward through the ranks, a captain at his side.

Aren bowed slightly from his saddle. "General Karpasic. An unexpected honor."

The general turned his gaze toward Captain Halik at his side.

"Hardly unexpected, Captain Bennis," Halik said. "General Karpasic has come to accept the surrender of the city of Opalis from its rightful sovereign lord. Where is he?"

"*He* is sitting on this horse in front of you," Aren replied.

"Wh-what?" Karpasic sputtered, glaring at Halik. "What is he talking about?"

"The Titans of Opalis and its city elders convened yesterday and surrendered the city to me," Aren replied, ignoring the general's snub. "I accepted their surrender on behalf of the Obsidian Cause just last night."

Captain Halik was in shocked surprise. "They . . . they surrendered the city to *you*?"

Syenna turned her own angry look at Aren. "What are you doing?"

"That's right." Aren nodded and then turned to face General Karpasic. "It's all mine. So, if anyone is empowered to surrender the city to you, General, it would be me."

Karpasic looked up at Aren with unabashed hatred.

"Oh, come on!" Aren rolled his eyes in frustration as he leaned back in his saddle. "General, what do you think I've been doing all this time in the city? I've been playing them. I bemoaned my fate, I appealed to their sympathies and asked for their pity. And they gave it! I showed them this ridiculous, lousy sword and convinced them it was some sort of sign of prophecy that the good old days before the Fall were coming back. I even talked them into walking away from their city with their personal trash and leaving all their legendary treasures behind. And now they're even going to do it. The Obsidian Army doesn't lose any more men at arms, and everyone gets rich on the spoils. I'm here to hand all that to you, so how does that make me your enemy?"

Karpasic stared at Aren, struggling to think through everything he had just heard.

"Look, all I ask is for a piece of the plunder," Aren said, flashing a brilliant smile. "Is that too much to ask? I mean, I *already* own the city and all, so I don't *really* have to share. Just accept my surrender, give me, oh, say, a tenth of your take, General, and we'll just forget about everything that's happened and get back to the business of conquest."

Karpasic's eyes narrowed in thought and then his face relaxed into a smile. "Why not?"

"Captain!" Syenna's voice shook in anger. "You cannot do this! You promised the people of Opalis . . ."

Aren ignored her as he smiled back at the general. "A wise and reasonable bargain, General."

"Indeed, and I'll be happy to hold it for you, Captain," Karpasic finished.

"Hold it . . . for m-me?" Aren stammered.

"Why, of course." The general nodded, placing his gloved hands on his wide hips. "Perhaps you have forgotten, but your orders still include leading these people to Hilt for—what did you call it—resettlement?"

"Wait! Surely someone else can nursemaid these people back to the Obsidians," Aren objected. "Captain Halik, for example, is perfectly capable of—"

"Oh, Captain Halik will be going with you, but only you can

lead this column back to Hilt, Captain Bennis," the general said with no small delight. "Perhaps you forget that the Cabal of the Obsidians is also most anxious to examine that 'ridiculous, lousy' sword of yours. I'm afraid there is no one else as uniquely suited to the job as you."

Aren drew in a long breath. "So, you'll hold on to my percentage of the city's plunder?"

"Absolutely." Karpasic nodded, he mouth breaking into a grin. "And when the Obsidians are finished with you, you can come right back and get it."

† † †

The stream of refugees coming from the North Gate of Opalis had been going on for more than an hour. It already stretched for miles to the east across the South Paladis plain. Now the column snaked eastward, trailing both Captain Bennis and the scout Syenna. She had spoken of a little-used track that could lead them more quickly across the prairie to find the Broken Road and then bring them northeast to the pass through the Blackblade range and to Hilt.

When the last of them was clear of the city, Aren had promised Karpasic, the mystical, glowing dome that protected the city would vanish. That would signal the end of the city's defense and the open invitation to enter the walls and strip the spoils from Opalis.

Yet before that could happen, each of the refugees, their carts, and their wagons had to pass between several ranks of satyrs whom General Karpasic had ordered specifically to the duty of inspecting the column for contraband; in this case, weapons or, more important, treasure. It was a unique quality of the satyrs that they could "smell" gold. Their cousin fauns could even use their high-pitched voices to "call" to gemstones. Their voices would reverberate and resonate within the crystal structures in ways that they could hear. It was a specific talent the Obsidians had concocted for each of their races when they were reshaped from the humans they once had been, and one of the few that had worked out better than the sorcerers had anticipated.

It was their task to insure that nothing of value was taken from the city, hidden among the refugees. Their reward was that they could be the first to enter the city.

"Halt!" bleated the satyr as he stepped in front of a large wagon. It had just crossed the causeway from the North Gate and was moving between the jittery ranks of satyrs.

A stocky man with broad shoulders walking beside the oxen coaxed the team to a stop with a long, willow goad. A woman sat on the seat at the front of the freight wagon as it lurched to a halt, her boots pressed against the footboard and her hands clinging to the edges of the seat in a white-knuckled grip. Both the man and the woman wore long cloaks, their hoods pushed back. The man turned to the satyr and quietly asked, "Can I help you?"

"Inspection," the satyr screeched. He had forgotten everything about who he had once been, and the language came hard to him. His hind hooves clacked against the stones protruding from the ground as he moved back toward the wagon. He gestured up toward the wagon seat. "This your woman?"

The woman with the thick, curly hair at the front of the wagon glared with her large, dark eyes indignantly back at the scrawny creature striding in her direction. "In point of fact, I am most certainly not his woman, or anyone else's for that matter! I'm the loremistress of—"

"She's my sister," the man interrupted with a broad grin, his face outlined by a circle of white beard and a fringe of hair. "You know how they can be!"

In point of fact, the satyr had no idea how they could be and was about to say so when two other satyrs and a faun scrambled up to him from behind the wagon.

"Well, Simeus?" the satyr asked. "Do you smell anything?"

"Not a single nugget," the thin satyr answered.

"And I sang 'em, too," the faun offered. "Not a gemstone in the whole box, Gargo."

"Well, they got to be carrying *something*," Gargo answered. Thus far they had not found a single thing worth confiscating. "It's a mighty big wagon for hauling nothing!"

"I checked the box," Simeus said. "Figured it might be worth a look."

"And?" Gargo demanded.

"Nothing but fruits, dried meats, water, bread," Simeus answered, shaking his horned head. "And stacks of them . . . What do they call them . . . books?"

"Books!" Gargo snarled.

"Aye." Simeus shrugged. "Books, scrolls, and the like."

"All day, nothing but paper." Gargo spat on the ground between his hooves. "Every wagon we've looked in is full of writing. It's all barely worth burning, and that's what they bring with them. No wonder we conquered them so quicklike! Bunch of fools!"

"Excuse me?" the man standing near the front of the oxen asked. "Is there a problem?"

"You're the problem!" the satyr screeched back at him. "You're blocking the road! Get this garbage out of my sight!"

"As you wish," the man said, urging the oxen forward to follow the line of wagons stretched before him toward the eastern horizon.

† † †

The last of the wagons left the North Gate just before sundown. It had barely cleared the causeway when, in the failing light of day, the dome over the city flickered and then vanished.

Every member of Karpasic's army—from the general and his captains, down through his warriors and archers, his elves, fauns, ogres, and satyrs, and even to the teamsters, smithies, and cooks—could see at once that the city was instantly defenseless.

The refugees were, in that moment, forgotten.

The warriors poured across the causeway through the North Gate. They flowed into the wide avenue of Muse Way that ran as a circle inside the city walls. They were soon met by others in the army who had charged through the rubble of the collapsed Fields Gate and were pouring into the city from that breach as well. The Storm Gate to the southeast was discovered to be left open and, in a moment, the army was pouring into the city through that gate too.

Everyone's eyes were fixed on the obvious prize: the towering citadel of the Titans near the center of the city. They converged on its outer wall, searching for its gate, for a way in so that they might find the treasure for themselves.

So quick was the rush into the city, for each member of the army determined to take as much as he could for himself from the citadel, that the encampment of the Westreach Army was completely abandoned. . . .

Including the supply wagons.

† † †

Three men stood at the crest of the hill, gazing east toward the towers of Opalis that stood shining in the last light of the setting sun.

"They're pouring into the city," the scout reported between gulping breaths. "They've posted no pickets to guard their perimeter. Even the encampment appears to be abandoned."

"Boreus was right," Tribune Marcus Tercius observed with a nodding grin. "They are not expecting company."

Legate Planus Argo could barely make out the stream of refugees moving slowly eastward beyond the city. He could see movement within the walls, but none outside.

"Then I believe it is time for us to come calling," the legate said, setting his jaw. He looked down the hill to either side. His legions were facing east as well, their eyes, too, set on Opalis. "The order is given. Tell the commanders they are to charge and surround the city and then prepare to lay siege to it."

"By your word, Legate!" the scout answered, smartly slapping his scabbard against his leg in salute. He then ran down the hill toward the ranks of warriors over a mile long in each direction, waiting for word.

"How long do you think they will be able to hold out?" asked Marcus Tercius as he, too, looked toward the distant city.

Legate Argo folded his arms across his chest, considering. "If we can confiscate their supply wagons, and if what Boreus told us is true . . ."

"He has proven to be correct so far," Marcus observed.

"Then this shouldn't take long at all." The legate smiled.

CHAPTER
27

Epiphany

General Karpasic pushed his way through the group of confused and listless satyrs. He choked suddenly, coughing from the dust that filled the corridor from the collapsed wall he had just climbed over. He had "liberated" a lantern from one of the city's shops earlier in the evening. He now held it high over and to the side of his head, trying to pierce the darkness of what had been an enormous, elegant hall.

It had taken the greater part of the day to break into the citadel. The flood of warriors into the city through the open and broken gates had, predictably, resulted in considerable chaos for the first few hours as such discipline that had existed dissolved into cutthroat greed. They poured into the abandoned buildings of Opalis all along Muse Way and down into the back alleys among the smaller shops and homes. The warriors spread over the city like locusts devouring a field. The crashing sound of ransacking each building grew with every moment.

That sound was soon followed by a growing howl of anger and betrayal. There *was* gold and even a few gems to be rutted out here and there among the buildings, but the legendary wealth of Opalis was not evident in the shops, stalls, or homes of the city. The scavengers washed back and forth within the walls of the town like water in a bucket suddenly jarred, desperately seeking the hidden trove that would make their hardships and spilled blood worthwhile.

It was just before evening that the focus of their frustrations fell on the towering citadel near the middle of the town. General Karpasic had been considering the problem since they first entered the city, but he had become increasingly puzzled by it as the evening wore on. He had personally circumnavigated the outer wall of the citadel a number of times, somehow unable to accept that there could be a defensive wall around the towers that had no gate at all. He considered the possibilities of a hidden gate or an underground passage. He had only two kobolds at his command—the latest of the reshaped creatures from the Cabal of the Obsidians—and he directed both of them to search for any subterranean access. Unfortunately, he had not heard from either of them since. A number of the elves had scaled the wall, only to report that there was no access into the tower from the top of the wall either. As the sun set to the west, the rage of his own army was gravitating toward the marketplace at the foot of the citadel and Karpasic. Growing frustrated himself, he knew he had to act.

He commanded the remaining ogres into the marketplace.

If he could not go over the wall or under the wall, then he would go *through* the wall.

The ogres were particularly adept at this sort of work, although the masonwork of the citadel's outer wall was particularly smooth and well fitted, making it difficult for the ogres to get a proper grip on the stone. In the end, they resorted to brute force, punching the wall to break up its surface and allow them a proper hold.

Now, Karpasic made his way into the interior of the tower, illuminated only by the lantern in his hand. The dust was settling, and his vision down the hall was limited but clearing. The hall appeared to end in a larger, round space. He could see the shadowy form of a great statue on the other side of the rotunda.

There, he thought, his smile broadening. *There it is!*

Piled in the center of the rotunda were stacks of chests, nearly filling the central space. Many of them were filled to overflowing with coins spilling out onto the floor. Their warm shine winked back at him in the light of his lamp.

Karpasic rushed forward, stumbling slightly over some debris scattered across the polished floor of the hall. Behind him, the satyrs stared at him in confusion. He gained his footing in the tomblike darkness, turning back to scowl at them.

"What are you waiting for?" he bellowed. "We're here! We've found it!"

The general caught his balance and stepped quickly down the dark hall. The pool of light from his lantern swung shifting shadows over the walls, floor, and ceiling. He came quickly into the expanse of the deserted rotunda. Three statues stood at equal points at the perimeter of the curving wall. They each looked down on him, their features shifting in disapproval with the movement of the lantern light. The illusion startled Karpasic for a moment, but then he sneered both at the figures and at his reaction.

"Ghosts," he said. "I've beaten you, and now you're nothing at all."

He turned to the treasure stacked high in the center of the room. He could see the glint of gems interspersed with the warm color of the shining coins. He smiled, reaching his hand forward, trying to plunge it into the pile. The coins moved at his touch, creating a small avalanche.

The coins rang brightly as they cascaded to the floor. The sound echoed through the hall as several of the coins rolled away.

The general frowned.

Gold coins would have dented as they were dropped onto the marble floor. They would not have rolled away.

General Karpasic curled his fingers around several of the coins as he pulled his hand away from the treasure. He pulled the lamp closer, keeping it slightly behind his head as he peered at the coins in his hand.

The color of the metal was golden in the light of the lantern, but duller than he might expect from gold. He could see engraved on its face the symbol of Etceter, apparently where the coin was issued as currency. He slid several of the coins through his fingers. Another had a symbol he did not recognize, but the third was definitely the crest of the Lords of Resolute. Then there was another from Etceter.

The general slipped a coin between his teeth. He was

surprised by the bitter taste. The metal did not bend between his teeth.

He suddenly understood why the satyrs were standing at the end of the hallway, confused. He had sent them in to sniff out the gold.

He looked down at the coins in his hands.

"Brass," he murmured. "They're all brass."

He suddenly cast the coins to ring against the floor and reached for the nearest of the obvious gems. It appeared to be a ruby of unusual size. He drew it close, turning it in the light.

Scratches marked the surface of the facets.

In a rage, Karpasic turned, throwing the object fiercely against the wall.

It shattered into dust and small shards.

"Glass!" he yelled. "He left me glass?"

Karpasic charged back down the hall toward the satyrs, who, seeing his approach, drew back against the walls.

"Bennis!" The general's breath was ragged as he charged down the hall. His voice rose with every step. "Keep my ten percent, he said. Give us safe passage, he said. Now he's left me here with a pile of brass coins that are good only for trading with enemy kingdoms while he rides, laughing, across the plains toward the protective arms of his sorcerer conspirator!"

The general stopped in the hall, his shoulders shuddering in rage. He raised his fist, shaking it at the ceiling overhead. "I'll see him drawn and quartered first! I'll run him to ground on the plains before he even makes camp, and bleed his followers until the ground refuses to soak up their blood! Not a dog will be left alive among them before I'm—"

"General!" Captain Odman was struggling through the rubble of the tower's breach. His voice was considerably higher and more excited than Karpasic remembered ever hearing it before. "General Karpasic!"

"What!" the general screamed.

The captain might have quailed at the sound of the general's rage any other time, but panic overwhelmed his fear. "An army, General! An army has surrounded the city!"

"An army!" Karpasic's eyes bulged slightly. His mind was still fixed on Bennis's betrayal and was having trouble forming an understanding around the captain's words. "What are you blathering about? What army?"

"No one saw it c-coming," the captain stammered. "The victory had been won. . . . Everyone was within the city walls. . . ."

The general grabbed Odman by the front of his breastplate just beneath his chin, dragging his face within inches of the general's own.

"What army!" the general demanded.

"They come under the standard of Norgard," the captain replied, sweat breaking out on his forehead. "Our scouts had reported them far to the west, at the base of the mountains . . . the Pillars of Night. No one saw their approach—"

"Call to arms!" the general shouted, and he shoved the captain toward the gap in the citadel wall. "Get the army to the walls! If Bennis thinks he can trap *me* here in a siege . . ."

"We cannot outlast a siege!" Captain Odman shouted back at the general.

"You idiot!" the general snapped. "We *own* the city! The food stores here alone—"

"Are useless," Odman interrupted. "I've had several reports

over the last hour of warriors becoming violently ill from the supplies they've liberated. I believe the citizens here poisoned their food and drink stores before they left."

"But our own supply wagons—"

"Are *outside* the city walls," Odman reminded the general.

General Milos Karpasic, Supreme Lord of the Westreach Army, fell silent. His eyes shifted back and forth, his mind racing, but he was somehow unable to comprehend anything but the distant laughter that came, imagined, to his ears from across the prairie to the east.

"Then we have to break the siege at once," Karpasic said at last. "We have to break through the enemy lines while we still have the strength! Bring the captains to me! We're about to show these Norgard scum what fear is all about!"

† † †

By dawn the next day, General Karpasic had those of his troops within the town who were not still posted to the walls prepared to charge out of the city's North Gate. He was determined to lead with the ogres to break the Norgard line, followed by the satyrs and fauns at their flanks to open up the gap even farther. Elves would bolster those lines to help widen the gap while the bulk of the army charged through the opening to the plains beyond. Karpasic told himself that leaving the city gates open behind them, the Norgard army would abandon pursuit of him and his forces in favor of taking the town just as he had done the day before.

Karpasic ordered the North Gate opened.

Beyond, he could see the Legions of Norgard waiting for them.

Karpasic smiled, telling himself that his enemy had no idea what was about to hit them.

And, for the last time, he was wrong.

The Titan Boreus had told them exactly what to expect.

The Legions of Norgard were prepared.

† † †

Aren sat astride his horse, a cloak pulled tightly around him as he looked down the slope to the column of refugees winding in his direction from the south. They were following the trail Syenna had marked out for them along the east bank of the upper reaches of the West Jaana River and into the long mountain bowl known as Highvale.

It had been a difficult journey. They had made an abrupt turn to the north in the middle of that first night and traveled with barely a rest for the horses and oxen before pressing on into the next evening. They wound their way around the Middle Downs and eventually through Monk's Hood Pass into the southern parts of the Highvale. There, they found the upper reaches of their familiar friend, the West Jaana River, and followed it northward, higher into the long mountain bowl.

"We should make camp." Syenna sat on her own horse side by side with Aren, gazing back at the approaching column. "We'll need to be rested for the climb tomorrow into Resolute, and I don't think we're likely to find a better place to stop before nightfall."

Aren turned around. They were both stopped just short of the tree line. The air was scented with pine from the forest to the north behind them. "Will we make it tomorrow?"

"To Resolute, certainly." Syenna nodded. "Sequana has made

all the arrangements with Marshal Nimbus. You do realize that the Titans surrendered their people to Nimbus, not you."

"I may have been mistaken on that point when I addressed the general," Aren said through a loud, exaggerated sigh. "I promise to apologize for that error the next time we meet."

"And when do you expect that to be?"

"Not soon, and certainly not in this world," Aren replied as he turned his gaze back down over the long mountain bowl beneath them. "He got the treasure he deserved, and the Titans got to keep the treasure they wanted."

"And what about you?" Syenna asked, turning in her saddle to face Aren. "What did you get out of this?"

Aren grinned back at her. He reached down, patting the sword that hung at his side.

Syenna gazed at the sword for a moment, and then her eyes widened. "The pommel! All three of the symbol's blades are shining!"

"Yes." Aren nodded.

"When did that happen?"

"Not long after we left Opalis," Aren replied, his gaze returning to the mountain bowl before them.

"What does it mean?" Syenna asked breathlessly.

"I asked the loremistress that very question," Aren answered. "She said it had something to do with the ancient Virtues . . . that somehow I had honored them, and the symbols had responded. Maybe it was supposed to empower the sword, or maybe it was just a way for the Avatars to know they were on the right path. Given the circumstances at the time, she believes they each had something to do with things like truth or courage or compassion. However, she also pointed out that there are a number of other symbols on the sword that are still dull and have yet to shine . . . so I guess I'm not yet perfect."

"Hardly." Syenna chuckled.

"Well, the loremistress says she will have to do more research before she can say for certain," Aren said through a smirk.

"It's not very complete, you know," Syenna said.

"What isn't complete?"

"Their knowledge of the past," Syenna said quietly into the still mountain air. "So much was lost during the Fall of the Sky. I was speaking with Loremistress Lanilan earlier today. Despite the Titans' struggle to maintain the knowledge of their own machines, for all their searching, they have not been able to find or even piece together what it was that the Avatars brought to the world. They still don't know what caused the Fall, let alone how to prevent it from happening again. They could not even tell you now whether the Avatars were trying to prevent the end of the world that was lost, or if they caused it."

"Then what has been the point of all this?" Aren asked, continuing to gaze down on the refugees streaming into the meadow below them.

"The Loremistress says that the Titans have a plan," Syenna answered. "They believe they can use what they know of their ancestors' machines to build a great device—an oracle of such power that it may be able to recover the wisdom and knowledge that was lost . . . perhaps even find a way to bring the Avatars back into the world . . . if they still exist."

"Or whether their return would be good or bad." Aren sighed. "I've got the blade of an Avatar—and I still don't know if it is a blessing or a curse."

Syenna turned in her saddle, looking at Aren with searching eyes.

"You saved my sister from dying by my own hand," she said. "You saved the knowledge of the past so it could be preserved. You saved the people of Opalis from death and misery."

"And, while you're about it," Aren said, shaking his head, "do not forget to include that all these things I've done will no doubt also prompt the Obsidian Cause to react in a most unhealthy way. All these currently grateful refugees may reconsider their opinion of me once the Obsidians realize that there are forces in South Paladis that can oppose them. Let us see just how heroic I appear when the full strength of the Obsidian Army falls on them because of what I've done."

"You wield a blade of the Avatars," Syenna said with a smirk. "Something about you must be right."

"Yes, I am indeed such a magnificent hero," Aren agreed, suddenly flashing his broad grin. "And would you be so good as to explain that to our guest? My old friend Nik Halik seems a bit skeptical on that score since I forced his surrender the first night after we left Opalis."

"Well, you can't really blame him." Syenna smiled at the thought. "All of us had given up our swords."

"All of us except one," Aren corrected, resting his hand on the pommel of his sword.

"All except one," Syenna agreed, her smile broadening into a grin.

CHAPTER 28

Thundering Silence

vard Dirae stood at the crossroads of the Broken Road and waited, just as he had waited for twelve days. In the evenings, he would prepare a meager meal and contemplate the gathering darkness. In the night, he would lie on the ground, a stick propping up his robe over his head to shelter him from the wind across the prairie that never seemed to stop. Then, in the morning, he would awaken, prepare his breakfast, and again wait with watchful eyes looking down the Broken Road to the south for some sign of his old friend's approach.

Evard was, he knew, hardly alone. A detachment of warriors over two hundred strong, each he'd handpicked, was encamped near the mountain pass that led through the Blackblade Mountains back to Hilt. The captain in charge of them was awaiting only the sign from Evard—a homunculus that Evard had reserved for the purpose—before ordering the marching of his command to capture the refugees as they approached. They were prepared on short notice to march northwest and southwest, so as to encircle the approaching column of weary Opalis citizens. In that moment, their flesh would be sealed to the monstrous fate that Evard had planned for them in service to the Obsidian Cause.

Yet nothing had come up the road from the south. It was not just a matter of missing the column of refugees—that could easily be explained as simply being slowed by the weakest from among them—but no rider, no trade wagon or caravan, no pilgrim wanderer had appeared from that direction either.

Certainly, Karpasic would have dispatched someone with the news, someone crowing about his captured city and its treasures by now.

As the twelfth day drew to a close, Evard stood up and whistled softly. The leather-winged form of the homunculus appeared as though it had risen from a shadow on the plain. It hopped once and, beating its wings, lit upon Evard's shoulder, its hand resting upon his head as it craned its flat face around, peering at the sorcerer.

Evard started to whistle a familiar tune to the homunculus.

Aren's tune.

When he had completed it, he reached up. The creature stepped onto his forearm, its claws digging into his flesh as it turned to face him. The creature was already anxious and agitated, driven to find, in the gathering night, the notes it had just heard.

Evard spoke simply to the creature.

"Where are you? Do you need me to come?"

Then, with a sweep of his arm, he released the dark, winged creature, sending it into the twilight sky.

Through many nights to come, wherever Evard journeyed in the service of the Obsidians, he would repeat the ritual. Sometimes with one creature, and sometimes with dozens, but each time the creature would return exhausted and silent.

Those notes were never answered.

The song had gone forever silent.

THE END OF BOOK ONE

ABOUT THE AUTHORS

———————

TRACY HICKMAN has been publishing game designs, books, and stories for more than thirty-five years. In addition, he is a *New York Times* bestselling coauthor of many novels, including the original Dragonlance Chronicles. Hickman lives in Utah. Visit him at www.trhickman.com.

RICHARD GARRIOTT DE CAYEUX is a video game designer, collector, and private astronaut. In 2006, Richard was awarded with two industry honors for his work in the games business: selection into the Academy of Interactive Arts & Sciences Hall of Fame and the Lifetime Achievement Award at the Game Developers Choice Awards.